# TRINITY LAKE

# TRINITY LAKE

❖

A Story of Departures and Returns

# Richard S. Monkman

Library of Congress Control Number:      2016913898
ISBN:           Hardcover               978-1-5245-3684-8
                Softcover               978-1-5245-3683-1
                eBook                   978-1-5245-3682-4

Print information available on the last page.

Rev. date: 10/10/2016

**To order additional copies of this book, contact:**
Xlibris
1-888-795-4274
www.Xlibris.com
Orders@Xlibris.com
742486

We do not want you to be ignorant about those who fall asleep or to grieve like the rest of men, who have no hope. We believe that Jesus died and rose again and so we believe that God will bring with Jesus those who have fallen asleep in him. According to the Lord's own word, we tell you that we who are still alive, who are left till the coming of the Lord, will not precede those who have fallen asleep. For the Lord himself will come down from heaven with a loud command, with the voice of the archangel, and with the trumpet call of God, and the dead in Christ will rise first. After that, we who are still alive and left will be caught up together with them in the clouds to meet the Lord in the air.

# CHAPTER 1

Fire refines.

"Zell . . . donnn . . ." It was a refining cry.

A young man's agonized face appeared on the second floor and disappeared in billowing smoke, his eyes wide with fear and his mouth desperately forming Zeldon's name. To the paralyzed onlooker outside, it was clear there were sheets of flame between the suffering figure and the window. In the brief moments when visibility permitted, he could see fists pounding on the wall, the face shouting. Zeldon stared up, his own young man's heart twisting in anguish, every instinct reaching upward, but his body stayed, unable to move, rooted to the ground. Flames ate at the house, licked increasingly at the upper floor. Bryan's contorted features possessed all of Zeldon's consciousness. He strained further forward, helpless. His senses dismissed every stimulus—other men shouting, sirens screaming, fire engines roaring, and disgorging firemen as they braked. In the remembrance of that misshapen, staring face, all other impressions receded. The disappearance of sound turned the scene before him into pantomime. Nothing registered but the one image of Bryan's plight and his own impotence. Behind his friend's face, he conjured the flames browning the edges of their shared textbooks, slithering along the floorboards, melting the plastic of Zeldon's computer. Undulating, they would be toying with the keys of Bryan's accordion and devouring its box, killing the possibility of any joyful sounds he might have brought from it. Bryan, joyful Bryan and all his joys, was dying.

Once more, Bryan appeared, gesticulating wildly. Then the twisted face was gone. The cries stopped. Zeldon knew there was frantic activity about him, but it left no impression. In the presence

1

of that terror, he entered a world where no one else existed. He was completely alone. It would be a world in which Zeldon would live for a long while to come. For that moment, his own body's functions became paramount, the beating of his heart and dryness of his mouth. His body was a stony weight, making it impossible to lift a hand. Worst of all was the paralysis of his will, knowing as in a nightmare, that he was seeing death and could not intervene.

At the back of his mind, something dark approached, a muffled figure, unrelenting, not to be denied. The phantom impulse left no room for him to move in his own defense. If he could fly into the flames and join Bryan, he would escape, but he could not. What was this shadow on his brain? Whatever it was, he knew somehow it would capture him, own him, but still his fear would not let him act. He could feel his own personality melting, being smelted down. Over time, it would congeal into a different form entirely.

Finally, it was forced upon Zeldon that gawking neighbors were being ordered aside. Mrs. Rodgers, his landlady, was being herded along with them. He, too, was shoved roughly away, stumbling into the supporting arms of a young woman who looked into his face with an expression of deep sorrow. She was framed by the flames leaping behind her. In the confusion, she faded away.

Zeldon tried to blurt out Bryan's plight, but by the time anyone paid attention, it was much too late. In time, the walls of his home were engulfed in the fire, then fell into the basement in one mighty burst of orange and yellow. Chest constricting, heart protesting, he peered into the burning pit, sure he was at the edge of hell.

"What happened?" From his state of shock, Zeldon noticed the fire chief's overhanging belly and one open buttonhole just above his belt. The buttonhole jumped. "What happened?" the chief insisted. Zeldon was speechless. Hoses sprayed water over all that remained of the house and its steaming ashes. An engine snarled. One of the trucks edged its way into the street, heading for the firehouse. Neighbors began returning to their homes. Mrs. Rodgers and Zeldon stayed with the few remaining firemen. Still he was silent, settling into shock. It was as though he had been rendered lastingly still with no prospect of recovering motion, dead in fact.

"It was their coffee ring. I know it was. I told them any number of times. They kept . . . kept blowing my fuses," Mrs. Rodgers answered for Zeldon when he couldn't. "They're nice boys, lovely boys . . ." then she stopped. Only one of the lovely boys was accounted for. "They're . . . they're . . ." Drawing her housecoat around her, the devastated woman broke into loud sobs as the full force of her loss came upon her. Her home, her belongings, one of her college-boy tenants—all were gone.

The burly chief turned back to Zeldon, impatient for a response. Haltingly, Zeldon said, "I don't . . . I don't know. Maybe it was the coffee ring." He swam in a sea of guilt, ready to accept any accusation. "I was upstairs in my room. I . . . I thought Br . . . I thought Bryan was downstairs in his. I'd heard him moving around." Gathering strength, he spoke more quickly to get this over with, "I smelled smoke. Then I saw flames coming out of my closet . . . It was all so fast." Instinctively, he looked around for Bryan to confirm what he was saying, but the huge fact of Bryan's absence made him nauseous and forced him into silence again. The gray impulse and the muffled feeling weighed him down.

"OK, son, go on." The fireman spoke with a surprising tenderness and waited for Zeldon to recover.

"I met Mrs. Rodgers in the downstairs hall. We were both choking on the smoke. We came out the front door together. I thought Bryan was already out. His room's right by the front door . . . I guess . . . I guess . . ." he was ashen; his mouth had turned to cotton. "He was upstairs in the b . . . b . . . bathroom." He stopped. There was no more to be said. Bryan was dead and he was not. But the cries had settled deep in his heart. Zeldon would hear those cries for the rest of his life, accusers, calling out his name, calling out his cowardice.

"Don't worry, boy." The chief laid a hand on Zeldon's shoulder. "They die from the fumes before the flames do much harm."

Zeldon had his doubts about that. Mrs. Rodgers walked over to a cluster of neighbors and returned to invite Zeldon to spend the remainder of the night with an older couple willing to put them up. "This is Zeldon," she said to the sympathetic twosome.

"Poor boy, you're in shock," the woman offered. "We all are. Come and stay with us while you catch up with yourself."

"We're the Grouts, Emily, and I'm Steve." The old man shook Zeldon's hand in both of his. Mumbling his thanks, he followed after them. He felt he would never catch up with himself, didn't want to.

"Can we call anyone for you, your parents?"

"Zeldon's on his own, his parents aren't living," Mrs. Rodgers intervened. That fact increased their compassion, but the wise folk knew better than to press themselves further on the traumatized young man.

His stay with the Grouts lasted for several nights. Their sensitivities, and those of Mrs. Rodgers, helped him drift through Bryan's funeral service. Bryan's father's firm had taken both parents abroad; they lived in England, so Rockwater, New York, with its natural beauty, provided as good a cemetery location for their son as any. They were a reserved couple. That and their sorrow allowed little exchange between them and Zeldon. They flew back to England within a few days.

*     *     *

It was several evenings later when Zeldon drove to the edge of the town's Trinity Lake and turned in at an old New England sign reading, "Ye Olde Burying Yarde, Rockwater, New York." The sign had been there the day of the funeral, but its finality struck him that day. He entered its solemn property and walked from the car with heavy feet, then stood before the grave of the dead man, - boy – youth, Bryan. Bare earth surrounded its rectangle, emphasizing his forlorn emotions. Bryan was just a name on a stone. Yet Zeldon heard again his dead friend's voice ring through the yard, "Zeldon, Zeldon! Zell . . . donnn . . ."

Bryan's anguished expression now belonged to him, the guilt-filled living man, transposed from that haunted memory to his own unhappy face. He lifted his head to the sky, arched his back, spread his arms wide, "Bryan, I'm sorry, so sorry, so s . . ." He cried the words aloud to give reality to them, to lend them a power he had no hope of making real enough. The darkening sky looked down upon him. Nature confirmed its cruel neutrality, the lake's water reflecting the vast indifference about him, but trauma had given Zeldon an almost palpable alertness; all five of his senses stretched to their limits, a symptom that would stay with him. He heard a bird's lonely evening call. The sound of a car passed without pause, grass stirred at his feet, but no one, nothing, gave voice to the response he so desperately needed. "Forgive me, Bryan, I couldn't help it, I . . . I couldn't move. I was so afraid." It was the first of many such scenes. Zeldon returned the next evening and the next. Gradually he took to frequenting the graveyard, where he wrestled with those ogres in his mind that kept Bryan alive as an unpardoning judge.

\* \* \*

He rented a cottage on a Rockwater estate and as much as possible avoided his new landlord. It was an easy next step to stop attending classes at the Danbury campus of the University of Connecticut. He did that even though the term was almost over. The days following were spent in shocked reverie and failed efforts at diversion. Movies couldn't hold his attention. One day he traveled into the city to see the new exhibit at the planetarium, but it couldn't arouse his interest. He walked into Central Park and trudged all the way down to the Park Zoo. Instead of seeing a collection of animals, he saw merely many ways of being alive. Bryan was not. He returned on an early train.

Former college friends found him hard to trace and unresponsive to their overtures. One did manage to trace him through the ever-helpful Mrs. Rodgers. "You can most likely find Zeldon down at the lake, in the local cemetery," she said in a worried voice, "probably reading a book." The puzzled young man did find him there and as predicted, reading.

"What in hell . . . ?" He stopped, staring at his fraternity brother. "Ye Olde Burying Yarde?"

"Bill, how did you find me?" Zeldon's voice was flat, unenthusiastic.

"By asking around. I heard about Bryan. Jesus, Zeldon, what a bummer." No answer from Zeldon brought another attempt from Bill. "Well, how are you? What are you doing here?" He looked around as if he had just been told a bad joke.

"Nothing, just passing the time." The intense interest shown by his friend emphasized Zeldon's indifference in stark relief.

"Come on, Zel, what's going on? I know what happened to Bryan was crappy, but you can't go down with him. I mean Jesus, Zel."

A nod.

"You remember that English course in our sophomore year, when we were reading James Joyce?"

"Yeah."

"OK, remember Joyce's remark about how we live and die while an indifferent God cuts his fingernails? That's my religion."

No answer.

Trying again, Bill changed his tone. "Did you really drop out just at exam time? I mean, Jesus, Zel."

"I need some time."

"The guys are asking about you. Mandy wants to see you. What should I tell them?"

"Tell them I need some time."

"Yeah well, graduation is on Thursday, and we'll all go with the four winds, sort of. I'm, like, a little short of facts, you know? What should I say to Mandy?"

"Leave me alone, Bill. I just need some space. Tell them that."

"OK, pal, your call." Then making one more effort, he said, "You want to go get a Starbucks or something?"

"No, thanks."

"A walk along the lakeshore?"

"I don't mean to be gnarly, but I really do need my distance."

"Right well, good luck. Sorry about Bryan." He was feeling offended.

With that, he walked out of the Yarde and with him went Zeldon's social ties of the past four years. Only the Rockwater cemetery offered him a place where his real self was engaged. He held internal monologues there, which he hoped might bring some response from Bryan, and his friendship with the silent absentee deepened beyond what it had actually been, appreciating Bryan more than he had before, idealizing him, pandering to him. Without awareness, Zeldon was allowing Bryan to become transmogrified into an indication of his own mortality. A consciousness-expanding thought came. For the first time, he felt the darkness that surrounds and encircles the living. "Maybe Bill and James Joyce are right. Nature certainly is indifferent to our troubles, lots of evidence for that even though we don't want to believe it." The live man was slipping into self-mourning, a young man's bit of melodrama. All the small guilts accumulated in childhood, products of having disappointed adult expectations, became an assemblage deposited at Bryan's feet, a propitiation that failed to buy the desired result. The continued hope for a signal from Bryan brought only silence.

After two weeks of those, his visits to the cemetery fell into a routine. One afternoon, he sat on a bench, reading one of his textbooks. A voice spoke but not the awaited voice of Bryan.

"Becoming a regular here, aren't you?" Zeldon recognized the speaker to be the caretaker; he had avoided him several times in the past days. The man, although not young, showed mighty arms, a barrel torso, and legs like two oak trees.

"Yes," he answered, hoping to return to his reading without further conversation.

"What's your book?" There were exploratory words, removing Zeldon's hope. "Must not be much good, you haven't turned a page in fifteen minutes."

Zeldon showed his discomfort, unhappy to be so closely observed. The old gentleman continued in a not unfriendly tone, "You've been coming here a lot."

"It's quiet. A good place to have lunch."

"It is quiet. I've noticed you. I could see you wanted your privacy."

No answer from Zeldon brought one more remark. Recognizing true grief, a quality familiar to him in his line of work, he said, "Something wrong, boy?"

*     *     *

And so the boy stood on the early margin of manhood, having met his first adult trauma. In time, grace would come to him as his visionary moments came and went—life-changing moments of high emotion and clarity of mind in the onrushing history that would become his. Being in love would become an ingredient as would other unique encounters; unfolding insights would play a part, at times becoming unsure of the distinction between himself and the outside world, seeing sunsets and their repeated return in matchless sunrises would contribute as well as commit to danger on behalf of another. Grace would show itself, grace that could produce a powerful, focused mind worthy of those visions, a mind able to retain them in memory by recognizing their importance. Thus might the immature young man preserve their vividness, and them as one would a summoning finger, ultimately growing into a power in his own right and once again a young mind leaning into life.

# Chapter 2

On a bright, sunny morning four years later, Zeldon Wade stood beneath the featured tree of the Burying Yarde, a distance away from the day's proceedings as befitted the cemetery superintendent. Before him unfolded a scene that had by then become familiar. Another of Rockwater's citizens had arrived at the Yarde for a last entry through the gates. In preparing such a scene, Zeldon's role was to make the arrangements for the ritualized farewell, and do it unobtrusively. One of the dead resident's surviving friends approached.

"Nice morning."

"It is." Zeldon's manner was friendly but not easily drawn forth, coming seemingly from a deep recess of stillness.

"You must see some interesting groups come here in your line of work." The visitor was obviously avoiding the crowd behind him, probably a family misfit looking for a place of social safety. Zeldon didn't really want to oblige him but was incapable of rudeness

"Yes, quite a variety."

"Worked here long?"

"A few years." Beyond that, he said nothing. The question opened a memory he didn't care to share. Dan Shipley, the former caretaker-superintendent, had hired him as a groundskeeper and then gave him a rapid progression of responsibilities. The old man didn't indicate that he was laying plans for his own retirement. Zeldon could hear his solicitous growl then, "Something wrong, boy?" It had opened a friendship between them that was marked by mutual respect and yes, love. He had loved Dan. The memory saddened him. It was Dan who was being buried just that moment, a few yards away.

He reviewed in his mind one defining conversation he had had with Dan, telling him feelings he had never told anyone, not even Bryan. Bryan knew of the double tragedy of Zeldon's parents' deaths but not of their true cause. He also thought they had died in a traffic accident in Cairo, there on a vacation. After the added horror of Bryan's death, Zeldon had been carrying a double burden.

One dismal, windy winter day in his first year on the job while Dan and he sat on a bench at lunch, he blurted it out, "I need to tell someone about my parents."

"What about them, son?" Dan had begun to talk to him like a parent himself. In days to come, the young man would learn to feel that talking with his companion was like throwing open a window to the fresh air but not yet.

"My dad worked for the State Department. He traveled a lot, and sometimes Mother went with him. They combined his assignments with vacation time when it was possible." After a pause to gather his feelings, he went on, "They were caught in Damascus during the civil war, and before they could get out of Syria, they were both killed in a car bombing. They sent a department man to tell me about their deaths."

He stopped again, taking deep breaths, gulping for air. Dan put a hand on his shoulder. "All he said was that they were victims of a terrorist attack and . . . and there were no remains to care for."

Dan lowered his head in sympathy, nodded slowly and repeatedly and said nothing.

"No remains." The two of them sat in silence for long moments, and Zeldon repeated it once more. "No remains." They gazed together at the gravestones surrounding them, the remains of generations of Rockwater's residents. Zeldon reflected how his only people were buried in a secret place in his heart, a place without comfort and without companionship.

"And then came your friend, Bryan," Dan murmured, showing how he understood.

For nearly a year, Zeldon had closed down all avenues of connection. Then he opened himself just a crack. "I need this job," he said after another pause, "to stand in for my family, to make a place for them along with Bryan."

After his unburdening with Dan, things were different between them. It was not that they hadn't been cordial, but then they became more than that. Zeldon remained quiet to others, disguising his distress. He lived in flashbulb time, in stopped time more than in action time, adjusting himself only when it was necessary. Dan kept a careful eye on him, recognizing a young man in deepfreeze.

When the short committal ceremonies for Dan were ended, the small knot of people dissipated into their vehicles, exchanging murmured remarks. Last to leave was a tall figure, standing before a drop in the ground, which left him silhouetted against the horizon. Behind the man, large, chesty white clouds strode across a blue sky—Tap Andrews, the local clergyman, nodded in Zeldon's direction. Rockwater had one church, a focal point for Christian believers of many denominations. Andrews was their dispenser of reminders and encouragements.

Zeldon, feeling his own loss, approached him. "A dark day," he said, belying the sunny backdrop.

"Dark, not black," Andrews said.

It was typical of the man. The two met often in their capacities, yet habitually exchanged few words. Both were quiet men, the older one, Andrews, always leaving something memorable despite his reserve. Zeldon registered again his tall slender form standing in outline before the green of the Yarde, the looming trees, blue expanse of sky above, and the lake below. He embodied his own remark, "Dark, not black." A sober man dealing with sober commodities yet alive himself, Zeldon admired him. He was ambivalent over his own attitudes about Andrews's faith. Andrews spoke of the soul as more than a ghostly extra and not something to be located below the left armpit. "If you can locate envy in your body," he once had said, "then maybe I can locate your soul." But then he had asserted himself enough to quote Thomas Aquinas as saying, "My soul is me, able to articulate myself astride the grass line." That impressed Zeldon, who would keep the conceit as central to his arsenal of convictions. Yes, he found an ever-receding God and a country in spiritual retreat. All politics, he thought, was fear ridden and Andrews apart, Christianity he believed to be all smiles and no bite. On the other hand—there was always the other hand—there had to be more to the soul than the visible and the obvious. That fed his spiritual curiosity and permitted his borderline what ifs.

He glanced about his chosen ground, his place of work, place of working out meaning for his unfolding life. It was truly a place of beauty. The Yarde was on a wooded, elevated plateau, looking down at Trinity Lake on the Yarde's eastern edge. Adjacent to the burial ground to its south, the Rockwater Town Park reached in an identical view of the lake, presenting itself a changeable face of beauty.

Zeldon had inherited as Yarde superintendent the title of park governor as well, but the town fathers saw the park as a place of nature, that is as a location that should produce itself from out of the earth, unassisted. Translated, that meant it foresaw no prospect of funding for improvements. Nevertheless, the young superintendent/governor saw the properties as a unity, which in scope and topography they were. That was important to him because he had begun to see life and death as a successive continuity and portraying the properties as one property only emphasized the message he wanted his work to suggest. What did the two share?

The view from the Yarde was commanding. Zeldon once wondered why towns seemed always to give one of their best prospects to the dead. He had learned it was as much for drainage as for esthetics. In any case, it afforded, as one might expect, a sensation of tranquil quiet, removed, self-contained, yet proximate to the living. He remembered standing before the first open grave he had prepared after Dan's retirement when he was the sole administrator over the property, flying solo as it were. Looking into its shadow, he had seen only an emptiness but then stepped into new space himself by considering it rather as a temporary home containing many varied guests, an invisible hope . . . . a departure wrapped in a sunset, another step in the young man's walk toward resolution.

As Reverend Andrews drove away, Zeldon was reminded again of how he valued that removal. It was quiet, with the town reduced to a distant hum in the consciousness. But he was aware, too, of how contradictory that was. He fled social hysteria, seeing it as a destruction of all that life promised. Yet there he was, seeking life in a place of death. Where was life? Where was death? Many of his belowground residents had come here directly from hospitals, which he called God's hotels. Others were from centuries earlier. Things needed redefining. He was determined to find life, to live, and he would. But to do so, he couldn't proceed without any questions asked. What was he learning? Flat earth people knew the abruptness of death. Must he, knowing the earth as a sphere, see departure as gradual? Had he begun?

The scene just disbanded came to him. Positioned as he always was beyond the participants and just after the idle conversationalist had wandered off, he watched a uniformed nurse caring for a child. Soap bubbles floated above her efforts to entertain him, circles of blue and green and purple. The child watched a colored sphere land on his hand, pause, and burst, leaving behind it only a dampness. "Yes," the young superintendent thought, "that's exactly what the child will learn," what he himself was still having trouble with—relationships, not only bubbles, didn't last.

His thoughts ran along those lines a good deal. The four years working with Dan had been eventful. Begun in a habit of hovering among the gravestones hoping for some smoky encounter with Bryan's spirit, the obsession had grown upon him that he must hear, just once, his friend's forgiving voice. It hadn't happened. But in the preternatural sensitivity his trauma had given him, he saw the Rockwater Burying Yarde yield up an unexpected direction to his life. Dan's retirement brought Zeldon the superintendency and with it the privilege, as he came to view it, of living in the quiet world. His work kept him primarily in the Yarde. A house adjacent was provided, along with an adequate salary. On the opposite side of the road from the cemetery, his windows looked out upon the lake, the Rockwater Town Park, and on extended acreage where wooded paths, ponds and ancient trees afforded him freedom to roam.

How he had come to love the grounds, cicadas in summer, grasshoppers, butterflies, insects. There were chipmunks, rabbits, foxes, coyote, hawks, owls, skunks, woodchucks, and raccoons. Wherever humans slowed down, the animal kingdom exults. He relished it all. There were flowering trees for spring, fire-red euonymous for fall, boxwood in quantity. On some occasions clouds, it seemed, loved the Yarde too much to leave, and so they had a foggy day. Nights ingrained themselves in his memory, watching rippled clouds underlit by a rising moon, grasses waving a gentle greeting or a goodnight. Reliving it all, he drew a deep breath, drinking in the distillation of the day.

It was on just such a day that two schoolteachers came to him cautiously with a request made nervously. Would he guide a group of young high school people about the Yarde with a description of the place and of his own work in it? He appreciated the imagination shown and saw the value of forming young attitudes toward the subject. Those thoughts overcame his first hesitations, and he agreed to try it.

The appointed day turned out to be one where nature could be proud of itself. In preparation for their coming, he combed his hair in temporary obedience and walked the acres in respectful contemplation. Seeing the assembled fresh young faces before him, he understood them to be carrying in their hearts the dust of their dead ancestors. Addressing the youngsters, he riveted their unfocussed attentions by beginning, "First of all, I want you to consider the content of what you're seeing, not the container." Then he mastered their puzzled thoughts by explaining, "For most of you, this is a family gathering, your family, most of whom you've never met. Your own history. Maybe not your parents, I hope not, but maybe your grandparents, aunts, maybe uncles, ancestors. Look around. Say hello to them."

The children were serious then and cast furtive glances about, embarrassed, some of them then more confident.

"OK, that's the content of this place. And then there's the container. The Yarde, the Yarde is supposed to be a suitable container, a good environment for its content. I'll leave it to you to decide if it does its job."

He smiled at them, pleased with their respectful attention. "Take a deep breath now," he said, "then another one. Does it feel good? Nature gives you the air to breathe. It gives you the sky, too. Look up. Look through the leaves of the trees and up high, way up there." They gaped and staggered, enjoying themselves. "Pick out a cloud and watch the wind push it along. That's nature doing its job. Find some water. Look at a tree or two, or lots of trees. Check out the sun. Spot a bird, some flowers, a bug or a creepy-crawly thing. The earth itself, all that's nature, doing its thing. Mother Earth, the container for your ancestors' bodies, what do you think? Is she doing her job?"

Then looking up, he pointed to white pillows floating across the blue sky and called their attention to a copper beech tree that was proving its identity with richly colored red leaves. "Check out the colors, red, white, and blue. It claims to be an American sky. But it belongs to everyone who breathes."

Murmurs of approval, of pleasure, thoughtful expressions moved through the group. "My job here is just to mow the grass," he concluded. "There's soda and pretzels under that big tree over there. Thanks for coming."

Without realizing it, the Yarde Superintendent had established a Rockwater tradition.

\*    \*    \*

Thinking on his pleasure at reminding the schoolchildren of their ancestry, Zeldon made a decision about his nearest ancestors, his parents. Because he cared so deeply for them, because they moved so freely and widely over the globe, and because the Yarde had become a place of meaning and beauty to him, he felt moved to leave a mark somewhere on the globe to commemorate their time on Earth. And where better than that very place? So using a small part of his escrow funds, he had placed in the Yarde a water fountain in his mother's memory. Astride the fountain as though to embrace it, he had constructed an elegant clock tower remembering his father. Symbols governed the young man's thinking. It was easy to see water as the source of his gestation and time spent living out his duration to be appropriate statements. Consequently, the base of the water fountain encased a plaque reading, "FRANCES WADE, Wife, Mother, Ebullient Spirit." The clock tower read, "BURBAGE WADE, Husband, Father, Servant of the Public." Satisfied that he was underlining lives well lived, time well spent, he asked Tap Andrews to lead a modest ceremony before an appreciative gathering of residents, responding to his announcement in the Patent Trader. Thereafter, the bubbling water and the twice-daily clock chimes became a familiar part of Zeldon's workaday world.

*     *     *

He took to running in the early mornings over the pathways and neighboring roads. His young body wanted to celebrate his health, and he wanted his mind to move more sedately through the days. At first he ran because he felt that motion and emotion were linked, so he played a game in his mind, running to stay ahead of entropy and the despair it engendered, to break the immobility of his depression. He ran to create change as a challenge to inertia. He ran to breathe. He ran to create new scenes, new experiences and to distance himself from the pursuing memory of the fire, as a sacrifice to Bryan.

He just ran, and the winds carried for him a secret alphabet; the sounds of nature spoke to him in a private language he could only have learned through his new, stilled mind. He heard new sounds, different sounds that revealed hitherto invisibilities.

During those days, expediency slipped gradually into habit, then preference. Zeldon's life was thus projected off into the future, a life of silent removal from further calamity. One of his college texts had quoted a Frenchman, Alexis de Tocqueville, who visited America in the 1800s, reporting on the national habit of mobility, "Citizens of the United States," he had marveled, "have a habit of building a house in which they mean to spend the rest of their lives. Then they sell it and move elsewhere before the roof is on." Perhaps, he thought given great good fortune with a decision to abandon that instability, there might come a remission of his consuming sense of guilt. He would not be forever governed by the coward in him, and he would face the memory of his father, whose courageous service overseas he had always admired. And if such relief were not to come, he would at least attend his friend's grave and his parents' memory as atonement—a lifetime's atonement.

In a further development, the months following the fire had seen a slow evolution in his personality. What had been an intense immediacy at the scene of the fire became in him a continuing undercurrent of behavior. As he had then felt himself removed from all about him, he came to purposely hold a part of himself in reserve. He came to see the public attending those occasions in the Yarde as Little Red Riding Hoods moving through the lair of the Big Bad Wolf, doing their best to whistle their way through the obvious.

He was helped in that by watching Dan. Dan was like an eagle; he observed everything as though from a distance and from an inner stillness, never missing a detail. He held an unassuming yet commanding posture, mesmerizing to his young subordinate. He had taught Zeldon more than the practicalities of burial and proved to be a wise tutor in many ways. Once early in his apprenticeship when a grieving party seemed to be lost in an excess of dramatic gestures, Zeldon looked at Dan's passive face for guidance. There were no signals, no criticism, no sympathy, only attentiveness.

"Does this ever get to you?" he asked.

"Not so as to throw me off my balance," Dan said. "They're like cats in the night. They all look alike to me." That sounded uncharacteristically cold to Zeldon, not like the man. "I don't mean they don't matter to me, but one thing about living in a cemetery, you don't have to worry about relationships."

That shocked the younger man. How could his mentor be so engaging with others and be so disengaged then at the time of their deaths? Were those only small knots of mourners, taking a brief timeout to recognize they had a past before quickly forgetting it again? "So long, Joe." He would be sent off with his only gift, a casket? Deep compassion, which came naturally to Zeldon and which began early in childhood, showed itself indelibly in the nascent adult. Hence, he was surprised at Dan's remarks. But Dan went on, "Back when they had a future, these folks were still in the game." He went on by way of explaining himself, "Things were important to them, and maybe I could have given them a hand in their troubles. But by the time I meet them here, they're all boxed in." He gave no indication if he recognized his own pun. "The possibilities are over, and their childish quarrels are finished . . . no more of their sandbox warfare. So it's over. We solve our problems, son, one grave at a time."

Zeldon had been both enticed and repelled by that great secession from normal life. Just then, in his bruised retreat from living, he found himself attracted to it, and yet something didn't fit. It was then that he saw the enormity of the choice he was making in that promised career. He had looked at Dan—large, strong, reserved, and lonely. Time for Dan wasn't registered on clocks and calendars but on shrub growth and floral blossoming, seasonal bird songs and ground cover, precipitation and behavior of the sun. It would be a different life.

On another occasion, Dan said to him, "Watch your first impressions of these folks. Impressions have a way of blurring into an attitude then the attitude becomes a posture, a stance. And the first thing you know you have that good old cliché, a lifestyle. So watch that first step, how you sort out your impressions."

One morning, the sun rose in a watery bed of clouds, dimly lighting the curtain of fog hanging in the air. Zeldon shivered his way to work where Dan met him, saying not, "Good morning," but simply "Find a woman." He said it without prelude, and in that utterance, a world of deprivation had been revealed. It all came down to that. Relationships did matter, supremely. With that they began their day's work. After their conversation, Zeldon, in his injured inadequacy, had planted a directive cry deep in his heart.

Hereafter Bryan's cry of "Zeldon!" and "find a woman" would together locate the man's mind. And of course, there was Andrews's "My soul is me, able to articulate myself astride the grass line." His latest insight, would determine his future.

*     *     *

On another midsummer day, a group gathered at a graveside dressed in plain, everyday apparel, minus clergy, minus transportation. They had walked into the Yarde, preceded by the hearse carrying the deceased. When a funeral director had made all ready, the casket beside the burial location and a green tarpaulin stretched over the fresh mound of graveside dirt, he nodded to a young woman in the group. Plain, earnest, confident in herself, the woman began her speech.

"Indians lived here long before us white people took it. If we're going to take things from Indians I would rather we took from them some of their wisdom. For instance, they believed that a dwelling should be a continuation of the outdoors, so their ceiling had a hole in it, where the Great Father could enter to protect the floor, the earth, the Mother, who will ultimately embrace us in death. This is my mother we are returning to nature." She gestured toward the casket. "You also know how she loved you all and how we all loved her."

Others were then invited to tell of their love for the woman in the casket. There were long, emotional testimonies, brief, choked comments, many tears, and many silences. After that, the young woman picked up a drum she had stored in a backpack, shook it, and explained that she would perform a shaman dance pointing in each of the four directions of the compass. "It would," she said, "express respect for the world of nature in which we live and to which we all return." She beat her drum. After some minutes of that, she began a keening accompanied by bendings from the waist, rising with arched back, and shuffling of feet all to the sound of increased wailings and moanings, rising and falling in conjunction with the body motions. That went on for some time in each compass direction, finally falling to a slower rhythm, a lowered pitch and lowered volume until it faded into silence. The group, which had been following that with swaying torsos and weaving shoulders, also quieted. Then they silently and slowly walked from the Yarde.

The transparent ingenuousness of that display moved Zeldon with its honest statement of a perceived fact without embellishment. The woman was dead. Her daughter rocked and reached in physical appeal to be rocked and held by her mother once again as she had been in childhood. It was articulate and without any expectation of the privations being satisfied. It was a stated fact without hope of restoration—a loss, pure and simple. Tap Andrews came to Zeldon's mind with his spiritual sophistication, his highly complex, interrelated convictions, and the emotions they evoked and strengthened. The shamanistic acceptance of finality and on the other hand, the church's high expectations for holding a faith in resurrection sounded a contrast in the dance of death. Zeldon felt stupefied in wonder, like a cow staring at a gate. The seismic power of nature called to him; old structures began to shift under his feet. Social constructs faded, politics receded, and nationhood meant nothing. The land, the sky, and water gained in ascendancy, and he questioned his place in the general setting of his world. He felt he had no place in what the world had made of itself, and yet he would not withdraw from life.

It was only a few days later that he once again listened to the local clergyman conducting his ritual before a grieving family with all the familiar proceedings. For the first time, he recognized that the scene was older than Christianity; it carried echoes of Greeks burying shepherds, Egyptians laying pharaohs to rest, hunters with their gathering wives, cavemen with their brutish offspring. Old, old, distant customs still observed; human loss frozen in time.

A sports car sped by.

What had Andrews to say to those impulses? Zeldon's thoughts became trumpets, introducing a sense that he was designed to be too large for the world he inhabited. Andrews would agree with that. There was that irrepressible frustration quotient that could only encourage further searching. Dan had been right to feel removed. Alienation somehow seemed to make him a larger man. Loneliness would be inevitable, and struggle was a surety. "Find a woman" sounded hollow and unpromising. The loss of close relationships, like that with Bryan, would continue until his own death ended all losses.

No sooner would he settle into his stoicism before so much surrounding inner pain than he would be forgiving himself for wincing before some especially poignant moment. "Can I run my lawnmower over these experiences and cut them all to the same level? That's the path to complete insensitivity. Dan was never like that."

In days to follow and in all of those stupefactions swirling in his head, his consciousness overlapped the situation, but throughout, he insisted that he himself was distinct from it. Despite his reasoning to the contrary, his distance increased. The habit showed itself when one day he met Mrs. Rodgers in the local post office.

"Zeldon, my boy! Oh, I've thought so much about you. How are you, Zeldon?"

"Fine. I'm fine. How are you?" He was able to hide his discomfort and placed his attention on a part of himself that would not enter the dialogue.

She studied his face. "I guess you know I'm having the house rebuilt with the insurance money. It's almost finished."

"Yes." No subject was less welcome to him; he wished she would go away.

"When it's finished, you must come to tea. It would give me great comfort."

A cold shudder made as if to pass through him, but it never quite formed. When she finally left, Zeldon had returned to his remembered self, never having really left it. He had met his civil requirement; he had been polite but never actually been engaged. To his own traumatized center, all such intrusions were borrowed and temporary conditions, not of himself and therefore secondary to him. Those social invasions gradually dimmed in importance. He was learning to regain his damaged self on the far side of every experience.

While he struggled with his slowly forming interior, he also adapted to his daily surroundings. His favorite time was early morning, with night mists staying late among the trees and stones, smoke sculptures in a memorial garden of life/death. A hooded man's figure became a rabbit, a column became a dragon, and flying pelicans became dancing leaves. Soon they were all gone, defeated by sunlight. In the spring, it was the faint/strong smell of garden growth in his nostrils, the earth itself speaking to him softly. In autumn the trees turned to flowers and the flowers to memories.

He learned to love winter, a season that had never been his favorite. On some mornings, awakening, he would find that snow had been falling secretively all night and left his day's work outlined before his eyes. Often unfallen snow, awaiting orders in the clouds, would add to his duties. The lake stretched as a large wet patio out before him. If it weren't iced over, he could enjoy the waves dashing and pitching in their wind-driven celebrations. And when there were no expected burials so the weather didn't matter, he preferred not to know the predictions. The unexamined future made it more interesting, so he didn't check weather reports on his TV.

He also learned the milieu of the dead. His loneliness evolved, and the Yarde became an embracing home. He in turn formed a welcoming feeling toward those interred there. He hated news of cremations, the cleansing fire as they were called. Cremations seemed to signify to him an unfocused death. But chiefly, they brought too much association with Bryan's death. With all those strong marks of individuality, his social position in Rockwater took its place as a peculiarity. He found that acceptable; it gave him the privacy he needed.

The Yarde had its own peculiarities. It was shaped like a shallow snap-brim hat. The hat band circling it outlined the inner road and its accompanying stone wall. Along the wall, Zeldon had placed a row of asparagus plants, his favorite vegetable. The center of the Yarde held the chiming clock and the water fountain he had appointed as his parents' memorial. He meant for the memorial to be a private statement made all unnoticed in public after his own style of understatement. Next to the fountain, he had placed a large boulder, hauled in at some expense to imply to the discerning alone the proximity of a rock and water, quietly making tribute to the town that would locate his parents' memory. Also at that stage of his evolving philosophy, he looked upon drops of water as individuals, living and not specks, droplets flung through space, thrown through time for a short while with no goal and no purpose. Time and experience would enrich that perspective.

The view from under the snap-brim hat that was the Yarde looked out over a steep embankment with an unbroken view of Trinity Lake and the town park before it. Unseen, below the embankment and skirting the lakeshore, ran a paved road coming a short distance from the hamlet over the viewer's left shoulder, and to its right was found the bulk of the Yarde and its two ponds as well as the town park. To the right of the Yarde's circle entrance and across a side road lay Zeldon's residence.

The scene had a personality of its own, as though it had denied its inanimate quality and joined the interred with its assertive presence and why not? The variety of the funerals on its premises revealed the instability of the culture from which they came.

They almost insisted on an external response, if not always on the immediate moment of the occasion, then in the vicinity of its time. For instance, a local murder, a blatant scandal involving racism, a wartime victim's remembrance—each must have its redeeming interpretation. Nature agreed. And so sometime thereafter, the Yarde would show itself in dark clouds, tumbling over each other, scuttling across the partially-hidden moon, and clashing in the sky as they traveled toward their different destinations. Or an angry night wind punished its resisters, trees whistling, twisting, horizontal rain gusts slamming into the figure of its superintendent, obliging him to hunch his shoulders into the blasts.

Other occasions prompted quite different responses. A health care failure, transportation mishaps, poverty extremes, suicides, euthanasia desperations, stillborn births—those sorrows might evoke a compensating encouragement with days of wonder. The ponds might change the nature of the air and the quality of the light—evenings of pink light and mornings of gold. Rainbow autumns, mirrors and mists from the water, and earth music were finding comfort in the beauties of life still to be lived, never consciously analyzed by anyone, only absorbed by everyone like skin tone.

After his style, he stood one afternoon, arms folded and smiled as the sun rose higher in the branches. Shadows worked their way up the tree trunks. There it was again, the environment indirectly, subtly reinforcing its intention not to abandon the living in favor of death. He felt the Yarde showing nature's alliance with human experience, as though to belie the common conviction over its indifference. Always the drama carried on with its raw unassuageable sorrow often coming to those trivial pro forma good-byes with such a spectrum of hopes or lack thereof, a spectrum because the departures were so varied. Some were soft, exquisitely beautiful, and strangely consoling. Wit, not necessarily disrespectful, also asserted itself. There seemed no pattern, only secret circumstances, deeply buried in the private past. They yielded emotional kindnesses and punitive guilts willy-nilly. The public wept and evaded and loved and resisted as their diversities led them. In the meantime when the wind was right, the church bell in the hamlet called for rumination, and when the wind reversed, the Yarde clock told the hamlet of the time. In between, the Yarde told the truth.

One day it told the truth in the voice of Tap Andrews. A young resident of the town, a high school athlete much loved and full of promise, was killed while serving in the Middle East. His family and friends appeared in the Yarde much as they all did, deep into sorrow and mute with their collective shock. Andrews was brief; his prayer rose like a soaring plane climbing on hidden thermals in an unnoticed atmosphere.

Then he concluded, "You're here to mourn. I want to advise you how to do that. Focus on holy dread, the fear of the Lord. Work on these emotions, your *yearnings*." He emphasized the word. "The *majesty* that George is now meeting. A sense of *wonder*, you can only do that in deep solitude." He kept stressing his important words. "George's *astonishment* at what he is now experiencing, how he has *approached the unapproachable*. He's in touch with *transcendent power*, and he's *safe*. He's *forgiven*. Focus on these things."

That was it. He closed his Bible and was gone.

\*     \*     \*

Newer areas of the grounds favored grave markers either level with the ground or of a low profile as though in denial of death. Nineteenth-century stones were more visible, with their romantic sentiments expressed in couplets and statuary. They and the even older markers revealed the presence of a large proportion of children's graves unlike the later years. Wartime years also listed a disproportionate number of brief lives, mostly those of young men.

Absorbing these impressions quieted Zeldon and drove him deeper into his thoughts. His remote detachment gave him impressions and suggestions not always familiar to the dot-com mind. In fact, thought became more a part of him than activity. He had always had, then it occurred to him, distant longings although he had never noted the fact. As any young man would, he had reached for things beyond his grasp and peered at things dark and indistinct. "Thought," he concluded, "is timeless while activity has a terminal point." The boy who had played soccer with Bryan was changing.

Dropping out of college actually accelerated Zeldon's education. He read everything. His college years had met their main purpose, that being the disciplined organization of knowledge, whatever its source. The Rockwater Public Library was an excellent one, and he used it liberally. His musical tastes tended to jazz and the classical. His readings were selective, drawn from serious writers of the past and present. Mrs. Rodgers and her townspeople, decent folk all, could be held at bay, with his experience of them limited. The name of their town, Rockwater, came to have special meaning for him with gravestones and Trinity Lake denoting its origin. Not what the founders had in mind, he was sure.

He rarely turned on his TV and used the Internet purposefully, never for browsing entertainment. More and more, those media persuaded him the world, the larger world was losing its moorings. "All right, give it to them," he decided, "I'll make a world of my own." That was when he allowed his inner imagination more scope.

It was not so much, however, that he could ignore that mantra he had forged from Dan's remark, "Find a woman." Given his age and temperament, he permitted himself to dream. Over some evenings as he surveyed his workplace, he came to observe walkers strolling about the grounds. One single recurring figure marked herself in his mind. He recognized her, always at a distance and many times after dark as the wife of the town supervisor, Mrs. Glover. He had seen her in the village, sometimes in the company of her husband. They both presented themselves as self-possessed although differently. He was all bonhomie while she was reserved and distant, not necessarily spatial. There alone in the Yarde as she always was, she was no different. It was that quality that attracted him particularly—individual, apart, especially at night and after dark.

There were other times when from the corner of his eye he could feel a cloudy perception, almost a sound, almost a movement, no more than a light wind of restless air. One experience though was not so easily dealt with. For several days, he had smelled a scent he couldn't capture. Then there came a clear, crisp sunny winter morning, much like its predecessors. Zeldon surveyed the scene before him, stones long wept over with storms of tears; others faced with stoic heartbreak. He saw an ocean of snow; broken by markers, surfaces rippled with white waves sculpted by the wind. His unusually sensitive hearing picked up a sound of murmuring voices in a remote part of the yard. Drifts of snow piled high in that section muffled sound; he crossed to the area and found nothing. Some days later, it happened again, again nothing. A third time, that day with a strong wind blowing, he heard, carried on a gust of snow, the sound of voices. The tired lonely boy let his mental self-control slide into a manufactured plurality of presences, if for no other reason than to be part of a community.

'He said my skirts were too short. Too much ankle above my shoe buttons,' he said.

'Your ankles showed?' Incredulity sounded in a different woman's voice.

The wind dropped. Puzzled, Zeldon examined the area and found no trace of anyone, no tracks in the snow, no vehicles in the distance, and only whiteness and wind.

The phenomenon repeated itself in the days that followed. Voices but no one was present. There were two female voices, sometimes clear, more often muffled, and occasionally lower male voices as well. The fearsome hallucination became common. Once the conversation was longer.

'I remember my grandmother's breasts. They were like great loose pillows to us children.' It was a girl's voice with a smile in it. Frightened, Zeldon paced the ground, his eyes everywhere but nothing.

'My grandmother never held us. She were harried enough by her other chores that she made no time for our little squirmings.' That was a more mature woman's sound with sadness in it.

'But you did.'

'Oh, I did. Yes, I did.'

Seriously alarmed by then, Zeldon was sure he was having an attack of some sort, a stroke perhaps. He had thought his way too far into the other world. The voices faded but continued. When they returned to an audible pitch, he heard the younger one again, 'My grandmother always wore black. Never gray, only black.'

'I was a breather when your grandmother lived. We all wore black. Hid the dirt.' That was a man's voice, an old man.

Laughter came from the older woman. 'Oh, the dirt, so much dirt, we fought it with a godly cleanliness.'

Zeldon did his best to pinpoint the sound. Each speaker seemed to be in a different location, close together sometimes in midair, sometimes on or in the ground.

The occasion faded to nothing, leaving Zeldon an alarmed and worried man. He slept little in the nights following, had no one to confide in. At first, he avoided that part of the Yarde, but one day, highly nervous and feeling a fool, he ventured into the area. He knew it well. Slowly he traced the ground, studied the tree branches overhead, and read the gravestones, Sarah Lockwood 1793–1821.

One stone defaced by weather had no name. A short distance away another, with a more modern headstone, read, Hope Fancher, 1902–1919.

With nothing to lose but his sanity, Zeldon said to the empty air, "Hello?"

Air movement sighed in the branches; snow shined blue in the sunlight. Embarrassed, he retreated to his pickup truck and ate his lunch. When he finished, he returned to the spot. "Hello?" He couldn't have been more tentative. He walked the ground, restudied the stones, listened.

'Who's there?'

Zeldon jumped, nearly fell backward. Shaking, he remained silent. He dared not answer, in part because there was no one to answer to. The sound had come from a particular grave that time, several yards from his earlier focus. "I'm losing my mind," he said to himself but trusted his senses enough to approach the grave and read the stone, Harold Foster; 1912–1943. Expecting trickery, he looked about him in every direction, sure he was about to make a fool of himself.

"Who is that?" Zeldon said. It was an enormous act of psychic courage. "Who is that?" Then he waited.

For a long while, there was silence.

'I'm Harold.' Silence again. Zeldon was too terrified to move or speak. 'Are you a newcomer?'

Zeldon watched his hands shake. Not wanting an answer this time, he repeated, "Who is that?" It was all he could get out.

'Are you new?'

That bordered on low comedy. "Zeldon. My name is Zeldon."

'I'm Harold. As conversations go, this isn't exactly spellbinding.' Zeldon felt the irony of that. 'Tell me, Zeldon, where do you lie?'

"Lie?"

'Come now, Zeldon, let's upgrade this talk. Where do you lie?'

"Where do I lie? I guess you mean lie down. I'm not lying down."

Now occurred the longest of the silences.

'Zeldon?'

"Yes?"

'Zeldon . . . . you aren't a breather, are you?'

"A breather. I breathe, yes."

After that, there was nothing. Zeldon remained too distraught to make any attempt to reenter his monologue/dialogue. It entered his mind that he should quit his job immediately, get out of this work. It was too isolated, too lonely and the damage it could do had just proven itself. The trouble was he had seen no sign of that coming. He liked the privacy his work afforded, the exposure to the elements. Beyond that, he wasn't sure what he was doing. Social isolation had taken its toll. That phenomenon would work its way into Zeldon's mindset for an extended time, becoming more vivid then less so. Was it whimsy runaway imagination, the result of social starvation, that dipping into the fringes of derangement? With never a decisive, conclusive resolution, the shadowy presences would become a factor in his history.

But he could go mad, he had thought, might be doing just that. He knew how to do it. If he were to speak to tombstones, he would cut away his anchorage in reason. He *was* speaking to tombstones, for god's sake, and worse, the tombstones spoke back. He tried avoiding the suspect area, spent more time in the vicinity of Bryan's grave. He would not quit his job, only get a grip on himself. For a week, it worked. The hallucination became a troubling memory, appeared to be a one-time delusion. The breather began to breathe again.

Then it happened once more.

'Zeldon.'

A voice, a sound meant only for the wind, a private utterance Zeldon had no reason to hear. Clearly that time, it flew into his hearing unbidden, telling its secret without invitation. By it, he was to learn things he would rather not know despite its absurdity.

'Zeldon, is that you?'

Zeldon crossed a line that day. Lost in his pathological solitude, he admitted that imagination filled in the blanks in everyone's world, why not in his own? And children gave voices to their stuffed animals, animating them. But that wasn't enough. There had to be some more civilized, rational approach to that kind of lunacy. Otherwise it required an admission of babbling lostness. Reaching further, he pointed out to himself that lots of sane people speak to their pets. A dog for instance—he could easily talk to a dog. That was it, he would talk to his dog but a dog that talked back? Can a man talk to his dog and presume his answers then hold a conversation? What the hell, he was desperately lonely then. What was the harm in sharing his deep solitude with a handful of interior exchanges?

He answered Harold's fine courtesy.

"Hello, Harold."

# CHAPTER 3

It seemed to Zeldon that a cemetery is a landscaped plot of ground where the human rape of nature is denied, but also a place where nature is avenged. The rapists are gathered to her bosom and held fast. Zeldon's particular clientele were not many, as graveyard occupants go, the contents of about eight hundred plots spread over four acres. It seemed to him the containers appeared to be disturbingly porous. Harold, for instance, managed to emanate from his allotted tract to an undefined area closely surrounding it. Above ground, his space grant reached somewhat beyond his stone marker and plot but only a few feet beyond. That range was for spirit-extension only, of course. Physical remains stayed where they belonged. He was after all only toying with his mental creativity. That day, Harold seemed to dwell above his headstone.

'Zeldon, I can't believe this. I can hear you.'

"Is that a good thing?" Zeldon wasn't at all sure about that, being torn between fear and wonder.

'I don't know. It's never happened before.'

"I should think not." Another long silence filled the time between them. Lengthy silences appeared to be frequent.

'Are you really a breather?' Harold sounded more unsure of himself than Zeldon did.

"I am. I breathe. Are you really dead?"

'Yes, good and dead. I don't know for how long.'

"About seventy years from your grave marker."

'Has it been that long? It seems like yesterday. For us time has turned into just a progression of postponements. All Saints' Day, Easter . . . may be a question of readiness. Who's to say there has to be a sequential progression in resurrection. Don't ask, just remember that time is no longer a factor in our world.'

"I can't do this." Zeldon was overtaken by the insanity of his condition. His private game was becoming too real. He ran shaking to his distant pickup truck and raced from the Yarde. The short drive to his house took no time at all; he still shook as he put the key to his front door. Inside, he flopped into a chair and sat, ashen-faced, sure he was losing his mind. But unable to act as though nothing had happened, he rose, paced the floor, muttered to himself about his fears, and promptly returned to the Yarde, that time on foot.

He went straight to Harold's stone in the southeast section. The southeast section was filled largely with older markers, but Harold's stood squat and low nearby.

"Harold, Harold, are you here?"

'He's resting.' He heard an old voice from a short distance away, male. Zeldon had heard it once earlier when the two women talked about their grandmothers. 'We're not always on call, you know.' The voice was rich and gravelly with a smile in it.

Zeldon suspected that mental turmoil would become his constant state. Sure enough, things had gotten out of hand. But the foolishness had its comforts, another person, another spirit. So determined to play his new mind game, he accepted that he was only meeting a new dog in the neighborhood. "Who are you?" he bluffed.

'I hope you'll be able to tell me that. Harold says you're a breather.'

"I guess I am."

'Well, are you or aren't you?'

"Yes, a breather." He might as well accept it; that was his designator.

'I'm glad to meet you. We're all very excited about you. I'd introduce myself, but I don't know my name.' Zeldon's head swam. 'Some of us have lapses in our remembrance. It's time, you see. Time does uncommon things to our memory, and we have these lapses.' He sounded sad about that.

"I'm Zeldon."

'Yes, we know. Maybe you'd have a look on my stone, Zeldon, and tell me my name. It would mean a lot to me.'

"Where's your stone?"

'It's over here.' The voice moved in the direction of a slender piece of sandstone, tipped at a precarious angle and weather-worn almost to indecipherable smoothness.

Zeldon knelt down with his face close to the stone. There were several like it in the Yarde, with names erased by rain and lichen and smoothed by wind and sand. Faint irregularities were visible on that one, but no tokens could be read. He ran his fingertips over the surface as if to read in Braille. Where the name should have been was no imprint at all. In the place of the dates, he was able to feel the hint of two digits to the right side of the span. "Eighty-eight, that's all I can make out, the last two numbers of your death year, '88."

'Of course, '88. That's when I died, in the blizzard of '88.'

Zeldon was becoming used to those extravagant circumstances, and that worried him as much as anything thus far. But there was no time to drive them away.

"You died in the blizzard of 1888?"

'Froze to death . . . but you can't make out my name?' There was enormous disappointment in the question and resignation.

"I'm afraid not."

'We'll call you '88. God meant for us all to have a name. Now you'll have a name.'

Zeldon dropped from his knees to a sitting position on the ground. The new voice, a woman's, caught him entirely by surprise. Was he in a crowd of ghosts? What was going on? He tipped his head back and slipped into a deep sadness, mourning his lost sanity. He was no sooner invested in that emotion than it was taken from him.

'I'm Sarah. Hello, Zeldon, it's wonderful to be able to meet you.'

He had had enough and gave no reply.

'Don't be afraid, Zeldon, we be friends. And you be not losing your senses. We be real people . . . or we were real people . . . no, we be real people, aren't we . . . ?' She stopped then apparently addressed the nameless male presence. 'You must have a name.

It's been too long a spell not to have one. You will be called '88.
It's too hard to have no name.'

''88.'

'Yes.'

''88, It has a certain ring to it.'

'It has. That's settled then. You have your name from your
marker. That's as it should be.' The voice, by its tone, turned back
to Zeldon. 'So now, Zeldon, we be real people. We won't admit to
anything less, will we, '88?'

''88, that's me, '88. Yes, no, no, we won't admit to nothing else.
I have a name!' The old voice trembled with delight. ''88!'

'I need rest now,' Sarah's voice said. 'But we can talk with a
breather!'

'Me, too, I must rest. I've got a name!' The marveling voice
trailed off into his personal plot. Zeldon sat on the ground before
the eroded marker, his hands in his lap, the picture of a drunk
wondering where he had lost his hat. He truly felt as confused and
lost and overwhelmed by events as any drunk could do.

In the weeks that followed, Zeldon succumbed to the communal
invitation offered by the presences. He felt it was safer to invest
himself in what was happening than to precipitate a mental crisis
by challenging it, so he took the line of least resistance, opting out
of a fight for normalcy.

As soon as he made this decision—a long-term surrender he
knew it to be—several comforts closed in to reassure him that
there might be a life for him in his reclusiveness. His dubious
social position in Rockwater became resolved in his mind. Of
superior intelligence himself, he had rebelled at being identified
as a blue-collar gravedigger by the townspeople. That no longer
mattered. His social group would not be found among them in
any case.

Probably the greatest advantage stemming from his new
world was the renewed hope that it would lead him to some union
with Bryan, which in turn could bring him to the forgiveness he
required and a recovery of his self-respect.

Those whispering walkways of the Yarde would tell him of
intimate histories. He would have converse with beings ready,
obviously needy, for soul-to-soul exchange. By degrees, he would

learn to live in other precincts and become a man not afraid of groping thoughts and circling apprehensions. Every mind carries on an internal dialogue; he knew. He could at last give identity to the other half of his internal dialogue. Was that not integration of the profoundest kind? Reasoning further, he pointed out to himself that the very stuff of stories was environment, scenery, exposure, solitude. It shouldn't be surprising then that those life stories, stories of the Four as he was to call them, should grow from enciphered stones, his daily companions. As the days became weeks and the weeks months, he came not to mind living in his ghost culture. Slowly asleep and awake, he began to appropriate a tendency to find certain intangible things holding more reality for him than the visible realities. The young man knew better, however, than to slip into complete mysticism. He took seriously the hard immediacies that governed so many lives without allowing them to dominate. He saw the workaday world as derivative, a created thing with a Source to whom it is accountable. He had but to accept influences from earlier times that might preserve important attitudes trendy people never meet. There wouldn't be any more foolishness about talking to his dog.

*    *    *

But it wasn't to be easy. Things were serious then, desperate even. Bryan was dead and voices claimed a place in Zeldon's mind. He was finding it hard to look in a mirror. In that severe outline where impressions were solidifying rapidly, there was no avoiding it; he was being forced to choose—suicide, madness, or a rock-hard determination of what world he would call real. And so it came about that Zeldon committed himself to the Yarde as his lifetime home. From there, he would hammer out his most personal notions—nothing derivative, no borrowed philosophies, his own and only his own. His starting point was the plain fact nearest at hand, the fact of death. Everyone would die. If he lived long enough, the entire town would come to him for their send-off. No sophistries could spin the truth away; no fogging could hide it. Dying presided.

Not all his relationships were of the amorphous kind, however. There were substantial ties as well. Once he reached his new perspective, he found it easier to sympathize with his fellow residents of the present time. It wasn't long before that capacity for sympathy was called upon. One day, a crestfallen man wandered into the Yarde, seemingly aimlessly. By his appearance and manner, that was a man accustomed to having others serve him, but that day, he approached Zeldon in an apologetic way and said, "I wonder if you can help me."

"Any way I can," said Zeldon with all courtesy. At that time, he had no idea that the solicitor was the famed attorney and investment manager Dalton Sumner, who had made a fortune in the paper trading of the 1990s.

The stranger introduced himself by name and Zeldon knew his record and place in the public eye. Sumner said, "My wife has died, and I . . ." Controlling himself carefully, he went on, "It would mean a great deal to me if she could be buried under that copper beech tree over there." He pointed to a specimen of great age and beauty on the crest of a prominent rise in the ground, the specimen tree near which Dan was buried. The view overlooked Trinity Lake and an expanse of sky that amplified the emotions it evoked.

"I'm very sorry about Mrs. Sumner, sir. I can see why you would choose that spot," Zeldon said, "but you see why it hasn't been used before. The root system of the tree makes it difficult to excavate without doing a lot of damage."

Walking over to the spot, Sumner studied the ground then looked up at the tree branches. "No way, are you positive about that?"

"I've considered it before. It's pretty out-of-bounds. You see how it's surrounded by other plots."

The dignified man knelt on the location then sat awkwardly on the ground, gazing forlornly into the distance. It was as though a lifetime's achievement was erased by a woman's death, and the titan of commerce was reduced to the humble survivor before him. Zeldon was moved by the sight and walked around the tree, studying the area. Sumner was sitting all the time on the damp ground.

"Get up, Mr. Sumner, let's look at the problem." The two of them prowled the area, viewing the spot from every angle and conferring together over the desirability and the difficulty of a solution. In the process, they shared a growing recognition of a mutual love of natural beauty. Confidences flowed, confidences that under normal social circumstances would never have been permitted. Sumner spoke candidly about his wife's irreplaceable companionship and Zeldon countered with his affection and admiration of his parents and of their deaths. "Thank you for listening, Mr. Sumner," he said.

"Call me Dalton," answered the older man.

"Thank you." Zeldon avoided any chance of embarrassment by adding, "I think there's a way we can manage this, if you're willing to accept an idea that's just come to me. If I excavated at an angle under the tree roots, I could create a two-plot space, one for now and one for you at a future time. Would you approve of that?"

Sumner jumped at the idea, after which, Zeldon, with great skill and delicacy, developed the site without damage to root system or to surrounding plots. The episode resulted in a lasting friendship.

A further advance in Zeldon's depositing his ideas in local history came when as a result of his effort with Sumner; he purchased from the local nursery three copper beach trees of some advanced size and had them planted in a row facing the lake. He made sure they were large enough to be limbed above a standing man's head so as not to block a clear view of the water. Accomplished without announcement and without interpretation, it was one of his ways to plant symbolic statements about the Yarde for those equipped to uncover his secret enrichment of their environment. Trinity Lake, born of three ponds expanded into one lake by a dam, would have its living echo in the leafy trio standing opposite its shoreline, deciduous representatives frequently changing in color, hue, leafage—reminders of passing time which spoke to the populace much as the clock and fountain pointed to birth and tenure.

And so Zeldon found himself living in two worlds, his live man-dead man dichotomy. Following on that admission, a strange release came over him, a quirky disrespect for life's dramatic ending yet with a residual seriousness over the somber business. All his future effort would be to overcome, truly escape the fear of death. Achieve that and all other fears, being secondary, derivative, would fall away. He couldn't know his specific future apprehensions, but he might dare look them in the eye once that supreme challenge was brought to heel. Of course there was arrogance to his quest, but the fear of fear drove him on.

He was helped by the voices. They served a dual purpose, first in the immediate reminder of their below-the-grass-line status but also in the way they allowed a gradual construction of tested values. Death had acted as a filter for them, straining out everything that was insignificant. An early example of that came one morning in March when the rumbling voice of '88 sounded without preamble.

'I was a peddler in my time.'

"How did that come about?" Zeldon was in the habit now of picking up conversations in mid-thought.

'My horse, my horse was the cause. The ornery cuss never was any good. Bucked and shied all the time and nipped.'

"That made you a peddler?"

'Hold on now. I'm getting to that. You damned breathers, always rushing things. Where was I?'

"Peddling."

'Peddling, yes, my horse threw me, broke my consarned leg. Laid me up lame for a full winter. It was my horse told me that my body wanted to be fat.'

"So you became a peddler."

'You're still pushing me, but yes, it was then and there I took a mind to take up peddling. Make my living on my feet, walking, for the rest of my days. To hell with horses.'

"A thin man."

'I died an old man, but I had strong legs and a straight back. Ladies liked that.'

"Were you a ladies' man?"

'I walked three states on a one-year route. Had quite a few rewarding stops, if you get my meaning.'

Zeldon the breather at that point needed a breather. He was learning too much, too fast, not yet easy in his alternate dimension of living, if that was what it was. '88, however, was just warming up.

'I could boast of a big nose. It gave me authority.'

"Like Cyrano?"

'Who?'

"A man with a nose."

'Where was I?'

"Peddling."

'Can openers were a fine product. It was just about the end of the war, I think, when cans came in thin steel. So somebody right then invented the can opener. For me, they were easy to carry in the pack, and everybody wanted one.'

"Which war, the Civil War?" Zeldon still had trouble placing those dwellers of the past in their proper time slots.

'88 showed his scorn for the question by ignoring it. "I never carried canned goods, too heavy. And the women did most of their own canning anyway. Thin steel and can openers started to change that though. I sharpened knives." It was clear the old fellow, not having had one for over a century, needed a willing audience. He proved to be a loquacious spinner of tales with many to tell. Working to the north and east of Rockwater, he seemed to have known people over a surprisingly wide area and known a good deal about their circumstances.

'Safety pins were a good seller. They came in a little earlier. The ladies loved them, and I could carry a couple of hundred in the pack. Came in about the same time as chewing gum, about the time of the gold rush, I think it was.' A chuckle sounded then a lengthy pause. 'The gold fever left a lot fewer young men on the farms. They left behind some golden farm girls for me, if you know what I mean.' There was another happy growl. 'That's why I never went West for my gold. Got it right here, New York and Connecticut. Some golden memories from Massachusetts, too.'

'Your past was my future,' came a woman's voice. They had a way of doing that, the Four, dropping into a conversation as from nowhere. 'For us, the biggest improvement in fifty years were the invention of the new oxen yokes. They made burying the rocks easier. And shoe ties were a wonder to us, about 1814.'

'Muskets, 1814,' said '88.

Zeldon was sure there was some time wisdom in that overheard exchange but not certain of what to do with it. Before he could give it any thought, he lost the moment when the voice went on, 'Yes

yes, but we had our comforts, too.' The voice was Sarah's, Zeldon recognized it then. 'The fireplace were the center of everything. It were where we gathered. We got warm there, cooked our food, beautiful conversations. When I were a girl, I sat by the fire with my father, and he told me the stars were left over from making the sun. Sun-scraps, he told me. I went outside to see, and there they were, millions of sun-scraps.' The piece of spirit poetry brought silence and prompted more. "He said feathers would fall from angels' wings and janitor angels would sweep them up along with stardust and sprinkle it over little girls like me.'

'Mother told me the moon was a hole in the floor of heaven,' whispered Hope, introducing herself to the exchange. Not to be left out, Harold added, 'The harvest moon meant more to us than harvesting.' All that encouraged Sarah to pick up her narrative again, 'Took our baths by the fire when we were alone and dressed there.' There was a pause, 'Made love there, too,' yet another silence then 'We read by the fire and wrote letters, those of us could write. And always the talk, that were good, the talk . . .'

'I guess we came out of the womb talking.' Sarah grew quiet at that, and '88 added, 'I calculate all the reading and writing weren't for unrefined people.'

'When I was a breather, I never knew unrefined people.' That was the young voice that had talked with Sarah about the scandal of exposed ankles. 'Except once my father called my mother unrefined. That was because she stopped wearing her tightest corsets.'

The Four had crept up on him with their numbers. At first, it was the startling discovery of their presence then the fear of surrendering to a dialogue with unseen people. But then they were the four of them, becoming bolder in their conversation. In for a penny, in for a pound, was Zeldon's new attitude, and there he was chattering away like a fifth ghost at a Halloween party.

'They were whalebone corsets, and they made mother breathless, even faint.'

'Hope is our springtime girl.' That was '88. 'We have a rule that we can be ourselves, warts and all. But she likes to keep us from too much rough talk.'

'Well, you see, I never had my white hour with a man and my parents brought me up to be a lady. So you might say I have tender ears.'

"What's a white hour?" Zeldon showed his ignorance although he had an idea.

'We don't ask rude questions of the girl,' interjected '88, 'that's rough talk.'

"I understand," said Zeldon. "It's refreshing to know you, a pleasure." Rewarding, too, he thought, those very different dwellers in time. "I'm sorry you weren't given your full years."

'Yes well, Daddy's dream for me just didn't happen. He meant that I should marry well and never have housemaid's knee. Mother's dream was that I should vote. For myself, I wanted to be a poet. But . . . the influenza scrubbed it all.'

"I'm sorry, my dear. I'm very sorry." Zeldon felt as though he were talking to a child although Hope wouldn't have been much younger than himself. And there she dwelt on the lip of eternity.

'Thank you. You're nice.'

"Tell me about yourself." He felt an unjaded air about the girl, clean, unused. It left him glad to be in her company, expectant over what she would have to say.

'It's a sad story, I guess, but it isn't over. My family was rich, thanks to Daddy. He made things in factories. I'm not sure just what, iron things. We lived in New York, on Park Avenue in a big house. The servants said it was about the best house in the city.'

"Was it a happy house?" Zeldon was having trouble sorting out the mixture of tragedy and buoyancy in the child's telling.

'It was very strict. I laughed a lot, and I loved to play, but it was mostly with the servants. Josie, she was the cook. She was the best.'

"Why?"

'Well, she giggled, and then I learned to giggle from her. With the others, I could laugh, but I only giggled with Josie.'

"About what?" He probed the fresh sensibility like a vein of silver.

'Anything. Mother got angry once when a guest left his doily on a dessert plate and the butler put blanc mange over it. Josie giggled in the kitchen when the butler told us. So did I.'

"I'll bet you were a good kid, fun to be around."

'Yes, I guess so. I used to dream of the man I would marry. When I was sick, I did that a lot. He was like a beautiful ghost waiting in the future.'

"What a lovely dream."

'I was sure he'd give up being a ghost and become real and marry me. But I never met him, and he stayed a ghost. And now I'm one.' Her voice trailed off, not laughing then.

"Not to me, you're not. You're young and lovely and full of the future."

'You think so? You think so?'

"I think so."

Of course there was the inevitable question of what things were like in Zeldon's world. He sensed it would be wise to describe the twenty-first century piecemeal, so as not to overwhelm those delicate spirits with an avalanche of challenging facts.

"We walk much less than you did. We have machines that carry us about so that we can go greater distances and much quicker." Harold murmured his agreement.

'Is that a good thing?' A frequently asked question, that was one from Sarah.

"Well . . . it's a mixture, I guess. We miss a lot of the details around us."

'That's not a good thing.'

"No."

'How do people pick flowers from a machine?'

"We don't, much." There were murmurs of disapproval over that.

'I wouldn't want one of those machines.' That was Sarah again.

'Daddy had one of them,' Hope said cheerfully, 'when I was sixteen, a Chevrolet 490. He said it was a cut above a Ford Tin Lizzie. But of course we had few flowers around us.' She was less proud of that. Uncharacteristically, she went on quite volubly, 'It was called a 490 because it sold for $490. But Father wanted electric lights on his show-off machine. And he didn't want to break his arm cranking it, so he bought the one with a starter. He didn't have to go out in the rain to start it up. These good things cost $60 extra, so we never called it the 490 the way everyone else did. We called it the 550!'

There was applause. Zeldon noted that he could hear the clapping of hands from identities that were mostly smoke, but he went on, "The machines, we call them cars, put us much more in touch with other places and other experiences. In fact, our world has grown very small."

'Very small?' '88 sounded puzzled at that. 'It was pretty big when I walked on it.'

That was getting hard for Zeldon, but he ventured on. "We drink coffee from South America in cups that come from England. We wear clothes that were made in Italy and watch moving pictures on Japanese machines. We write letters on another machine made in California. We eat Australian lamb, French pastries, and Chinese soup. You get the idea."

'I don't. Write letters on what kind of machine?'

"A computer—don't ask."

'More,' said '88.

'More,' Sarah said that time.

"All right, it's pretty fantastic, really. We've seen the far side of Mars, and we've walked on the moon . . . ."

There were shouts of disbelief at that. 'Walked on the moon?' gasped the little romantic from a century ago.

"Really, and we've pretty well wiped out diphtheria and smallpox and typhus and polio."

It was Sarah's turn to gasp. 'Smallpox and all those things, truly?' Everyone caught their breath, so to speak at those reports. 'It sounds like heaven.'

"Not quite. We kill each other by the millions, wars and a new thing called genocide."

'What's that?'

"Picking out a race or a group and killing them all."

'Killing them . . .Why?' That was really a question from all four of them, but Sarah asked it.

"I can't really say why, Sarah. We're proud of our knowledge, but we live in the jungle."

'I can't . . . I can't . . .' she stammered, 'Zeldon . . . sin and salvation, heaven and hell. There be a symmetry there, all is gathered in a balance. It looks like to be that you have tinkered that away . . . never to have that balance again. Zeldon . . . a blood-soaked globe . . . it be a darkness caused by them who control the lighting . . . Maybe it be good to be dead.'

Hope's tender voice whispered, 'It looks like a world full of wonders.'

But Sarah, still in shock, wasn't finished yet. 'A world filled with wonders, but none of it is like to tell you how to live. Or what you should live for? We Four live in displacement, but you're not alive, you're just undead.'

After that, no one spoke. Harold must have known some of what they had just heard, but he, too, remained quiet. Zeldon sensed their departure, one by one, realizing he had overdone it with too many facts too closely distributed. But maybe not.

Shaken himself as he felt the calamitous absence of his shadow-friends, Zeldon realized that he needed an image of each of the vaporous people. So he gave '88 a bald head over a big, stocky, shaggy bear of a man with lots of energy and charm. His beard would look like a brush pile after a snow flurry. Probably he would have a sharp eye for a person's weakness. He was, after all, a traveling salesman. To Hope, he gave cascades of golden blonde hair, shy. He remembered her telling the others of being afraid of her mother's gramophone, thinking there were little people in it doing all that talking and singing. She would think thoughts born in morning mists and evening shades even before her death. Harold, the son of Dust Bowl heroes, Great Depression parents, and a hero himself of the Great Adventure, obviously deserved a muscular body. He had indicated as much. Lingering over the impressive Sarah, he envisioned a lovely figure hidden in voluminous clothing, high button shoes, and a white bonnet, plain without ribbon, and with a proud carriage. Her face he left in shadow, but he thought of it as beauteous, unmarked by smallpox. A keen intelligence shone from her despite the shadows. Their shock and sorrow over his revelations left him longing for some way to bring comfort to their hungry waiting for a spiritual integrity.

The smoky friendships developed rapidly, more soberly then, giving Zeldon an increasing sense of richness in his previously isolated world. In time, they became presences, which could not be eradicated, archetypal, recurring, and defining. Sarah was clearly significance, wrapped in a veil, '88 was élan, Hope was visions and dreams, and Harold was perspective. He saw their indicated identities inscribed on the four stones like thoughts draped over them much as Salvador Dali's clocks, undulating histories of four small people. He came to need them, to benefit from them. And he was coming to admire their spiritual courage, made so necessary by their being held as they were in their purgatorial suspense. That made them additionally lovable. They showed him how courage purchases a triumph over anxiety. Yes, he needed them.

# CHAPTER 4

### The Yarde Superintendent

There were, of course, the other relationships of a more substantial nature that also developed. Those mourners who would appear in the Yarde, visiting gravesites, absorbing the atmosphere, or walking about the grounds aimlessly, continued in their habits. Some of them he recognized over time and developed with them a nodding acquaintance. Mrs. Glover didn't exactly become a relationship as much as continue to be an observation. His curiosity deepened, but he kept his distance. Good manners and her diffidence ensured it.

In his midnight wanderings, he had long before become friendly with the nighttime world overhead. Stars, clouds, and the dark became companionable. Like the raccoon, he developed a night vision. He walked quietly, paused often, and breathed in the stillness. What soft night sounds there were became old friends— the wind, of course, but also the low-pitched murmur of distant voices, the scratch of a dog moving among dead leaves, and a sleeping bird's peeping. On that day, he had mowed the grass and could smell its perfume, the earth with its green hair cut short. Such was his way of thinking. Gradually, stillness had become his nature, and he revealed himself to be one of those rare sensibilities who hears the background music of creation.

Sometimes the music took form. On that particular night, he saw the inscrutable figure standing among the trees that lined the lakeshore. For ten minutes, he watched her silently under the black night sky. He liked the way she held her head, proud, alert, and willing to deal with the world. Tiny jewels of light galaxies away winked down on her silhouetted outline. At last, she stirred, moved like a child, clearly taking pleasure in sheer movement, indulged in it unselfconsciously. She had seen him.

"I'm sorry," he lied, "I didn't see you."

After a silence a soft, whispering voice said, "In a place of death it's only prudent to be self-effacing," and she was gone, still a part of the dark.

In the weeks that followed, he saw her again several times. She came only at night, always alone. By her behavior, she continued to show her seeking privacy. He respected the need and kept himself at a distance. Never did she acknowledge his presence although on some occasions, she must have known he was there. In fact, like moths circling one another, they floated into and out of one another's presence without acknowledgment. One stormy night, a roaring wind whipped leaves around the graves, sending them upward, upward over the treetops into the upper spaces until they disappeared in the dark. She strained upward herself, ready to follow. Was she reaching for death, was she reaching for life? It was never to be revealed because in the shadows, she saw his deeper shadow, standing, watching her. He disappeared, but she knew who it was.

They never spoke. On one evening, he didn't see her slender figure, but knew she had been nearby from the scent she had left behind. That time, she must have seen him without his knowing. He came to look on her as a regular among his breathing constituents. The time would come when their breathing would commingle.

*       *       *

In Zeldon's work, agility and comfort meant a lot. A favorite pair of boots needed attention, so one cold December day, he walked to the hamlet carrying them in for repair. The shoe shop was located below a small coffee chain store with its aromas swirling about the doorway. As he descended the narrow stairway below it, Zeldon was struck by a different scent of leather, pastes, and polishes. The whirr of a brushing wheel continued well after he stepped up to a scarred counter, obliging him to wait. He knew the stooped figure at the machine had seen him enter. After some delay, the sound stopped and with his back still turned, the operator snapped, "Yes?" Only then did he turn to face his customer.

It was a basset hound face with sagging eye pouches and generous jowls, stared into the dim lighting of the workspace. "What?"

Undeterred by the brusqueness, Zeldon nodded toward his boots on the counter. "These need help."

"Everybody needs help." The short shape of an overweight grizzly bear lurched into range and lifted one boot from the counter. Turning it over, he showed the same disdain for the pair as he seemed to feel toward his client. Zeldon wondered how the curmudgeon stayed in business with the public relations style. Lifting his face for the first time with a beatific smile lighting the disaster of his countenance, he agreed, "Yes, they need help." Without another glance at either goods or customer, he said, "That'll be forty-five dollars. Ready next Wednesday" and went back to his wheel. Soon it was humming away, announcing that there would be no negotiations. The deal was done.

Two days after he met the shoe man, a younger man about Zeldon's age sprinted into the Yarde while he was making his first round of the grounds. "Best way to warm up a cold morning," he huffed, jogging in place. Running shoes and sweats told what he meant.

"It's cold," Zeldon agreed.

The young man stopped his motion and looked around. "You work here?"

"Yes."

"I'm just starting a running program. Would you mind if I made this my turnaround point?"

"Be my guest."

"Well . . ." The youth grinned, looking around. "Just for two minutes a day." They laughed together, and Zeldon decided on the spot he liked the fellow. On several succeeding occasions the runner would appear. He and Zeldon greeted each other briefly while his guest huffed his way through their exchanges. Zeldon referred to him in his mind as The Jogger.

By Wednesday, when he returned for his boots, he had come to refer to the repairman as Shoemacher. Not everyone deserved a title. The Four, of course, and then those two. It was hard to say what accorded that honor to some and not others. Something intuited.

When he entered Shoemacher's shop, Zeldon felt at home despite the mixed signals from the proprietor. It may have been the smells. Added to the earlier shoe smells, there was today the strong smell of cigars. Funny, he hadn't noticed that last time. It must have been the unexpected welcome or non-welcome of the shopkeeper. That morning the basset hound features were arranged in an extravagant welcome. In his absence, Zeldon must have met some kind of testing and been found acceptable.

"You are the young man who works in the Yarde?" The man spoke with a heavy accent, Eastern European it seemed, maybe Polish.

"Yes, that's right." Zeldon wondered if Schoemacher had asked about him from some next customer. Shoemacher said no more. Zeldon paid his forty-five dollars, offered his thanks, and left.

On a later occasion when Shoemacher called him by name, Zeldon thought to ask how he knew him. "I knew who you were by the dirt on your boots."

"My boots?"

"They have deep dirt on them, not street dust."

"Deep . . . ?"

"Two types of soil, Rockwater loam and Rockwater hardpan. You are either a well digger, I say, or you are the Yarde man. Well diggers are out-of-town people, and I see you walk by many times." His glance lifted to the small windows looking out onto the street, windows that showed only passing feet.

Startled, Zeldon said, "You should be a forensic detective!"

"I am a foot detective."

No more was said between them, but Zeldon found himself examining his footwear more closely and wanting an excuse to learn more about the strange man.

Among the many events of those days, an unconventional circumstance arose when a different elderly man with a Central European accent approached him with an unusual request.

"My wife and me, we came to America, the Great Melting Pot. But we found the heat it was turned down under the pot, so it was not so good." He scratched his head, sniffed loudly, and went on. "Then she got sick, and we got worried. So I asked my brother in Hungary to send me some dirt from our farm."

"Dirt . . ." Zeldon wanted to help the old fellow. He was having trouble telling his story, but obviously wanted it told.

"He sent the dirt. Now you have to put my Schmiza in your dirt." He gave a long look around, avoiding Zeldon's eyes. "I want . . . I want to mix my dirt with your dirt. Now she has to go in the dirt." Moved as he so often was by those idiosyncrasies, Zeldon shook his hand in both of his own and promised that could happen the next day. It did, and the young man received the blessings of the ancient widower for the few months he survived his spouse.

Sometimes sympathy didn't suffice. He came upon an elderly woman staring at a marker without moving for long minutes. He approached her, expecting another touching story when the woman spoke without looking up. "He lived in a medicated twilight for eight years. I was a stranger to him while I acted as his nurse around the clock." Then she glanced at Zeldon. "Everyone praises doctors. Goddamn medicine is what I say." Duly shocked, he waited for her to explain herself, and she did so gladly. "If someone, some old somebody you love has a crisis, make sure you don't call 911. It's a sure way to send them through hell before they get lucky and die." Without another word, she picked up her flower basket and departed, not looking back.

In a more poignant moment, a woman won his sympathy from her unusual appeal. It was to be only one more of those early accommodations, a kindly deviation from the commonplace as taught to him by Dan.

She entered the Yarde alone and on foot one cold autumn morning. "Sir, can I speak to you?" She had loitered nervously among the stones before speaking, and her question was asked tentatively.

"Yes, good morning."

"I don't know how to ask this. I hope you won't take offense." Her cheeks were wet with tears, maybe from the cold, maybe not.

"I won't take offense. What's on your mind?" He did his best to appear unthreatening. He certainly didn't feel himself so.

"My son has died," she said it simply and without follow up.

"I'm sorry. I'm very sorry."

After a moment's effort she continued, "My son is fifteen . . . was fifteen years old." Another pause while Zeldon waited. "My son had." She nodded at her capturing the right tense that time. "My son had bone cancer for a long time." Zeldon registered with his features his complete attention. "He couldn't stand. And he wanted to stand up so badly. But he couldn't. And he tried so hard."

"He must have been a courageous kid."

"He was. And we wanted him to stand as much as he did. But he couldn't." Then she gave up and let her tears flow.

When her sobs had subsided a bit, Zeldon said, "Is there anything I can do?"

"My name is Samantha Gibbs." The woman inserted that information gratuitously as though it might make a difference. "Yes, actually, that's why I wanted to speak to you. There is something."

"What can I do?" As willing as he was to be cooperative, Zeldon was taken aback by her request.

"Will you bury him standing up?" The pleading look on Samantha's face was enough to reduce the oddness of her wishes. "Can you . . . could you . . . could you dig his grave . . ." She stifled a sob. "So he could be buried standing?" Then she hastened to add her assurance. "No one will be at the burial. Just Harry, my husband, and me. The marker is a small one. It's all strictly private." She stood leaning toward Zeldon, frightened beyond speech at what his response might be.

Zeldon's mind raced. He knew how life was porous and grieving was filled with intermediate states and no man's lands. That was a chance to ease some of her pain. He also knew how his preparatory work for an interment was seldom observed; he could make the excavation as for a normal burial, only deeper at one end. At the moment of burial, he would do as the woman asked. But first, there would have to be a collaboration arranged.

"Who's your funeral director?"

"Murphy and Soberman."

"All right, don't say anything about that to them. Just ask Mr. Murphy to call me." He was sure Murphy would roll with the punch and keep his silence. "After I've talked to Murphy, I'm sure it will be all right. I'll let you know."

He could see the woman's emotions were adjusting. Her sorrow might be marked with a secret gladness for her remaining days. As things turned out, it happened just that way, and Zeldon had two grateful friends for many years. Her parting words to him were "Anyone can dig a grave, but you gave us a piece of art. We love you for it."

Kindnesses like that, silently and privately bestowed, evoked nevertheless a growing respect among a slice of the public. As time passed slowly despite his wish for anonymity, Zeldon became known as an agent of healing, to the degree that such sorrows were ever assuaged.

Later, much later, Samantha was quoted in the town's gossip as saying, "He gave us a place of beauty during our lifetimes and a location to honor us after our Great Transformations!" Indeed, the waters of the lake taught him its silence, and what words he spoke were filled with poetry. His days were suffused with so much public sorrow that he knew he would not escape his own. It seemed that others hadn't enough happiness to spare

After the upright burial experience, he had his next extended conversation with one of the Four. That time, it was with Sarah.

'That were a kind thing you did there, Zeldon.' Her voice came to him on a morning when Samantha and Harry had come to the Yarde to thank him once again. As they walked away hand in hand through the gateway, he felt her presence before she spoke. The fragrance of lilacs—that in late fall—told him of her nearness. It happened that way often, that he sensed their persons even when sometimes they were silent and merely came and went without remark. That time, however, she seemed to want to talk.

"I felt sorry for them." Slowly, unobtrusively, Zeldon's identity was being formed and not by psychic devastation alone. Admiration, appreciation, and finally love became tributaries of emotional input that shaped the young man.

'Tell me about children,' said Sarah.

"Children? You mean now in my time?"

'Yes.'

Zeldon cleared his throat self-consciously. "I don't have much experience with children. I guess you know that. But I know they're TV watchers, every one of them."

'TV?'

"Pictures in a box. Pictures that move."

"'Pictures that move?'"

"Yes."

'Pictures that move . . . .is that a good thing?'

"If they move to any purpose. Most TV pictures don't."

'So why do they watch them?'

"I don't know. It's kind of a . . . I don't know."

'Well?'

"It's like alcohol. It's kind of a way to quiet down your brain."

'Like whiskey.'

"Yes, like whiskey."

'Ah, poor souls, so reduced. And they could have been alive.' She considered that for a while and then said, 'I wonder, Zeldon friend. I am in need of your help. Could you one day do me a great service?'

"What's that, Sarah?"

'My dying came in giving birth, you see, and . . .'

"You died in childbirth?"

'Yes, yes, I did.' And they both went silent at that, then Sarah sighed and said, '"My womb, the source of life, brought me my death, left me like blown chaff.'

Softly, respectfully, he said, "In 1821."

'My burying stone tells me so. Not like poor '88. Poor people couldn't afford a stone in my time,' she went on as though she needed to explain. 'In my last hours, I asked Mr. Lockwood to get me one, and he said he would and oh, how chuffed I were to learn that he had.'

'Yes.' He could feel the pathos of her story although she made no point of it.

'What I hope, Mr. Zeldon, sir, is that you might find out for me if my child lived.'

"Oh, I see. Well, I . . ."

'I can give you aid. I lived right here in Rockwater on the Salem Road. My husband were named Horatio Lockwood. He were the son of Major Ebenezer Lockwood. We owned a store in the Rockwater Hamlet.'

"I should be able to learn something about that, 1821?"

'Yes, 1821. That be the date when my remaining years were lost.'

"And you want to know if your baby survived."

'Yes, I do. It would mean a lot if I could know. It all starts in the womb, you see, expectation and dread, the two opposites. Then when you come into the big world, the battle starts. And it lasts till you reach these gates. I lived in expectation right to my last day, and ever since, I've lived in anxiety. I need to know, you see, if my baby became a child, even maybe a man or a woman.'

"I'll find out, Sarah, I'll find out. No matter how long it takes me, I'll find out." It registered with him that there had been cells dividing in her body, possibly giving life at the loss of her own.

'Blessings on you, Mr. Zeldon.'

Using the Internet, the local library and church records, Zeldon easily found that one Horatio Lockwood was father to a Seth Lockwood whose mother, Sarah, died in childbirth September 9, 1821. Seth Lockwood grew to raise a family of his own and lived to the age of seventy-three years. Two days after their conversation, Zeldon gave those particulars to Sarah and was moved to hear her happy sobs carry away on the wind.

# CHAPTER 5

## The Town Supervisor

Phil Glover served as Rockwater's town supervisor. He was elected on the strength of a remarkable campaign speech, short and persuasive. "Rockwater is a small town," he began, "it's not a suburb. A suburb is just a layer on the outside of a city, but a small town is a microcosm. It holds a little of everything, and that's what we are, a bit of everything. We're a small town.

"Now I'll tell you why you should elect me to supervise our town. When I moved here ten years ago . . . that was before I married Catia, one of your local girls, a real beauty . . . . but I needed a cleaning woman to look after my bachelor quarters on Stone Hill Road, so I put an ad in the *Patent Trader*. A woman called the next day and said she was interested. When she told me she had her own transportation, she put it this way, 'If I were to say I needed wheels, you wouldn't want me, but I've got my own.' Right away I said to myself, any cleaning woman who speaks in the subjunctive, 'If I were to say,' can't be all bad. So I hired her over the phone. And she was as good as I guessed. She knew distinctions. She recognized the difference between clean and dirty. She knew subtlety, she hunted out the dusty corners, and she liked light and washed every window in the house. In her second week, I gave her a raise. In her third week, she burgled my house of half my valuables and disappeared with them." Phil waited for the gasp of sympathy to register then he continued.

"Here's why I tell you this story. I want you to know I make mistakes. But I know distinctions, and I know subtlety, and I like to carry out my work in broad daylight. I may not speak in the subjunctive, but I won't rob the farm. I hope you'll vote for me."

They did, with a plurality of eighteen per cent. Phil had been in office for four years. He was fiercely friendly, which showed him as welcoming to the confident and made the shy envious. Having a winning political style, none of them knew that beneath the man's presentation of himself lay a void, darkness. Like an actor practicing sincerity, he had his image under control. They did know that he possessed a robust sense of self. In truth, it was the picture of a character positioned not up to his context or the faint echo of an idiot king placed on a magnificent throne.

"What do you know about this kid that took Dan Shipley's place at the Yarde, Wade, Zeldon Wade?" he asked Velma Nelson, his town clerk, as he burst into her office one morning.

"You know him. You've seen him lots of times." Velma was surprised at the question but not at the abruptness. Phil Glover had a hard face, self-satisfied, and he knew he held all the cards over the town employees. It wasn't easy to earn a salary under the boss.

"Of course I know him, but I want to know him better," Phil said.

"What's he up to now," thought Velma, "wanting to know the Yarde man better?" Aloud, she said, "He's OK. Non-political, you know that. Keeps to himself, you know that . . . lives pretty quietly in the Death House." The Death House was what townspeople, certain townspeople, called the Yarde superintendent's residence.

"Tell me something I don't know." He lit a cigar.

"He's strange. People say he talks to himself in the Yarde. But he's good at the job, even better than Dan. He's got the place looking like a park. He put in a fountain and a chiming clock at his own expense. You must have heard about his talks with the school kids. They're a high point in their year. And he keeps out of people's way."

Phil knew all that, but he needed to know if the gossip agreed. He knew that the Yarde clock chimed once at noon and once at midnight. When the wind was right, it could be heard in every corner of the hamlet. It had come to define the boundaries of the hamlet, much as Cockneys are defined as those within earshot of the Bow Bells of London. Wade was more well-known than Velma seemed to indicate. He walked out, puffing thoughtfully while Velma told herself there was soon to be a new twist to town affairs.

*    *    *

Zeldon was surprised later that same day to receive a phone call from the town supervisor. His job was too remote from town life ever to have had any significant exchange with the flamboyant politician. Phil Glover was known to live well and boisterously on his retired wealth, gained from some obscure career on Wall Street. In his four years in Rockwater, Zeldon knew little of the town, which was not surprising given his chosen detachment. So a request from Glover to come to see Zeldon in his Yarde house, as Phil called it, was startling.

The next afternoon, his visitor approached Zeldon's modest home with a critical eye. When he entered, however, he was surprised to find it well furnished with artwork, oriental rugs, and antique furnishings. He looked about, nevertheless, as though he were examining a town property, which it was. He noticed classical music playing in an adjoining room, violins and things. Despite Glover's presumed authority and despite the absence of any hint of deference accorded to his privacy, Zeldon felt no discomfort over the invasion. He lived simply, but his furnishings showed the advanced taste of a person who knew the value of a rich context. In his inwardness, the younger man was developing self-confidence.

Phil controlled his surprise. "Not bad," he conceded as his eye fell on polished wood floors with their coverings and the tasteful surroundings. "Not bad." He sat without being invited to, lit a cigar without asking, and got straight to the point.

"Wade," he said. Zeldon realized immediately he was to be treated like an employee, much like a minor member of the road crew. "Wade, I need your help." Already Zeldon was disinclined to give it. "We have a chance to do the town a big favor, and you can give it a lift."

Zeldon nodded tentatively.

Suddenly the supervisor stood and said, "Can we walk across the road and look the Yarde over?" Again he headed for the door without waiting for an agreement. As they walked, he continued to talk. "It's like this . . ." Phil's voice boomed through the quiet. "The town is growing, and we all want to keep its flavor as it grows. So many of these towns grow into little urban monsters, you agree?"

"Sure."

"Good, a growing town," he went on as though he now had Zeldon on board for whatever unmentioned scheme he had in mind. "Needs growing services, but they have to be introduced carefully. It needs planning. You're for good planning, aren't you?"

"I am." Zeldon felt the condescension.

"Good man. I thought so." He cast a sharp glance in Zeldon's direction. "Some of us are working to make a gift to the town, by expanding the town park." Who would pay for that gift he didn't say. Obviously, it would be the taxpayers. "We mean to put in a couple of soccer fields and a ball field. Enlarge the pool, that kind of thing."

"What can I do?" Already he felt uncomfortable, fearing what might be coming.

There Phil fixed a fierce glare upon his host, walked over to a grave marker, unzipped his fly, and began to urinate on the stone. "It means some property adjustments."

To Zeldon a tombstone was an irruption in the earth that sent up a piece of the past. The crudeness of that act, obviously meant to intimidate him, had the opposite effect, but even so, he felt the power of the man, showing just a hint of menace.

Confused and nervous, Zeldon said, "What kind of adjustments?"

"We have to move the road."

Instantly Zeldon knew what the man was getting at, disinter the graves for a soccer field. Before his discomfort set in, it registered with him that the town would never put up with it, and he eased his posture a bit. But then he tensed again.

"I know there's going to be opposition. There's always opposition to a visionary project. But I think we can handle that, and that's where I need your help."

"You mean to relocate the road and re-inter some of the burials?" Zeldon disguised his anger.

"Most of them, but not far." He nonchalantly waved an arm. "We can buy the residential properties to the west of the Yarde and just shift the whole shebang over a hitch."

"Move the Yarde a hitch."

"Right." Phil could see the guardedness in Zeldon's remark. "Not much gets done without breaking some eggs. So you can see where you could help a lot with your support. I know it's a new thought for you. Think it over. I'd like your help." His stare told Zeldon that was more than a request.

Needing time to organize his outrage, Zeldon said nothing, and the supervisor walked back to his car after a bone-rattling handshake.

*     *     *

"How can he do this? Move the Yarde a hitch! Just like that! Dismember all those past residents and put a bulldozer to the history of these people for a soccer field!" Zeldon stopped, surprised at himself. He had only recently come to that town, two years with Bryan and Mrs. Rodgers and a few more than that at the Yarde. And yet he was finding his young world splintered by the callousness of that lunatic idea. Cheap progress, it struck him, without a thought for the rich treasures so willingly surrendered, progress.

Reason began to return after his first outburst, but the outrage didn't lessen. He recognized that it struck directly at his shock over Bryan's terrible death and his parents'. Then he was driven to remember that pain as well. They left him with no more than a large inheritance. That pitiful legacy, money only, he had put in escrow with the help of his father's attorney. He would make his own way. Irrationally, his young, self-pitying mind felt the injustice of his abandonment more than the obvious suffering of his parents.

Zeldon had come to Rockwater already feeling as one left out of events, making his gravitation to the Yarde not altogether surprising. Lives once lived were real in their time. In memory, did they deny that once-upon-a-time reality? Solitude, careful study of local history, the arbitrary assignment of then-current habits—those meditations gradually added flesh to Zeldon's imaginings and his substantial characters. No doubt they were once real. Reassigning that reality fell easily into place. And so, what would appear delusional to lesser imaginations, pulsed with personality in Zeldon's private-most moments and flavored his more rational thoughts. Thus, did he absorb his strangeness and gradually the shadowed past melded into his real world. Living without love and abandoned, his role in the fiery death of his friend by his own cowardice, he felt had left him crippled and feeling unworthy. But his time in the Yarde, at first only an envelope of emptiness to him, might heal all that damage. Spirit friends and solitude had begun to do their work. He hadn't found the woman Dan had referred to—that was hard—but it could well yet happen. He was almost happy or saw the prospect of happiness. That in turn told him he had been dreaming small.

Early risings began most days with their own reward. The morning sun would light a beautiful world of trees and water, shrubs and grazing deer, but all its beauty would be shamed by the wonder and the splendor of the sky. Vivid colors streaked into one another, contesting among themselves for highest honor in their spectrum. From the horizon, gold would flow across the sky and spill itself at Zeldon's feet. Often he would stand allowing the grace of the moment to flavor his being. Such days had come to give him a sensation of something undiscovered, something yet to be understood that lived there. Whatever that was, it was at his fingertips, waiting to be embraced. Where else could a life yield up its secrets if not at that frontier of time and space? His plan was to probe the history of possibly richer times by way of his ephemeral spirit friends. He would read their attitudes and their values. He would follow their personal stories as they were following his. He wouldn't settle for a culture without substance. He had just begun to root himself in those stable values of yesterday. Order, the old order, and a place in it for him were beginning to look possible. And then Rockwater needed soccer fields and a larger swimming pool.

A long, interior silence began, grew, then prevailed in him. The violence subsided, and the fear lost sway. He was larger than that. His young strength took its first step toward mature power.

Without his awareness, all his lonely honesty over suffering had readied him for such a move. The boy brought into focus the hidden man. The Yarde would not move over a hitch. That town's past would rise from its grave and defend itself.

Even in his adopted lifestyle, Zeldon still held the common attitude that a cemetery made a gesture in the direction of sobriety. He was startled then after he had prepared himself to give the bad news to his vaporous friends at what greeted him on entering the Yarde. He heard the unmistakable sound of laughter as though from festive catacombs, unruly and joyful.

'We'll hold a Halloween convention,' Harold was saying with laughter in his voice. 'There's a town out west called Tombstone. That's where we'll hold it. Send invitations on death certificates.'

'Not on Halloween, on All Saints' Day,' corrected Sarah, warming to the mood.

'Dress will be formal, shrouds only. No naked bones.' Hope was giggling then.

"What on earth?" thought Zeldon, not noticing his peculiar reference. "If they had been alive in later years, they'd be giggling over hiring the grateful dead. What's going on?"

'Free drinks,' said '88.

'No drinks. Mr. Lockwood and me, we had a neighbor, he would pour whiskey down his neck. Said it would make him think happy thoughts.'

'I 'spect it did.'

'Didn't. Whiskey were found wanting. He took his own life.'

Hope had something to offer on the subject. 'Daddy told me all about alcohol. He said it was bad.' Then to add to her impressive sophistication, she said, 'And he told me about stomach dancers.'

'88's reaction to that was open-jawed silence. The boisterous mood was becoming quieter, so he, wanting to keep the party going said, 'Not me, the weather got me first.' Then he pushed the jollity further. 'Peddlers drink. Sometimes bein' out of it is better than bein' in it. It swallows up the miles and makes the next step easier. Why, I recall—'

'Daddy said you can always tell a drinker by the way he walks.'

'Consarn it, I know a thing or two about walking. The first twenty miles loosens up the ligaments then you start out.' He went on as though he had had some of his beer already, 'I had a prize pair of boots one year, they made me float from Hartford to New Haven. They got wet so I hailed a wagon ride to Milford. Drank beer all the way then it appeared I'd left the blamed things back along the road. Went back on foot in bad shoes and found some good soul had sent them on to me in Milford. Lost the damn things . . . sorry, little queeny . . . lost 'em. Walked in that poor footwear for three days, looking for 'em.'

'OK,' Harold persisted, 'that can be the motto for our Tombstone party: Do or die.'

"Can I come?" Zeldon spoke up, "I'll bring the wind chimes."

The Four had been so engaged in their banter they hadn't noticed Zeldon's presence, and all murmured their pleasure. By then he could easily reform a quartet into a quintet.

'Why, Mr. Zeldon, we didn't know you had come to our world for a visit.' Sarah paused then said with some embarrassment, 'We be a quiet lot mostly, not part of your prating classes. Before you came, only knew the privations of this place. We could go for months without a word being said. But make no mistake, there be a life of the mind below the grass line.'

"I know that, Sarah. I surely know that." Then hating to dampen their revelry, he felt obliged to include them in the threat to their peace and told them what he had learned. The effect was immediate.

'"This be my resting place," declared a distraught Sarah. "Move me to move a road! That can't be so. That can't be so."

"It won't be so," Zeldon answered. "It will take some work, but we'll fight it."

'Oh, I hope so. How I hope so. When I had my birth pains, those ones that took my life,' Sarah continued, 'Mr. Lockwood were out clearing the cartway. He had to keep up his patch, you see. Our roads followed the old Indian paths through the woods. The men widened them and kept them clear and that's how we paid our taxes. So these roads be ours as much as they be anybody's . . . I were bleeding and calling for help, and my only help were outside building a road. He came in at last and then went for help, but it were too late. And I died from it, I did.'

"Don't worry, Sarah, don't worry." Zeldon was sorry that he had shared his information and had ended so abruptly their happiness. "I'm going to do some things."

She answered sternly, 'We be a handful of dust, but we have met our material cares and transcended our sorrows before. We will again, and you will help us. We look on you, Mister Zeldon, as a living image of the Lord's benign watchfulness.'

"Yes, I will help, Sarah."

'You will tell them that it takes one acre to support a cow in pasture land. And here, on one acre, we crowd how many people? Hundreds and Harold tells us, if we be burned instead of buried, we fit into a two-quart can. You have to admit, we be inexpensive. You tell them that, friend Zeldon.'

Friend Zeldon wasn't sure the argument was compelling to modern minds, but before he could respond, he was interrupted. 'You say you will do some things. What kind of things?' That was '88's gravelly voice. The proud, battered old man conveyed his strength and resistance in its tone.

"I don't know yet. Talk to some people, make some noise."

'I don't see you as a noisy person,' said '88. 'But ask them if they don't think a man's grave should be a private place. Scribble it on my clean stone, "Knock, please."'

'I won't be anxious. Zeldon will see to it,' said Hope.

'88 consistently showed a solicitous manner toward the girl, whom he referred to as the wee ghostie, and he revealed it then. 'You're right, lassie, no fears.'

'This is our home. And it's a beautiful home. The flowers in the summer and the clean snow in winter . . . and the stars all year . . . No one will spoil our home.' The girl had wanted romance in her young life. Denied it, she had obviously found poetry, and the wanting had pulled her in the direction of unexpected discoveries. That being the way hope works, thought Zeldon, she was aptly named. He was touched by the child. On the Internet, he had examined the times of her life and of her death and discovered the nineteenth-century practice of painting mourning portraits of loved ones after their deaths. At that time of hers, the custom still survived among some upper-class families. The deceased, if female, was often shown holding a rose—upside down. He imagined such a depiction as the child Hope.

He felt the ambiguity of the line between himself and those spirits. They *were* real to him with real characteristics and real needs. As he had earlier conjured up images for their vaporous beings, he felt they needed further fleshing out, so to speak. It had struck his fancy one day, when he was envisaging them, to convert their characters to music. Hope was easy. She was a love ballad, soft and tender. In his brusque intensity and love of life, there was '88, the embodiment of the percussion section of a pickup band. Sarah was refinement, a string quartet, and Harold, rational, wide-reaching, and somewhat conflicted, Harold was a concerto. A knowledgeable onlooker following the same whim would have called Zeldon himself a symphony, complex, eventful, and working toward resolution. Yes, he was coming to recognize the spirits. And yet there remained the uncomfortable gulf. He could accept them as private companions, but could he take their needs public? It was a further test of his commitment to living on both sides of the grass line.

# CHAPTER 6

## Lazarus in Limbo—The Four

During this period of his growth, Zeldon welcomed and relished the Four. Their versatility enriched his days. He had come to feel that he could unearth their spirits by delving into his own. Thus did the surreal become plausible for him.

### Harold Foster

'Think of how many secrets this place holds. It's a five-acre secrecy farm.' That was Harold, lending to Zeldon his young wisdom. It was a windy day in mid-summer, six months after they had met, and single conversations between each of the Four and their new friend had become common. Zeldon, knowing full well he was conversing with voices long extinguished, chose nevertheless to continue that, his personal idiosyncrasy. More substantial relationships had a tendency to evaporate through death or departure.

"I know about that," he replied, "I only had to look at a few of your stones to find proof. There's the epitaph that reads, 'Joseph Kavanagh, MD, Office hours 8:00 a.m. to 4:30 p.m.'" Pretty obvious that was a tribute placed by an angry wife. It would have been appropriate for her to have used the one that reads, 'I meant to put the world right before I went to bed.'"

'Yes, and the dictated scolding, pretty clearly put there on instruction, "I told you I was sick!" We've got a lot of ways to send our messages.'

"Um hmm, Peter O'Toole said he would like to plagiarize his dry cleaner's business motto and have carved on his stone, 'It distresses us to return any work that is less than perfect.' It's an attitude worth pursuing. And now you're sending me yours. What's your message, Harold?"

Without hesitation he answered, 'I've only got one thing I'd like to say to people if I could talk with them. I didn't get to be too old, but I know now what I'd like to teach in my history classes. Did you know that I majored in history and meant to teach it? Well now, I can teach my one thing by saying it to you. If you have a tough mind and if you know something about history, you will know there will be some things from the past that are superior to your present. And you have to say so. You weren't born yet when I died, so that includes you. Say so. But brace yourself, Zeldon. When you speak out, brace yourself. That's it. That's my history lesson.'

"I hate to tell you this, but we don't always go by what you early birds learned. Our popular wisdom right now seems to say that money is muscle. And you should have seen our celebration of the millennium. There was a five-minute party, everyone worried about computers crashing, and then it was over, not a peep. The dogs barked and the parade moved on."

'A thousand-year milestone and that was it?'

"Yes."

'You people are doomed.'

"Maybe, at least here with you and the others, I can have some history at my fingertips."

'Toetips.'

"Oh, right."

'But it kind of denies my sacrifice, doesn't it? Idealism handcuffed by power. You above-grounders. You drive yourselves with no kindness to your better natures. Then I bet you find your success is strangely empty? Surprise! But I guess that was true of a lot of us non-breathers. It's all in the moral capital of your time. Some build it up by living by the golden rule, and others spend it down with their indulgences.' Then in the next breath, rather without a breath, he added, 'What's the date?'

"July 22, 2015, why?"

'No reason, I just wanted to know how old I'd be . . . what, I'd be ninety-five years old?'

"Sounds right."

'Most likely, I'd be dead anyway. But I sure could have done a lot of breathing that I missed out on.' He chuckled, paused, and then grew serious. 'Your world seems inconclusive to me. When you die, you don't end, you just seem to fade. Nothing decisive, nothing resolved, just the fadeout. My world, at least, ended decisively.'

There was no comment from Zeldon. After a moment, Harold spoke again, 'I feel sorry for people who can only talk to the ones they can see. All my buddies disappeared one by one, but I kept in touch with them till I fell, too.'

"Shot down."

'With my 50-calibers chattering. We had a song we sang in battle with those guns firing, "If I fall among flowers, I don't care if I die." That might have been a little silly.'

"Flowers or not, you went down a hero."

'Not so sure about that either. The brave ones, most of them, are brave because they're ignorant, unimaginative. They can't see what might happen.'

"But you could."

'Well, the world was playing ideological hardball and I was glad to be part of the side that said, "No more." I even shot down a Focke-Wulf that day. We went by the old rule, "Leave things better than you find them."'

Zeldon didn't mention his reservation about the Focke-Wulf pilot in some cemetery in Germany. His vaporous friend continued, 'If I had had time to do my doctorate in history, I know how I would approach it. You know how many possibilities stand before a person, especially a young person. Well, we know only the one that was fulfilled. And those other lost possibilities are never a part of history, or their history. We never know what wasn't chosen or what didn't happen.'

"Yes, that makes history sound pretty thin."

'And it makes hindsight pretty sterile. So I would like to have done more research on those conjectures over the what-might-have-beens either in individual lives or more generally. What do you think?'

"I think we lost a good man when we lost you, never mind shooting down Focke-Wulfs. I'm privileged to know you."

Harold had come to appreciate those exchanges with Zeldon, as had the others in their small coterie. They loved his intellect—a razor-sharp mind—and his emotions, perhaps most of all his instinct, an instinctive gentleman. It gave them the recognition they had not enjoyed since death quieted their relationships. Yes, they had one another, the few of them, but Zeldon was their reacquaintance with the affairs of the world conducted in sunlight. In that he gave them a lost vitality. The young flyer knew the shadow people were knit together by Zeldon's presence. The warm regard he provided them changed their isolation into an admittedly amorphous community.

Harold decided that was a good time to tell Zeldon of their collective appreciation. 'Have you ever wondered why you talk with only a few of us among all the belowgrounders here?'

"No, I hadn't thought about it."

'Why not? The place is a beehive of activity. Well, not exactly activity, but you know what I mean.'

"Ummm."

'I mean this is a heavily populated place. Don't be put off if it's also a self-contained place.'

"All right."

'Well, we've been talking together about this. By we, I mean us Four. We know that you want most of all to hear something from your friend Bryan. When I say this is a self-contained place, I mean it's managed under its own rules, and we don't know what they are. We know that things happen that can't be explained, eyes worn by years of watchfulness and tears. And things don't happen that we would like to see, like Bryan giving you a nod. All we know is that we seem to need a quiet time all too ourselves before we are aware of anyone else, sort of a time of seasoning maybe.'

"Think so?" Zeldon was all attention. He needed to hear that.

'What do I know? I just think so.'

"Seasoning, seasoning. Wow, seasoning." He couldn't get his mind around that way of thinking. But it could make sense in that nonsense life he was living. And Bryan's distance was caused by his needing a time of seasoning? Again, nonsense but maybe?

'So . . . you have a few friends here. That's because we find you simpatico. We call it soul chemistry. You see, we find our social relationships with more sensitivity than you're used to. The Great Leveler has made us a true democracy, no social distinctions. So to avoid boredom, we have to search out companionship on a more refined basis. With more subtlety, we're more nuanced than you are. That's soul chemistry.'

"You're right. You're different from us breathers."

'Well, there's no turning back now. A pickle can't become a cucumber again. I suppose I'm yesterday's wisdom, and yesterday's wisdom is like an old bicycle . . . nobody can think what to do with it. I wish there were some way to tell living folks what we know. I wish I could remind everyone how we can form our individual beliefs, but we need a deep culture to give them a structure. Preachy, I know, but we need more than our own generation alone to pull that off.'

"I'm learning that."

'I just had an idea to add to my history lesson. This is for you to pass on, OK?'

"OK."

'Don't feel superior to the past. Try to remember days of your childhood. A few details you will remember. More you will forget. History is like that. You only catch a small fraction of the truth then subtract what you can remember but choose to leave out and the fraction diminishes further. You know very little of my time . . . nothing of my life. So I'm the past to your people. If they have some subsequent details, like computers and such, that I couldn't know, are they my betters? Just think ahead into your future. There are billions not yet born, many of them stupid or selfish who will be your betters and mine, just because they were slower at getting born? The outrageous condescension of posterity . . . they call it period ego. Be careful, future. Can you tell somebody that?'

"You bet I will."

'Good, you know there's a difference between out of touch and beyond reach. We're just out of touch. You haven't met everyone here because some of us have been cremated, just urns full of ashes, really, and many more seem to be in deep sleep. Some of the locations are only remains with the true occupants elsewhere.'

"Elsewhere?"

'Elsewhere.' It was all he would say.

## '88

'I be weathered and pruned like an old apple tree, but I still could tell the part of the world that would listen that the body be a unfit instrument for the powerful music in a man. I didn't make that up myself, but it's what I'd say to the women I met on my rounds. I'd only see them once a year, so I always wanted to leave them with a thank you, something to remember me by, except one time, I was gut kicked by a mule. Laid me up during two months of my best peddling weather. Had a good nurse, had her own way of bringing back a man's manhood, if you get what I mean.'

That was '88, holding forth about his romantic life before his atop-the-grass friend. Zeldon was establishing for himself an uncommon attitude toward events, past and future. He was aware of the history of his own time. But '88 being gut kicked by a horse—how important for the future is the echo of a lost event as trivial as that? Important to him then, but the present, who cared? It was doubly diminished and insignificant, once to others even then, once again for those over a century later. Who cares? His entire life? Who cares? And all of us together, what importance have we to the stars, the galaxies, time? Who cares?

Zeldon cared. And he was sure it didn't end there. But as the Four kept saying, time would tell. In the meantime, '88 was going on. And Zeldon was listening, caring.

'Something else I rewarded them with, about a woman's body, the mouth be a chamber from which there flows great wisdom and unbounded foolishness. It can smile and it can devour. There . . . you thought I was coming out with something bawdy. Ha, ha, no shortage of that neither, but not all the time. In its right place.'

It was clear the old man was acting up for Zeldon, to their mutual good cheer. "I guess you had quite a few lady friends on your circuit," he said. Zeldon, who was largely reserved, could be playful as could his cloud friends. He laughed aloud at the old rake and encouraged him to go on with his yarns.

'Angels in waiting, you might call 'em. Summat like us here in the Yarde,' he added with his gravelly chuckle. 'Ah well, a dirty mind is a continual feast, as they say. Some of my lady friends was real ladies, though. If I was to meet them today, it being a formal occasion, I wouldn't be introduced as plain old '88. I'd be more proper, be presented as Eighty-eight.'

"Did you deal with proper people then?"

'Oh, yes yes indeed. My favorite part of the one-year circuit I trod was the prosperous Connecticut River valley . . . actually, from Litchfield, high up on its ridge to Hartford and then south down the river flatland. Beautiful country it is, whole land scattered with pretty villages. Beautiful homes, farms, and some beautiful customers, if you get my meaning.'

"I know a bit about that country. Tell me what it was like in your day."

'I'd whistle my way about the circuit. I was a good whistler, and people knew I was coming by my whistle, but the air on the Litchfield ridge was fit to make the lungs sing songs, which I also often did as I trod my route. I swore my songs could be heard on the wind all the way to Hartford, fifty miles to the east.'

"Ahem."

'Well, maybe in a hurricane. What is Hartford like now, in your time?'

"As a city, not so beautiful. Bit of a slum city, really, on hard times."

'You be foolin' now.'

"No, Hartford is Hardford nowadays."

'What happened to the factories, the hospitals, the famous schools and museums, and the money businesses, banks and insurance companies, and what about all the rich farmland to the east and to the south down the valley?'

"A lot is still there, but times have changed. Some of the old ways have disappeared."

'I dasn't believe it. Hartford was said to be the richest city in America. The railroads was making my trade harder, and the canals before that, but they made cities like Hartford full of bounty. Is the old Meeting House Yard still there then?'

"I think so, but it's not a part of the center of the city."

'Can it be believed? The Meeting House Yard made a square with the old church on one side, then the market space where farmers brought in the best food in the land and then came the side with the old pillory and jail. Only the jail was used in my time. The last side was the slave pen, but always it was a place to be *against* slavery, abolitionist country you know. Home of any number of prominent leaders, Harriet Beecher Stowe was one. Do you know *Uncle Tom's Cabin?*'

"Of course, everyone knows that."

"Be that a fact?" Without comment on his illiteracy, he changed the subject. "I had me a guest membership in the Seven-copper Club, lots of famous men and some not so famous. A body could belong if he could tell a good story."

"Seven-copper Club?"

'Don't interrupt . . . 'cause it cost seven coppers for a half mug of flip, no more allowed. The owner being Moses Butler, he set the limit and sent the patrons home every night at closing time. Said, 'Go home to your families.' You got to remember our time passed less in a hurry than your time. We all had time for Moses Butler and plenty of time left over for going home."

He paused as though taking time to drink a draft of flip. But he wasn't finished yet with his recalling. 'They made me a honorary member because I had all the news and gossip over such a big territory. I was the first to report to them about the new cooking stove. Things took a while to get around in my time. Weren't necessary to cook in the fireplace after that. Box stoves came soon after that, for heat, you know, and life got easier all 'round.'

"You're an interesting man, and you lived in interesting times."

'Can't say I have no history, really. Humiliations, sometimes, and failures. Maybe with a few tiny battles won, though.'

"Tell me some of those."

'I sold a thimble once to a woman who had all her fingers bandaged. A pair of scissors to a blind man.'

"Those were triumphs?"

'They was. They was people I saw being unkind to the ones they lived with. So I skun them for their trouble.'

"OK, sort of a travelling court of justice."

'It did some good now and then, and the years went on. I'm sorry I never enjoyed that little space between business and the grave called retirement. That could have been a rich time. In my walking days, I still had a lot of fire in the furnace for them that wanted to be warmed.'

"I know you had to be a robust old bird."

'No query about that. One of my angels in waiting, I forget her name, a great featherbed of a woman, large breasted, large bellied, large thighed with an expansive spirit to match. It would be hard not to love whatever-her-name-was. We made good women in my time, and some men to mate them. I knew another hardy-type fellow, a cattle drover he was, walked the farmers' cows to New York City at $2.50 a day . . .'

"Cows, four-legged Weedwackers."

'What's that?'

"Weedwackers, they're small machines that cut grass and weeds. I'm just making a little joke."

'Machines that . . . .huh. As I was saying, $2.50 a day, that was good pay, men called $1.00 a day high pay . . . anyway, rough as he was, he dropped dead to the ground one day, left the cattle to wander their way to the city if they were of a mind. Cows did him in, snow got me, war got Harold, babies got Sarah, bugs got Hope . . . who knows what'll get you, son."

"Can't tell that, can we?"

'Nope, look at Harold. In my time, he would have been a schoolteacher. But during my time, war changed. Used to be a tournament, in the '60s it became a slaughter. So he died in an airplane, for land's sake. What kind of way is that to go? Some crazy sky machine.'

"Beats cancer or AIDS." Zeldon wasn't in the mood for the way that was going.

'Don't know about that stuff.,' The old man wasn't going to be put off. 'But no matter how it comes, dying is a serious thing, tends to interrupt the breathing process. So you don't want to go asking for trouble. I never learned to read or write, but even I know that. I heard you and Harold talking about buildings over one hundred stories high. You know they're going to fall down, those things. And Harold's sky machines are going to bump into them. That's asking for trouble. Reading and writing didn't help you people very much, did it? Don't seem like as your crowd could see over your little decades in either direction, past or future.'

Zeldon was determined he wasn't going to let that one-on-one moment go to waste. He would get in his point, insisting on a lively jibe in the face of such heaviness. "Well," he quipped, "I hate to throw a skunk into your serious parlor, but if I have to go, I want it to be like the fat man said, 'My exit was caused by too many entrees.'"

'Hmmpff.' A silence then he gave his final comment, 'So Hartford be Hardford now, huh?"

There was a motive to his listening so closely to the attitudes of the Four. As a national politician would do, he was gaining a sense of the culture. He had an advantage, though. It came from that listening to the voices of the past, his ghostly friends with their seminal understandings of their own times. It was they supplied him with the roots of the present, his own time. It was late afternoon, time to cross the road and walk from one privacy into another—pink underlit clouds spoke to him as nature always did. He waved over his shoulder as to a visible presence.


## Hope Fancher

'I like Zeldon, but he makes me shy.'

'Why is that? He's very accepting of all of us, and I know he likes you.'

'Sure, I know, but he sounds so handsome, and he seems to be so sure of himself. It scares me.'

Harold and Hope were spending a summer day on the surface, chatting away like two young people with nothing better to do with their time. An irony, that, since they had no time at all or more to the point, all the time in the world.

'That's nonsense, kitten, he's open to all of us and only seems to be unapproachable to you because he's quiet. Really, he's as safe as pie.'

'Pardon me?'

'It's an expression we have. Don't worry, he loves you. He loves all of us.'

'Oh, you think so? That's so good to hear. Thank you, Harold. My mother used to say, "Dull and ignorant people are in the majority. So you can't assume anything when you meet a stranger." But Sarah says strangers are untapped gold mines. I think you are gold mines.' Then followed one of their silences.

'Hope, if you lived in New York, how did you come to be here in the Rockwater Yarde?'

'It was very good I did because of my friends here, you and Mr. Zeldon and the others. Every summer, my parents brought us to Rockwater for our vacation. Daddy discovered it first because he had relatives no longer alive who came from here. So he came here to see about that, and he found there was a Fancher Road named after his people.'

'And your name is Fancher.'

'That's right. He was so excited. He never became excited, but that day he was. He took us all to see the town the next weekend, and when we saw Fancher Road, he said we should build a house on his road. He called it his road right away. So we came to our Fancher Road house every summer. We all loved it. Daddy told us the clams and oysters we ate in the city came in baskets that were made right here in Rockwater. He said they made shoes here, too, and maybe some of our shoes came from here. Anyway, he called it our quiet home, and I guess when I got quiet when I stopped breathing . . . I guess they decided I should live here, and so here I am.'

After a pause, Hope's voice rose from their silence, 'I remember a day like this. It was just such a day. I was riding my bicycle and singing "In the Good Old Summertime" until I ran out of breath like I am now.' She giggled and went on, 'I had just got a box of animal crackers. They were new in the store, and we all loved them. Just then Daddy came from the city in our car. I saw him stop the car and step out. He was wearing a flower in his buttonhole and his favorite scarf pin, all diamonds and shiny. He was very handsome, like Zeldon, only he had on a stiff starched collar. He would get out of that right away. I rode my bicycle up and handed him a bear cookie. He bowed, took my cookie, and tossed it in the air, and it landed in his mouth! We laughed and laughed. Mother wouldn't have approved, but that made it all the more funny.' Then she grew serious. 'To pay me back for my bear cookie, Daddy gave me a lifesaver. But it didn't save my life.'

Harold let her reminisce for a moment, and then said, 'Tell me about some of the things you did with your dad.'

It worked. She brightened and said, 'We went to Coney Island. Mother said it was vulgar, but Daddy took me anyway. Did you know that Coney Island Dreamland has one mile of lights?'

Harold wouldn't tell her that her mother was right, and that it no longer boasts so much candlepower. Instead, he asked her to tell him more.

'What would you like to know?'

'Normal things. Did you have servants?'

'Of course, my nanny would wake me with my breakfast and then take me to my bath. We had a big iron bathtub with feet. Such big feet like a lion. Later. when I was dressed, Daddy would come in his smoking jacket, or if he was dressed, he would let me play with his gold watch chain. We always had fun together.'

That was looking a little strange to Harold. 'Did your Mother come to play, too?'

'Yes, but not so often. More when we were here on our vacations. But she rose later than we did. And she was more proper. Later, when I was more grown up, I wanted to bob my hair. But she wouldn't let me.'

'Tell me some more about new things.'

'They discovered a milking machine for the cows. I never saw one, but I got the new Crayola crayons when they came out. They were wonderful. I drew pictures every day for weeks after that. Oh, and one of the best things was when my nanny took me to see *Peter Pan.* It was Christmastime in the evening, and Ruth Gordon was Peter Pan. And Nibs wore a suit like a Teddy Bear with fur in never-never land inside a tree trunk. And Nibs came out and said something I couldn't hear, and everyone laughed and laughed. And I never learned what it was he said . . . When it ended, we went out, and all the men wore silk hats and white ties and tails, and the ladies wore gowns and jewels, and we went to the back and saw Ruth Gordon leaving the theater, and Nanny said it was the best thing she had ever done. I thought so, too.'

"Sounds tremendous."

'But things weren't good when the war came. We all waited for the boys to come home, and finally they did, some of them. One day I said to Daddy the war was made by people who like to throw things that go boom. When I said that, he said that he made things that go boom. I didn't say any more and neither did he.'

Neither did Harold.

'Anyway, when those boys came home, we were all so happy. But then there was the polio epidemic. Thousands of people died. So when the flu epidemic came, we were already scared. I had grown up, and I was nineteen years old, and without telling Daddy or Mother, I volunteered to be a nurse's aide when so many people got sick with the Spanish flu. That was even worse. And then I caught the sickness, and it ruined everything.' She looked crestfallen, and said, 'My name is Hope. When I breathed that was a natural name to have. Here it's . . . it's quite a useful name.'

The conversation had turned so sharply to Hope's sorrow that Harold knew it was time to have a rest. He took his young friend by the hand, leading her to her own resting place and bade her a quiet time. Hope retired.

Later, much later, Harold reminisced over what he knew about Hope's influenza epidemic. For one thing, he knew more of her time than she did herself. As a historian, he knew, for instance, that the frivolous girl had been transformed into a compassionate servant when twenty-one million died worldwide in 1918 alone, that while she was still a healthy youngster. Her name was Hope. She died of a bird virus, and a dove was the symbol of hope.

He knew that her illness called Spanish flu had actually begun in Topeka, Kansas, and that it would have begun with an attack of grippe then quickly become a vicious case of pneumonia. Very soon, she would have shown mahogany spots over her cheekbones, a few hours later, one could begin to see cyanosis extending from her ears and extending over her face. One could not have told the original color of her skin. Her death would come in only a few hours as she struggled for air. Trains carried corpses to towns in Vermont where they could be buried. There weren't enough coffins, bodies were piled up, laid out in rows. Barns were used as morgues. At least the little darling would have been spared those latter indignities.

The same trains that took corpses to Vermont, known as Orphan Trains, carried orphaned survivors out of the most dangerous areas. Members of the public would go to the station, pick an orphan and adopt them.

Her wealthy Daddy, for whom the lives of the poor were incomprehensible, would have seen to a favored treatment for his favored one, but a treatment that was irrelevant and too late in any case.

He went to seek out Zeldon. He needed comforting.

## Sarah Lockwood

Zeldon sat one rainy day under the tarp he had erected to shelter a group soon to arrive for their graveside service. The kind of rain was falling that marked what the Scots called a fine, soft day and what Hawaiians called liquid sunshine While he waited, he felt the presence of a quiet and self-contained spirit, knowing it to be Sarah. Greeting her in familiar terms he said, "I've got some people coming soon, Sarah. Talk with me."

They settled together into their rain-wrapped refuge. Sarah considered for a moment and then began in her measured and dignified voice, rewarding him with the following, 'I will tell you some of my story. When I were a child, my father went toward the sunset, saying he would find new farm ground and come back for us. He never came back.' She thought about that for a while and then went on. 'We were scratch poor. My sainted mother kept chickens and sold eggs, and we ate from our garden in the summer and fall. But then the overseer of the poor put my sister and me into service.'

"You mean he took you from your home?"

'It were the custom. We couldn't become a charge on the village, you see. That were the practice, to bind us out by indenture. We went to a family by name of Lockwood, Ebenezer Lockwood and his wife, Mrs. Purity Lockwood. They had a son, name of Horatio. The terms were that they should feed us and clothe us and give us lodging. We would be servants until the age of twenty-one. That would be a good thing, but my sister, by name of Rachel, died when she were about twelve . . . smallpox. Lockwoods were good to us, gave us their name even.'

"So that's how you were Sarah Lockwood. What was your own name?"

'I don't know. And we didn't know when I were going to be twenty-one years old, neither. Most people did not know how old they were or just when their birthdays were. I just knew that I were born in the spring. But we were very favored children because the Lockwoods were famous people and prosperous. Mr. Ebenezer were a major in the Revolution, and his home were the first in the colony. It served as the Continental Headquarters until his soldiers were defeated by Major Tarleton. The battle were in his very own garden. He were obliged to remove to Ridgefield, where Horatio were born. They come back, of course. All that were before we come to live with them.

'So then the years happened, and when the Lockwoods reckoned I were twenty-one or thereabouts, Mr. Ebenezer Lockwood gave me one dress of holy day clothes and two workaday dresses. I saw them as sumptuous affectation and an affront to plainness, but then I grew weak and come to love them. Also they gave me a new Bible . . . to keep me from pride and my freedom. And then came the best part.'

"You mean your freedom wasn't the best part?"

'No.' Zeldon felt her catch her breath, a subject they often made jokes over and pause for another moment. 'The best part were that Horatio, Mr. Lockwood junior, asked me to be his bride.'

It was Zeldon's turn to catch his breath. "You were Sarah Lockwood twice over!"

'Twice over, twice over, and it were twice as good as before. I loved Horatio since when I were a girl, and I thought to catch him. So one Easter time, I took the money I were saving to buy a cow for when I were freed, and I bought me a new frock. Blue, it were with white lace.'

"You must have looked beautiful."

'Well anyway, I had no money for a new hat and my boots were strong and shabby, but that frock were my dream. I even had a bath. I guess I looked a strange sight when I went to church that Easter Sunday. But it were enough to catch Mr. Lockwood because after that, he watched me, and when I got my holy day clothes with my freedom, that sufficed. He took my measure in a new way, and oh my, he were better than any new cow you could ever see.'

"Twice over, and you later married for a new life."

'A new life but it were hard.'

"Tell me more things."

'Very well, what next?'

"Horatio, was he a good man?"

'Oh, yes, a good man. I called him Mr. Lockwood. Hard working and tender to me. Not many men like that. He were the son of a great man, Mr. Ebenezer, but I loved my own great man. He were great, even if he were a grocer and a farmer.'

"I don't suppose things were easy for you in those days."

'Not easy. First thing, Mr. Lockwood cleared some land across from his folkses' house. People helped, and they milled the trees, and we built a house and a barn. Then we made some furniture.'

"You had some good neighbors."

'Everybody did. We wouldn't have lived if we didn't do it together. That were the rule, help your neighbor and get help yourself. And we had to bide with each other betimes.'

"We could use some of that nowadays."

'If you don't, I feel sorry for you. One time though, Mr. Lockwood had some trouble with the neighbors. They said he allowed his rams to pasture on the common ground during their feeding time. That were not allowed. It bred mixed breeds of sheep and made the farmers distraught. The poundmaster were willing to return Mr. Lockwood's rams, but there were a fine. Mr. Lockwood revealed his self-mastery and simply made a quarrel over some ear notches, and it turned out they wasn't his rams. They was mistaken for someone else's.'

"Much ado about nothing."

'Yes well, anyway, Mr. Lockwood had started the planting in our very first summer. Crops went in right between the rocks and the stumps. He grew wheat and some corn. Mr. Ebenezer gave him two cows, so I got my cow after all. Later, we got another one. And we had those sheep, twenty of them, a couple of hogs. My, those hogs did gather the flies. We never paid a mind to the insects. They was everywhere all the time, but those flies that summer almost hid the hogs from view. And then besides the hogs and the flies, we kept some chickens, of course. My land, we worked hard, sunrise to sunset. We had not clocks, you see, only the wealthy had them. We told time by the sun.'

"You helped in the fields?"

'Had to, it couldn't happen with just one man working. You can imagine.'

"You planted between the stumps and rocks?"

'You daresn't forget the endless dark forests that stretched westward. They only stopped where the imagination fell exhausted.'

"It must have been frightening living on the edge of that darkness."

'No, that were my country . . . a wild reach with only our small order to give it challenge. But it were *our* small order. We were pioneers, you see.' She sighed in remembrance. 'Mr. Lockwood borrowed Mr. Ebenezer's oxen, and each year, after crops were in, he pulled out the largest rocks. All year round, we dug out the ones we could manage. I hurt my back one summer, and my body defied my will so I wasn't much good in the fields the rest of that year. And Mr. Lockwood got bad headaches. I laid brown paper soaked in vinegar on his forehead. Didn't seem to help much. Some said they were his own fault. There were a belief that anyone who got a haircut in the month of March would have headaches all year.'

"Oh, Sarah, I feel ashamed at how easy we have things now."

'Well, be glad and say, "Hallelujah!" But we were uncommon fortunate, and life were good, oh, so good. We kept a store, sold dry goods and salt fish, whale oil and coal oil, guns and ammunition, hardware, apothecary goods. It were better than the first days till the bad time struck us.'

"The bad time?"

'Very bad, I got pregnant in January. There came a beautiful spring, one of the best I can remember, and we were so happy about our child coming. We wanted a child from the day we were married, but it just didn't happen. Then it did. I helped as well as I could with the summer crops and in the store. We always worked till full dark. And of course I kept the garden and made our candles and soap and canned the fruit and vegetables. That were hard, so when my term came on me, I were done in. Mr. Lockwood did all he could, and he paid the doctor $1.50 for attending my childbirth. He used lots of cobwebs to stop the bleeding, but it weren't enough. Little wonder, I didn't make it, I reckon. I guess I died more from the work than I did from the child coming. Well, I loved Mr. Lockwood and my child lived. So that were a good thing. Now I be waiting. We are not yet in God's full presence, but neither be you. Us ones in the Yarde haven't yet triumphed over time, but we will.' She laughed. 'It's only a matter of time.'

"Is that how it is?"

'We be in a customs house, a holding place. We be numbered among the dead, but we be not yet among the resurrected.'

"Why the delay?"

'Our trumpets be not yet sounded. I don't know. Curiosity becomes lethargic here in the Yarde.' Her wisdom only reminded Zeldon how he worked among dreams.

*    *    *

The deep background of America's history, as Zeldon was discovering, was being given him through those conjured friends from its past. They assembled an accumulation of memories over two centuries resulting in a priceless education for him. And for the nearer background, he was learning directly from experience. It led to his personal protest over a loss of relationships in his own digital age, a loss no one can afford to lose. Hence, his reaching for the companionship of the Four. He treasured them.

A caravan of cars began entering the circle, so the young spiritual explorer turned up his collar and stepped out of his shelter, moving to an inconspicuous place under a large maple tree. In the absence of Sarah's proximity, the sounds of a cemetery filled his awareness—wind, birds, traffic, human voices, a distant dog, an overhead airplane, and a police siren. Because of the rain, he didn't hear the familiar sounds of leaves scratching over the ground, a lawn mower, his backhoe, and the scratch of a shovel. But he could smell the earth, setting the context for the day. Rain made the world young.

# Chapter 7

Four of the five town council members sat like apprehended truants in the principal's office. Next door in the high school theater, seventy-five Rockwater citizens awaited the town hearing on the new road issue. Phil Glover, the fifth member and chairman of the council, hadn't yet arrived.

"Where is he? Let's get this over with." Toby Stanley tapped his foot and shifted his notebook to the crowded desktop.

"When did you ever see Phil, I mean like pass up a chance at a dramatic last-minute entrance?" That was Matt Purdue. Purdue served as the town's road commissioner. A striking figure of a man, he might have posed a competitive threat to Phil Glover's dominance, except that he was known to harbor in his handsome physique a brain that had trouble keeping track of its own sentences. They tended to trail off before a clear idea could be detected, ending in whatevers and like-thats and you-know-what-I-means. Those sentence fillers were needed to allow time to search for the idea Matt had originally intended to express. And the use of a cliché made it possible to escape his previous sentence without too much thought. The poor man had spent so much time swatting away ideas that often one would no longer come near. It didn't take a superior perception to recognize his line-of-least-resistance thinking, or that it made his every remark predictable, except for one. He was asked after an early experience as a member of the town board who he found to be an interesting colleague, he answered, "Well, I met a frown named Penelope." Concerning Matt, good manners demanded mercy. No one called him stupid, but some were heard to hint that his mind was often unemployed. "So like, I mean, he'll be here soon" was his next offering.

Toby Stanley said nothing to that since his question had been aimed at no one and expected no answer. Toby hated serving on the town council, and only suffered it because of his wife's social ambitions. Merle chaired the Garden Club, enjoyed the presidency of the League of Women Voters and was known as Rockwater's hostess supreme. She entertained. That was another of Toby's crosses, providing himself as host to balance her hostess role when his greatest desire was to fade into the wallpaper. Those many tiny social events left behind them little residue for thought, hence his common state of boredom. He was a cadaverous man, abstracted in appearance, which suited him just fine. It left him to his inner thoughts, invariably more substantial that those surrounding him. The greatest of his contributions to Merle's vision of social grandeur was his service as a town councilor. "It adds a certain cachet, don't you think?" was the tag line of her insistence that he run for office. As for himself, the accommodating cipher stayed largely indifferent to the local agendas that so exercised his fellow citizens. He referred to those quibbles as our affairs of state. While public debates raged, Toby worked his crossword puzzles, leaving the feverish public to believe he took careful notes of what went on. Secretly, he scorned his political colleagues as limelight-loving cretins.

Far from cretinous but a decided lover of attention was Penelope Hentoff, the only female member of Rockwater's governing body. Penelope was astute enough to foresee every issue of any importance long before it became prominent. If there were not a supply of such issues, she showed an adroitness at manufacturing a few. Above all, no day must be allowed to pass without contention, which was mother's milk to the woman. Contention bred conflict, and conflict bred intensity. Penelope fed on verbal violence; she excelled at it and was never known to have been bested in argument. Invariably, challengers were sent off either visibly trounced or cowed by her shrapnel-like vocabulary, discreetly retired before they were. She knew full well that she was feared and loathed and reveled in the knowledge. Invariably, Penelope kept reaching for the doorknob of a new possibility and just as invariably, she would hesitate just at the edge of adventure. It was the characteristic that guaranteed she would always be second-rate. She didn't know that Phil Glover referred to her as the cow.

Penelope had followers, more than a few, which explained why she sat as a community leader. For one thing, she had an eye for popular stances and employed her terrors in support of those she cared about. In addition, there was a sizable contingent who feared attracting her wrath, and those timid souls took refuge in being counted as *her* voters. It was her cynicism that allowed her to rationalize her tactics, telling her that there were no strategic villains, only clever opportunists. Having learned it, she had practiced it for years to her satisfaction. Another discovery told her that networks grow willy-nilly, like the root systems of weeds and systematically smother other claimants, so she was willing to be patient in her ambitions.

It was Penelope who picked up Matt Purdue's fatuous question, "When did you ever see Phil Glover pass up a chance at a last-minute entrance?" She knew he had spoken in a jocular vein. She couldn't pass up the chance to slip in the knife. "When did you ever see him do anything but grandstand?"

Observing that byplay and seating quietly in a corner, a small uncommunicative figure waited. He wore black shoes with a shine to match his pate and the black briefcase he always carried. He himself might have been called a shiny man from head to foot, a patent leather man, except for his moonscape face, which was decidedly textured. Beginning at the hairline, or where there should have been a hairline, a corrugated brow betrayed years of extreme concentration. Hooded eyes, like closed doors, denied there being any resident behind them. Rimless glasses said nothing about that but belied a steely-eyed heartlessness within which he quietly scorned the mental lockjaw he found all about him. Invariably, that posture posed as principled honesty, prompting his sarcastic amusement, sarcastic, not indulgent. Legal had all the good humor of a porcupine.

A cratered nose showed traces of a love of Scotch liquor. Below the nose lived a wide frog's mouth, prone to snap shut when small irritations buzzed by. Murray Hubbard was his name, but his colleagues called him Legal. Beside Legal, next to the omnipresent briefcase, rested a black umbrella, another constant companion. In fair weather, it served him as a walking stick. Legal served as Phil Glover's hatchet man. That allowed his sponsor to stay clean and smiling. The all-but-invisible assistant was electable only on Phil's coattails and never said anything to arouse interest in himself, thus ensuring his anonymity. The man lived his life in the midst of fugitive thoughts and secretly he carried the bureaucratic insolence harbored by minor figures in small slots of control. He was, in the last analysis, a camouflaged man with a seething center. He was North Dakota with a New York subway system. His vote invariably doubled that of the town supervisor.

Loud laughter came from the parking lot outside. It told the small group that Phil had arrived, casting his jovial net over the voting citizens outside. Joviality came natural to Phil, often harnessed, as it was to his ambitions. Soon the extroverted man entered the room, booming voice and all. He tossed aside a cigar butt. A shade of seriousness stole over his features, showing the iron will beneath the joking manner.

"Well, boys," he said, "and madam . . . the loyal opposition" with a nod to Penelope which irritated her. "We have to go in there and harness public opinion to another great thought. Just remember, the little man multiplied is a mob. Rule number two, they're like a school of fish, one organism, and they'll mindlessly follow their instinct of pocketbook protection, real estate values. So shall we get right to it?" He waved his handful of papers in the direction of the theater. Details of their positions had all been worked out previously. Purdue could be counted on to go along with Phil's proposals, having none of his own to venture. It made him appear as one of the idea men of the town. Toby Stanley couldn't care less and would support Phil gladly in order to go home to Merle. Legal was a certainty as always, and the Cow was equally sure—a statement against. Like Legal, Phil never made a move without knowing the ground he stood on. Often that ground had been surveyed by Legal.

The dignitaries entered the hall by a stage door and took their places while the assorted audience watched them, studying their mannerisms and trying to read their thoughts. For those who knew him, that wasn't hard in the case of Matt Purdue. There weren't any. The Hentoff woman was equally predictable—she would be waiting for a savory morsel to oppose. The First Selectman was always interesting; one couldn't know just what he might come up with, and Legal of course, would duplicate him. Toby, strangely, was already taking notes although nothing had yet been said.

"Good evening, good citizens," began Phil. "This is an important evening in our town affairs. We're here to consider establishing a tree-lined boulevard from the hamlet to the village center with a walking trail that will wind along the lakeshore and through the town park and the Yarde, safe for children, safe for bicycles, scenic, and healthy." He cleverly threw all his goodies to the crowd right away to put any opposition on the defensive from the beginning.

It took thirty minutes to dispose of routine matters, a police report assuring of the town's security, a costly expansion of the recycling center denied, a progress report on school construction, minor matters handled by the council members while the audience waited for their turn. Phil, being a political natural, handled those subjects routinely. It was common knowledge that he had built a financial base for himself in Wall Street brokerage and then sold the business for a large profit just before the 2008 bubble burst. Investing wisely thereafter, he was able to pick up his friendships in Rockwater and transform them into his ownership of the town's Republican Committee.

From there, it was an easy walk into the office of supervisor. People liked him. He showed conviviality everywhere and hid his claws well. "Phil is good at running things," his colleagues said. "Things run smoothly, a minimum of controversy." Actually, governing Rockwater was no challenge at all to a congenial man with basic management skills and with Legal's groundwork. Only one issue, fundamental and perennial, dominated town politics, real estate values. Just then that issue needed careful nurturing, to keep taxes low, make zoning laws strict, and make schools well budgeted, and real estate sang encouraging songs to homeowners, homeowners who quickly reelected their smiling champion, Phil Glover. They liked his intelligence, and they liked his frankness. "I was born at night, but not last night." He was famous for wisecracking. Another of his crowd-pleasing remarks was "Craven leaders won't do. We need people-loving social geniuses, and there aren't any. But I'm trying in that direction on your behalf."

The chairman brought the evening to its purpose. He stood up from his seat at the dais, expanded his chest, spread his arms wide, and smiled his most winning campaign smile. "Friends, this is the moment. This hearing is the moment that will further a vital act of progress for our vital town. We'll do it together, and we'll be proud of ourselves for years to come. On May 14 we're going to vote on the bond issue to make it happen. A bond issue, by the way, that will cost us, in total, one million three hundred thousand dollars. That sounds like a lot but amortized over twelve years will hardly be noticed in the mill rate on our taxes." His expressions were as engaging as his features, assured of the intimacy between him and his listeners. "You know my hopes for Rockwater. And you know my actions in pursuit of those hopes . . . our hopes." He made no mention of cost overruns or the interest absorbed in the mortgage.

"Tonight I want to tell you what I base my actions on. You see, I think there are only two forces, really, that we all have to deal with, dreams and brutality. Dreams and brutality, we shape our dreams and then straight off something pops up to kill them, kill our dreams. Well, you know by now that one of my dreams is to make Rockwater the prettiest, best run, most desirable town in the state. And we're on our way to doing that. The project before us now is one step in fulfilling that dream . . . not a huge step. It's easy to accomplish, but it will be one more improvement, and they all add up. We're going to build a lovely walkway from the hamlet to the center of town, a one-mile ribbon of beauty. And while we're at it, we will take out a couple of dangerous curves on the road running along the same route." The man obviously enjoyed the mere form of oratory, which was one of the factors that took his audience with him. He was having a good time himself and wanted them to do the same. It wasn't so obvious that he simply loved the sound of his own mellifluous voice as it soared out over their heads, heads with all those listening ears. The whole experience made him feel powerful; it always did. "So let's open the floor now so you can add your dreams to mine. Who wants to speak first?"

There was a hesitancy among the crowd. No one seemed to want to be first, but finally a tall, gangly man in his fifties rose and spoke in a quiet, apologetic voice. "My name is Harry Gibbs. This is my wife, Samantha." He nodded, indicating the uneasy woman next to him. "We've lived in town for thirty years and love it. We want it to be as beautiful as it always has been. But I have a question, is it true that moving the road would mean moving some of the graves in the Yarde?"

"Here it comes, right away," thought Phil. He noticed Zeldon Wade, the Yarde superintendent, stir in his seat near the back. If Wade meddled at that point the whole discussion could go askew early. It had to be damped down right then. He aimed for the soft underbelly of the group's concerns.

"A few," he inserted himself quickly, "but the benefits of greater attractiveness are sure to increase real estate values in town."

Harry Gibbs showed a surprising determination not to have his question diminished. "Won't interfering with our family members at rest be counted for anything?" He sat down.

"I repeat, property values will go up. That will put many of you here in this room to rest." Phil recognized immediately that the attempt at humor over a dangerous subject was a misstep. He retreated with "Yes, that is unfortunate. But it will be very few graves that are disturbed, and they will be moved carefully and reverently. And I'm serious. Don't overlook the relationship between beauty and real estate values."

Dalton Summer, the prominent resident of Zeldon's acquaintance, stood with a frown on his face and said, "Real estate values matter, of course, but I'm a little concerned here about addled judgment. I like this town because it seems to be straightforward about its zoning intentions. Are we sure we're staying with those intentions?"

That was the point at which Penelope Hentoff recognized an extended debate in the offing. And Glover had blundered with his little joke. "Trading our history . . . the Yarde is our history . . . trading our history for real estate," she said, "isn't that sort of fishing with dynamite?" Penelope was no romanticist about history, and she knew full well the arguing power of money in that town, she knew she could lose the forming battle in the end, but in the meantime, a position could be staked out with the many voters who had friends and family in the Yarde. It was a situation just to her taste.

It wasn't going well. Phil used his ability to cajole a crowd. "We all love Rockwater. Rockwater is a small town. It's not a suburb. A suburb is just a layer on the outside of a city, but a small town is a microcosm. It holds a little of everything and isn't that what we are, a little of everything? We're a small town. So we share each other's values, give a little, take a little. And don't forget the cost of the bond issue. I take that seriously, too." There he hoped by making the mild concession he diverted the discussion to less dangerous ground. He looked over his listeners, waiting for nods of agreement and saw several. "Give a little, take a little. One casket, in the ground, horizontal forever. Is that right that our loved ones would steal from us after they're gone? Do you think that would be their intention? We can share our space and violate no one. Give a little, take a little at very low cost to our taxes."

That extraordinary argument quieted even Penelope. A common town discussion had leapt quickly into deep waters in which no one was comfortable. That was to be about a bicycle path, a walkway along the lake, and there they were discussing eternity. Voters didn't vote on eternity. The room was heavy with unease.

Into that heaviness stepped Zeldon Wade, the Yarde superintendent. Zeldon was seen by many of those townsmen to be a wraith himself. He was all but invisible on the social scene, and no one looked on him as an unseen observer/analyst, which in fact, he was, except with the young people. They called him their Youngest Ancestor, from his famous tours of the Yarde. By then in his young life, he had passed through enough wonders, terrors, sorrows, and softnesses that he could feel poised before the next unknown development. He had learned to distinguish between situations that presented themselves as urgencies but were not and the truly significant. Consequently, he could present a deep inner repose while he weighed matters. Topical matters did not command him, but he looked on that as no topical matter. He showed that repose that moment. When he rose to fill the awkwardness of the moment, many were grateful to him.

"Some of us are strangers," he began, "but we're nearby strangers. In the Yarde are more distant strangers. They're the people who lived in town before us. When they were buried here, their neighbors gave their lives a dramatic finality. We should respect those strangers as much as we respect each other. Because . . ." he paused, dramatically, "because they are guides from the past." A hush swept over the room. Some of them expected that he would say something outlandish. Instead, he said something eminently sensible. "I mean that the Yarde is a space we've inherited from others, from citizens who lived here before us. And a space, just like people, can have experience. And that space can be conveyed to our unconscious selves if we will only respect it enough to hear what it has to tell us." Every person present felt that their discomfort had passed in favor of an ability to cope with unfamiliar, albeit important thoughts. And many of them had heard of Zeldon's popularity with their children. He had their sympathy.

He went on, "The Burying Yarde is a green place of beauty overlooking a picturesque lake. I love it. I love its flowering trees and its ponds. I love the lily pads in the ponds. I carry on a battle with the deer to protect those lily pads." There were appreciative chuckles from some who were familiar with those battles. "Below the ponds, this modest ribbon of black asphalt winds. We all hurry along that ribbon, but in the end, the destination it will take us to is the Yarde. We'll all be part of that community longer than we are a part of this one. It's our town history, that place. Cemeteries are history. They're visual memorials to our collective past. They're places of individual stability. Would we dismember that old order just to move a road a few feet? We can have our park path without moving the road."

When he sat down, there was a moment of stunned silence. No one present had ever heard the Yarde superintendent speak before. Certainly, no one suspected his articulate artistry. He was a master of crowd control, at least the match of their celebrated supervisor.

To the discerning, he appeared to be somewhat starchy despite the artistry, plain spoken before all regardless of position and not afraid to challenge those of high position. Inwardly he was aware of the social asymmetry among Rockwater's residents and had determined to reject such management. It helped to make him a stronger individual. Those critical of Phil Glover thought they recognized someone not timorous before fraudulent aggressions. The young man showed himself to hold integrity in positioning himself, unassailable. What even the discerning couldn't know was that he had learned from the Four a degree of communal courage, garnered with them, that allowed him to hold an opinion despite the opinion of others within the community. From the same source, he had learned to approach events as he did with people of about the same importance except as they showed a quality of true significance, inner significance. All else came to him as small comedies and agonies.

Not to belabor the point but to comprehend the force that was addressing Rockwater's historic issue, Zeldon might have been seen as a simple conservative with his harking back to the values of the Four, but also he was a rebel introducing his new thoughts, and in that, he showed himself to be liberal. Actually, he was revealing the best of both worlds, bringing the product of new technology to disseminate proven values, industry, civility, honesty, compassion, and dignity.

In short, he was playing the role of the rebel who refreshes culture by challenging its complacency. The perspective from which he worked came from recognizing the end of things, and when he surveyed the middle events, it was from that position. He was not fooled by the radiance of promises not fulfilled by subsequent happenings. He was tempered by that and depended strongly on mercy concerning human performance. For a young man, it was a remarkable resume. Not surprising, his fellow residents saw promise without yet the experience to substantiate it.

There were a few occasions in a lifetime when an important corner was turned. Usually the moment was unrecognized, sometimes realized in retrospect. There were also hidden moments when an entire community could be pulled beyond its intentions. That would happen through the efforts of a skirmisher who worked on the frontier, speaking to unspoken needs not seen by the lagging group. Although many spokesmen may address a citizenry, they were like spermatozoa—only one need hit the mark, and when that happened in public exchange, true leadership was displayed, though seldom recognized. Rockwater, New York, had just experienced such a moment.

Even with the opaque insight into the presentation they had all just heard, a resident stood up and asked to make a motion, assuredly one in support of the speaker, but Phil Glover quickly intervened. He had to punch a hole in Wade's argument. He'd start with a quote from the Bible. That would give them a jolt.

"Reverend Andrews says, 'The earth is the Lord's and the fullness thereof.' He's right. The cemetery is the Lord's. And so are the roads. What I'm proposing is to use part of the Lord's property to make safer another part of the Lord's property. It just makes sense. It's all for the Lord's people. What we're doing is borrowing from the dead to keep alive the living."

That piece of casuistry confused some and sounded acceptably pious. He could see that it was a dangerous argument and would be seen through if the forming opposition had time to get hold of it. There were enough nodding heads puzzling over that effort that he might just have purchased a pause in the proceedings. His habit when he had made a solid point was to borrow from the bright ones and use them to persuade the laggards. That night, though, he wasn't sure. He suspected his beloved project was about to be modified not to his liking and quickly asked for a motion to adjourn in order to further study the issue. The motion was made and a confounded Phil Glover lied his way through the rest of the evening with smiles and handshakes. He avoided the damnable gravedigger.

# CHAPTER 8

Rockwater phones were ringing the next morning with the name of Zeldon Wade prominent in many of the conversations. "Phil Glover has a good idea, but that young man handled himself very well. Says we might have our cake and eat it, too."

"He's no fool, that cemetery fellow."

"Build the path, don't disturb the graves, that's what the Yarde man says. Good thinking, if you ask me." Praise of the Yarde man was given substantial weight by the compliments of Sumner Dalton.

Most of the town's four thousand citizens wouldn't become too exercised over that subject. It did not, after all, loom large in their getting and spending, but the stir was enough to trouble Phil Glover. He had ambitions, and they reached out into the future via the graduated stages of his projects. Town beautification was, by and large, cheap and gratifying, with a widespread and visible payoff. So last night's setback, although no calamity, was embarrassing. And Phil couldn't afford politically to be embarrassed so publicly. Neither could his testy pride swallow it. That was the real cause of his anger, a nobody, a town employee, for god's sake, had made him look foolish. The footpath be damned; it was only a tool to curry favor, but no one was going to trash his ideas in full view of the voters, least of all a ditchdigger, godammit, one of his own employees. He'd have the guy's ass on a spit. The joker had just dug his own grave. He picked up the phone and tapped out Legal's number. "Legal, get yourself over here to my office. We've got work to do." His pit bull's ingratiating manner disgusted the supervisor; he was certainly no flamethrower, but he had to admit the fellow was a Machiavellian genius when subversive chores needed to be done.

In thirty minutes, he was in Phil's office. "All right, what's it to be this time?" Legal got right to the point as he always did.

"We're going to weed the garden. The opposition are the weeds and the Gravedigger is going to do our weeding for us."

"Ummm, who is this fellow? Is he smart enough to do more than move dirt around?"

"I've wondered the same thing, but he's not stupid."

"Seems to play to a small audience in the clouds from what I hear."

"Whatever, discredit the Gravedigger, and you discredit the opposition. I want some chatter put around about this shovel-wielder. Do it fast while last night's meeting is still fresh in everybody's mind. We need some sarcasm about his dream. Distinguish it from my use of the word. Call it a vaporous mind cloud. Maybe wrapped in a thought warp. You know the kind of thing. Don't let him get any momentum. Stuff like *immaterial essences* and *imagined images* and *smoky histories*. Really cream him with all this ancestor junk."

"That might be overdoing it."

"I wasn't asking your opinion. Just do it." Legal started to speak, but his superior cut him off, "Do it!"

The frog mouth snapped shut.

"Give them this stuff as our cemetery superintendent's alternative to a more substantial vision, a road improvement plan. Remind them of my speech when I first ran for office in their town. I promised I could make distinctions and work in broad daylight. Tell them, 'OK, Rockwater, you see your choices, misty word-play or some of our own homemade history.'"

In good courtroom style, the attorney pretended to be listening, nodded, and lied, "It'll be a piece of cake."

"It better be. Make damn sure you do a job on him. Dammit, nothing worth doing ever gets done with a show of hands."

Legal was sensitive about his role as Glover's lackey but played the part because it gave him the notoriety he required without lifting the heavy load of the frontrunner. Inwardly, he carried his own judgment of where the balance of usefulness was placed.

*   *   *

Uneasiness had followed Zeldon home after the town meeting. He avoided the Yarde, the eagle's nest where he most often overlooked life's transience and found his perspective. Consequently, he slept fitfully and awoke in the morning unrefreshed. Still, he had a busy day ahead of him and applied himself to it early. There was the usual mowing, and he had to do some clearing in the new section. It was hard physical labor.

"Good job last night." It was the jogger, making his turnaround.

"Thanks" was all Zeldon had time to say uneasily before the man was gone. In any case, he knew the Four would be after him for news about developments.

'Nothing happened, did it?' That was '88.

"No, how did you know that?"

'We knew you'd stop by if there was anything.'

"It was just a public relations thing in the first place, and it had a little setback, but it'll be back. Maybe in a couple of weeks."

'What was the setback?'

"A couple of people spoke up and touched some emotions. And then I made a fool of myself and said a few things."

'You shaped your thoughts and spoke in public?' That was Sarah, stepping into the conversation.

"Well, yes."

'On our behalf, of course.'

"Of course."

'My hero!' Hope became vocal.

'So what did you say?' Harold made the quintet complete.

"Not much, I just said I was against it."

'He's not going to tell us what he said. "Not much" is all we'll get out of him.' Harold sounded resigned.

Sarah, who was quicker than the other three at recognizing Zeldon's character, understood him and read his mind more accurately then appealed to him piteously. 'When I died, it were winter. I waited in a mausoleum until spring because the ground were too frozen to bury me. Even building fires over the grave place gave no satisfaction. So they held me, and that were no small matter. Then they moved me and being moved then were a comfort. I returned to my earth and felt welcomed. But to be moved again, for such a trivial reason . . .'

'88 picked up the lament. 'You know how important it was to me to have a name. You know how important it is for us to think that someone remembers us.'

'Yes,' said Hope, 'that someone remembers us.'

'With respect,' added Harold. 'You've seen how each of us is careful about having an identity. But you can tell we have trouble over finding . . . I don't know what to call it . . . a place, I guess. You know what I mean?'

The others sounded their agreement, and Zeldon added his. Harold continued, 'It's because we're travelers, something like '88, but more through time or no, not time, we're in transit . . . this is very hard.'

"It's OK, Harold, we're all trying to grasp it."

He struggled on. 'So we want a place we can call our own, and we're just passers-through, and every place seems to belong to someone else but not us.'

'That's it. You say it just right, Harold.' Sarah's voice was clearly meant to encourage.

'Well, I can't tell it right, and maybe we have borrowed identities and maybe we're stalled in time. Anyway, we feel like clouds in space or like fish in water. I think I've got that right.' He seemed to find it important for Zeldon to grasp his stammered meanderings.

"I guess that's why I can enjoy your friendships," Zeldon answered, "I kind of know what it must be like." Then he, too, searched for words. "You know I was pretty well destroyed when I came here. Well, until you find a nearby voice, you're pretty much in the ultimate solitary confinement. I value you voices."

He felt almost maudlin in that exchange, but by way of his imagination, Zeldon realized he had crossed the grass line. He also knew, in a deeper awareness, why such translators from the familiar to the unthinkable are few because so few dare employ the imagination to these lengths and ensuring rarity that those who are not afraid are not only labeled demented, but that they may well be. Never mind, something important had happened to him and to them his companions.

A collective sigh of satisfaction filled the air, and then Sarah picked it up and asked that all the effort had some public result. 'So don't let them toy with us, Zeldon,' she pleaded. 'Every life needs a position. We all have a point of view. Will you make defending our dignity your position?'

"You know I will," said Zeldon, "you know I feel pity for you."

Sarah's voice took on a steely quality he hadn't heard in her before. 'I won't accept your pity for the past. Your present sounds to me like a poor exchange. Defend us because we deserve to be honored, no other reason.'

'Sarah for president!' shouted '88.

Chastened, Zeldon agreed to do what he had intended all along, to fight for the moral ingredients of history the Yarde offered the town of Rockwater. His early fear of the Four had by then changed to respect. Their world was a compound of scraps and echoes, a pitiable world of inconclusiveness, but he felt humbled by their courage, and it left him determined to hold fast to his soul as defined by Sarah, a mix of smoke and eternity. He pulled the starter rope of his mower and accepted its motor's roar as his own driving force.

*   *   *

Zeldon worked for an hour or so, mulling over the intrusions into his quietude and what he might do to give substance to his promises to the Four. As he rode his mower over a rise in the ground, his eye fell on the expanse of the town park in the distance, and a dramatic scheme struck his mind in an instant. Ever since his job description had been expanded to make him governor of the town park, he had seen the two properties with a single eye. In time, he came to his own ideas of park design and cemetery maintenance. The Yarde had been laid out long before grid patterns were introduced. His ideas borrowed from the charm of its rambling paths and stately trees, imagining the park as a second location of beauty as well as function. That morning with the grounds stretched out before him, he devised his plan in considerable detail.

His first obstacle was a non-existent budget. The town fathers saw the park as a place of nature, that is, as a place that should replenish itself from out of the abundant earth unassisted. So that day, undeterred, he planned his end run around the town council.

Enter, in his mind, the person of Dalton Sumner, Sumner, who had spoken his prudent thoughts at last night's town meeting. When they first met in the Yarde, he sensed in the bereaved man's sober demeanor a quiet composure that impressed him.

He cut the motor, climbed down from his mower, and walked to his house where he placed his call. "Dalton, this is Zeldon Wade. I'm glad to catch you at home. I wonder if I could prevail on your time for half an hour. I'd like to share with you an idea over last night's town discussion concerning the lake road and the Yarde."

"Sure, of course," said Sumner pleasantly. "I owe you. I'm going to the John Jay for lunch with some friends soon. Can you join me in an hour for a short while before they arrive?"

"An hour? Yes great, see you at the John Jay."

One hour later, showered and presentable, Zeldon was ushered to Sumner's table at the John Jay Arms to find the polished dignitary with a drink in his hand. "Sit down, Zeldon. What's your poison? I'm having a single malt scotch. You should have one." He sized up Zeldon with a friendly glance. "I said I owe you. What's up?"

Zeldon ordered a club soda and said, "I didn't do much, but I think you should leave a legacy."

"I'm going to, one of the best damned investment firms in the city."

"No, something more lasting."

"What's more lasting than money?"

"Just about everything."

Sumner laughed. "Well then, the power of money."

"You can make some town history by constructing a town park in Hazel's memory."

The older man jerked back, put down his drink, and leaned forward, studying Zeldon's expression. "You're serious."

"Ummm."

"Say some more."

That was the beginning. That very afternoon, Zeldon walked Dalton Sumner through the park property as he had once accompanied him in the Yarde, pointing out the large oaks, copper beeches, birches, and dogwoods with extensive stone walls threading through them. Together they recognized the possibilities given by rock formations, ground contours, and water locations.

When they had finished, Zeldon said, "There's an African proverb that says the best time to plant a tree is twenty years ago. The second best time is today."

Excitement showed in Sumner's face. "Hazel's memory, hmm?" He stroked his chin, looking about.

Zeldon chose the moment to bring up the subject of official receptivity to his idea. "You can expect the town council to be glad to receive your money. They'd love to improve the town park, but if it's presented as an alternate to their plan for re-interring the Yarde burials, they won't be so happy."

"To hell with them. We can curve the road along the lakeshore at the park location and leave the Yarde alone."

"I hoped you'd see it that way."

"You knew I'd see it that way. I know how crafty you've been so far. But I like that. And you know they'll move Hazel's body over my dead body."

"That's a little complicated, but I know what you mean." They had a laugh together, and Zeldon said, "Here's something that's not complicated, the name of an honorable woman should be honored."

Hazel's husband was pleased with that. It was left for him to put his people on the proposal that would be brought for public discussion.

\*   \*   \*

It was later that afternoon when Zeldon had a call. "Come on over to my house for a visit tonight. I'd like you to meet my wife and talk over this road question. Can you do that about 7:00?" Phil Glover's voice was all charm, a charm that Zeldon recognized as fraudulent, but he accepted the invitation anyway. It gave him a chance to press the point of view Sarah had so recently enforced for him.

Wearing a shirt and tie but no jacket, he drove to the hamlet where the First Selectman lived. The distance was short. He knew their house from the roadside view, a large, dignified structure settled among other colonial homes in a cluster of history that included Tap Andrews's church, his eighteenth-century parsonage, and a forest of ancient trees towering over expansive lawns. It was a green and white page from past time.

Zeldon crossed the terrace in front of the house and met Glover seated on the edge of a stone well, smoking a cigar and on his cell phone. He gestured for Zeldon to wait and continued talking. "Don't con me. I can sniff the air and know where the power is." After listening for a moment, he covered the mouthpiece and whispered, "Wife's bringing a drink. Want one?" Zeldon shook his head then saw a remarkable pair of eyes looking at him. The eyes lowered, and their owner handed Glover a drink, nodded to Zeldon, and as her husband continued his conversation, turned and disappeared back into the house.

Zeldon was left uncomfortable, struck by that alluring vision that had so suddenly appeared and as quickly vanished. He wondered at the strange greeting given by his hosts. All the while he hadn't spoken. Finally, Glover put down the phone, sipped at his drink and scowled at his guest, muttering, "Armadillo piss" and poured the rest of his drink into the well. "Follow me," he said, "got to make another call, and then I'll be with you." Leaving Zeldon still to fend for himself, he gestured toward the door, disappearing down a hallway. That time, he was greeted by his now-you-see-her-now-you-don't hostess.

Stammering a greeting, he said, "He didn't like your drink. It went down the well." Mrs. Glover's reply didn't register. By that time, he was too disoriented. He had seen the woman about town many times and once at night but had never been the subject of her close attention. It was that, that so confused him. In a moment, however, he regained enough of his composure to hide his disarray.

"Hello, Zeldon," she paused, looked up, and smiled, "May I call you Z?" Z was destined to love a smile called Catia. For that moment, he would attend to the voice, mellow, cultivated, with attention to its enunciation, a hint of amusement in it yet a voice that caressed time as with its own fingertips.

"Yes, do if you want." He wondered if she had caught his initial embarrassment and that was the source of the amusement. He hoped not. Then in his embarrassment still and to make conversation, he said, "May I ask you a personal question?"

"That's usually an introduction to something impertinent but do."

"Where do you come from?" He cringed because he knew perfectly well from local gossip that she was a local resident. She, however, took it to be a cultural question, not a geographical one.

"My father followed a career that's best left in the shadows." That's all she would say on the subject, leaving her polished manners and expensive appearance unexplained. "I suppose you were wanting to know about my background?"

"No no, nothing so rudely personal . . . well, maybe it was, I meant it as a larger question than that. Don't answer it. Give it time to grow. Maybe someday you'll feel like telling me." He couldn't believe his assertiveness in those circumstances. Just being near her was like breathing smokeless air. It was an enjoyment he never realized he was missing until then. His eyes looked on her as after years of night. It was dark and then it wasn't.

She considered his suggestion. "All right, I won't." She considered again. "Maybe, someday." She was finding him worth thinking about in the future tense.

His restless eyes lifted, and his glance rose to a splash of color over her shoulder. There she stood again, duplicated, but she was in different clothing and enclosed in a frame. A portrait it was, a remarkable likeness commanding in its beauty, hung on the wall behind her. The image perfectly matched the intensity of the woman standing before him. The portrait woman wore a formal, low-cut gown of gold lame; the breather was dressed in simple summer clothing. The living woman drew him out of his guarded self with her blue-green eyes. The woman in the portrait gazed directly at him with a longing, vulnerable innocence. The woman on the wall reached for him. The one standing there assessed him. Confused again and rendered uncomfortably awkward,

Zeldon had no idea where to look. He knew though, in those few moments, he had met someone *alive*, very alive.

Seeing his distress, Mrs. Glover laughed in a voice of soft acceptance. "It's all right, Mr. Wade—Z— it does that to everyone. That's why I keep it there. It breaks the ice and gives us something to talk about." Nodding in its direction she said, "I don't sell my talent. I prefer to choose what I do with it."

He found her kindly assessment less intimidating but could find no words to lift him into safety, and remained abashed. Mrs. Glover read his expression and seemed pleased. He couldn't read her reaction.

"It's one of my self-portraits as you see. I don't mean to leave you standing here in the hallway, but if you'd like to look it over, I'll leave you to it while I look for Phil."

His focus entered fully into the portrait. In the very vestibule of her home, it seemed the artist was telling all comers who she was. She had painted that work herself? The exposure caused by the honesty of it showed above all her courage, maybe also her narcissism. He studied it again, that time more critically.

The geometry of Zeldon's mind drank in its contours, its control of the counterpoints of light and dark, textures, and colors, and yet he felt a countertrend. Somehow the effect was of stunning beauty held in an unbalanced tension. Was it in the way a blue cape draped over her left shoulder, catching the blue in those eyes or the placement of a flowering plant in the right background? No, the disturbance wasn't in composition. That was all cunningly correct.

No doubt about it, it was those pleading eyes. In only a hint of an expression, a silent message was being sent, easy to miss. The beauty was a powerful distraction, but the signal in the eyes was not unintentional, he was sure. The artist was too skillful for that; she had planted it almost subliminally. Staring, lost to good manners and entirely absorbed, Zeldon exchanged inferences with the messenger. Some unbalance was being confessed with a reticent appeal for understanding. The suffering secret took the dark come-hither look out of the realm of sex and went to a deeper call.

Zeldon turned to find Mrs. Glover watching him intently. His turn in her direction was easy with almost no transition. That was the breathing duplicate of the presence on the wall, and he was able to enter her consciousness without any segue whatsoever. What he felt for the painting, he felt then for her; what he understood from her oil-painted message, he then acknowledged to her. She, in her turn, knew immediately that she had succeeded in her secret call for the first time. Once was enough.

She shrugged and repeated herself, "I don't sell my talent. I prefer to choose what I do with it." Beyond that, no recognitions were exchanged, but each knew that their introduction would not conclude with that occasion. "Will you come with me?" she said in her coloratura voice. "Phil will be with you in the study in a few moments." She smiled and led him into a room down the hall. As they moved, she estimated his progress, studying his anatomy as though she meant to paint him in mid-stride. It was a sensual stare, and he noticed it but walked confidently on. She noticed that. It told her that they were in private communication already. She left him without further conversation; he was disappointed.

No lights were on in the room, but in the half-dark a fire in the fireplace warmed the cool evening. Zeldon was startled again, that time to find those walls lined with portraits of his hostess, some of them full-length. They were the same breathtaking image, each in a different expression, each in different costume as that which had so arrested him on his arrival. There was the suggestion of a smile, there a darkening to veil a shoulder, a path of light focusing on a breast. The flames of the burning logs danced, shadows wavered, and a crowd of half-concealed forms moved about the room, all with their mesmerizing eyes on Zeldon. Spellbound by the room's bewitching appeal, he cared not a bit that it might all have been stage-managed This was artistry, and if this artful woman could create such an impression of herself, he could only admire her powers of inducement. It wouldn't register with him until later that all this talent was self-referential, uniquely so, hinting to the perceptive of a vast loneliness. The room held a built-in potential for tragedy. Only a faint smell of cigar smoke indicated any other presence in the world. By the time she reentered the room, becoming one of its moving conjurers, he was a conquered man.

"Don't turn on the light," Zeldon said as she reached for a wall switch. She smiled her agreement and stepped toward him, arms extended in an invited embrace. They kissed and moved into each other. Zeldon ran a hand over her body and felt its firm muscles, soft curves. There was no flinching away, only the merest tightening of her embrace. It was the first beginnings of their pleasure together. While he wondered at the evening's astonishing development, she spoke.

"Sit down. I have something to tell you." He marked her loose-fitting white top and flowing navy skirt tight over the hips. That was how he would see her in future. "My name, by the way, is Catia. I'd like you to use it when it's discreet." He remembered he had heard what her name was. "Phil's still on the phone. He said he'd be some time, so we have a few minutes."

He noticed coming from her a scent that he found vaguely familiar. "I don't know if you remember, but I've seen you several times before." Of course he had seen her about town but always at a distance, in the company of others, and he was surprised that she would have noted him under those circumstances. He'd never seen her that closely or spoken to her this familiarly, and then it seemed they were intimates.

"Several years ago, you were involved in a fire. In the confusion, you stumbled into me, and for a moment, we held each other in our arms."

"I'm sorry, I don't remember that."

"You wouldn't. It was a very bad moment for you. But that wasn't our only time of meeting at least, sort of meeting. I'm in the habit of going for walks in the evening before going to bed. Sometimes I walk into the Yarde because it's so peaceful. I've seen you there sometimes in the distance."

Of course, she was the figure he had seen several times, the evasive silhouette in the shadows. And the scent, he had marked it in the air after she'd gone. And one night she had left behind her an undefined prompting that went beyond the normal interest a lonely young man might feel for a woman. He lived a cat-and-mouse game of the mind, a cosmic peekaboo. At times, yes, he thought an answer to his lostness might be found in the soothing proximity of a woman. Dan had suggested it. But more often, all his swirling emptiness moved into areas of remote abstraction. That moment though, because of the paintings and the woman their creator, he sensed that there might be hidden in her presence some hint of an arrival point for him. Something at least had become clear in the short evening, he needed to love more than he needed to be loved, if that were possible. Before that hour, his only fidelity had been to the satisfaction of his need for forgiveness, Bryan's, an untrammeled acceptance. His mind could leave him in a cul-de-sac, his will could fail, his character could lose all admiration of itself, but he never lost that hunger for forgiveness. Then Mrs. Glover, Catia, had revealed to him that his need was to love. That would be the vehicle of his forgiveness. He felt it, he knew it, and he would remember that day until his last day.

Holding a drink, Phil entered the room to find the two soon-to-be lovers speaking in low tones and in semi-darkness. "What's this," he shouted, "an intimate tête-à-tête with my wife in my own home?" He laughed loudly as he switched on the light, but the skilled politician knew just how much displeasure to express and just how much to conceal. "Oh yes, I see, the resident artist has found a new art student. She'll have you over here splashing oils all over her expensive canvasses before long."

Even with Phil's explosive presence in the room, Zeldon remained aware that the portraits on the walls and their painter were not diminished. Their power refused to retreat.

"Hello, dear, I've been entertaining your guest while you so rudely kept him waiting." Catia showed no embarrassment at the interruption. Zeldon sheltered behind it. She excused herself with "It was good to meet you, Zeldon. See you soon again, I hope," and then she was gone.

"Well, Wade, I see it's Zeldon with my wife already. I guess I'd better be on a first name basis with you, too, if I'm going to keep up with her. That OK with you?" His smile held no warmth. He didn't shake hands.

"That's fine." Zeldon wanted no exchange at that moment except empty formalities.

"Good. Well now, let's talk. Would you like a drink?" Without waiting for an answer, he walked to a sideboard and poured himself one.

"No, thanks." Zeldon wanted to ask for something, on the likelihood that it would bring Catia back into the room if only briefly but thought better of it. He was here for a purpose, and Glover was already uneasy about the two of them.

"All right then, Zeldon." That settled, he shifted in his chair. "First, I wanted to thank you for taking part in the hearing last night. That's the way we get things done in town, by kicking our opinions around. Then in the end, when we make our decisions, we know what's at stake." He spoke as though he were in a tutorial with a slow student. The student said nothing.

"But we hope, in the end, to get it right. Let me tell you a bit about this road question. I've spoken with my legal advisor about this. It's a state road running between the park and the Yarde, you know that. So it would be a state project in any case. I have friends in Albany, and I can bring this thing around." He looked more intently in Zeldon's direction. "I'm thinking ahead for Rockwater. Not many people do that. They think of what they want today. Traffic is going to increase on that road in the next few years, already is. It's part of a curve, a long gradual curve around the lakeshore right enough, but the sight distance isn't good. That spells danger, and you wouldn't want to bring any of our citizens into your workplace prematurely because of the road, would you?"

Zeldon recognized a half-truth in the argument, but it was only enough to disguise another agenda. Phil's ambitions were common knowledge. So was his skill at debate. The younger man said nothing, but let his manner show his being unconvinced.

"Allow me to say a few things about your work, Wade, about what you do. Permit me." He waved his glass in a conciliatory gesture. "There's a certain etiquette to dying. We break the etiquette often with a grisly corpse or bad smells or some unseemly behavior by survivors. But we have to keep up appearances, and this is where we do it, in your workplace. Our etiquette helps to hide the horror, you see? We make it all very formal in the Yarde. But it's not sacred. The Yarde's not sacred." He stared into the distance for a moment then looked up and said, "What do you think?"

Smoothly, by the change in tone and his posture of intimacy, Phil seemingly brought Zeldon into his confidence as two equals sharing a common problem. "Wrong ideas get planted in people's minds, and you know how hard it is to overcome inertia in the public."

Inappropriately but amusingly, Zeldon thought he knew far more about human inertia than his conversant, but he held his tongue.

Phil rose from his chair, "Sure you won't have a drink?" When Zeldon refused, he poured himself another. There was no sign of his having too much. "There are a hundred ways to improve a place, and there will be ninety-nine people who think it's safer to do nothing. And nothing is exactly what happens unless somebody pushes and pushes hard. That's my job, and I try to do it well." He took another draw on his drink. "I've learned that changes are part of the exi . . . exigencies of life, my friend, wiggles of fate."

He wasn't being unreasonable. That was his ability with others; he could sound so convincing. Zeldon was aware he was being unresponsive to that show of companionability, but he knew its motivation and wasn't to be taken in. Phil, paying no attention to that, did show slight signs of volubility by going on.

"I try to do it well. Hell, that means putting up with some real crap sometimes." He laughed. "Did you notice how the . . . excuse me, how good old Penelope staked out her position last night straight off? If I'm for something, she'll be against it. That's OK, you never have to worry about the enemies you know about. They can be handled. If I tried to butter her up . . . hah . . . that would be like pouring turpentine on a grizzly bear's ass. But folks know her. They know ahead of time what she's thinking."

It was beginning to sound like two drinking buddies in a bar, thought Zeldon, except only one of the buddies was doing the drinking.

Then Phil became serious, with an attempt at sincerity. "I felt like a fool last night, Wade. I hate that. It makes me feel naïve, and if there's anything I'm not, it's naïve. And you know why I feel that way?" He stood up from his chair, raised his voice in Zeldon's direction, and said, "Because it makes me feel ashamed of what's best in me . . . my sense of trust. My trust and it makes me cynical. I don't like being cynical. We're all too well trained in that."

Zeldon felt uncomfortable then and looked for a reason to leave, but his host was talking again, changing the subject. "I don't know what you gravediggers think about religion, but I think the spirit and the body are like this." He crossed his fingers. "And when one dies, they both die. What do you think?"

When a drunk starts talking about religion, Zeldon thought it was time to go home. "I don't know what I think," he said, "I'll have to get back to you on that. Anyway, you haven't had your dinner, and neither have I. I get up really early for work, so I'd better be on my way."

"Well hell, stay for dinner." Phil waved his empty glass.

"Thanks, but I'd better go. Thanks for the talk. I'm glad I came."

Glover looked surprised at the suddenness of his departure, but he recovered enough to stare intensely at his guest. "Wade," he said, weaving slightly, "watch out for my wife. She's a dove-serpent." He turned his back to leave his guest to his own exiting. Along the way, he called out to his wife, "I'm going to go out for a few drinks with Legal."

Awkwardly, knowing his host was being offensive, Zeldon took his leave. He did, though, pause in the hallway to stare once more at the remarkable portrait in the entryway, thinking, "I wonder why she squanders all that talent on just one subject?" In any case, her representation left him with a sensation of water washing over him or of air wafting around him, sound whispering, and making music through himself. Unquestionably the object, the portrait, left Zeldon, the onlooker, changed!

# CHAPTER 9

Zeldon went home, prepared and ate his dinner and followed it with his ritual brandy, always one and always Martell. After that, he crossed the road for his evening walk in the Yarde, watch the lowering sun lend its colors to the sky, and see the day putting itself to bed. The Yarde was where breathing was a joy, and the sky was his friend. He felt a wind on his face. The young man belonged there then. It showed in the way he placed a foot on the ground, the way his strong back arched to the sky, and the way his eye surveyed the ambiance. All said that was his true milieu. The place of beauty, set firmly in its rightful location, was his home. Just then the silence of the night was settling over the Yarde. Midway around the circle drive, he was not altogether surprised to see the then recognized figure of Catia Glover standing in the dark.

"Do I surprise you?" she said.

"No . . . yes . . . no," he stammered. "No, not really. I'm glad." The wind wrinkled the skin of Trinity Lake. It tousled the hair of Catia Glover and tossed the green world of leaves over Zeldon's head. He felt alive. Incongruously, two points of view formed themselves in his mind for just a fleeting second, were the two of them earthbound creatures or were they potentially celestial? He dismissed the intrusive thought with an unconscious tilt in the direction of Tap Andrews.

She looked about her. "Zeldon, why do you spend your life in a cemetery?" He noticed she wasn't yet used to using his new nickname Z.

"Because it's a tierra de la verdad, a place of truth," he said. "Think of how many secrets this place holds. It's a five-acre secrecy farm." Actually, he was glad for the first time to be able to explain himself to someone. So carefully, carefully, he reminded her of Bryan's death and his felt complicity with all its nuances of guilt and sorrow. Throughout he watched her closely for any signs of disrespect for his sensitivities on the subject. There were none, so he concluded, "I can't leave this place until I feel Bryan's forgiveness."

"But that's crazy. A friendship makes a gravedigger of you?"

"It's not just that he died. We had a relationship, not homosexual, don't think that. But our friendship was ended. Don't you see? It's not death I'm fighting, it's broken relationships." Then he told her about his parents' deaths and how Bryan's own death had compounded the trauma.

"Ridiculous, all this relentless scrutiny and self-punishment. I can understand the sorrow over your parents' deaths and your friend's. But you and Bryan were college roommates, for god's sake, that's all. Not worth throwing away another life."

"Catia, if I can solve this, I've got a lifetime of companionships ahead of me. If I can't, I'm alone till I die."

"What a quaint way of thinking. For what you see as a moment's failure, you will inflict this time injury on yourself, open-ended? You might already be dead, the way you're talking."

"No, listen, two people become close. Then for any reason, if they become distant again, that's the calamity. That's a real tragedy. You were aligned with someone then you're alone again, you see? You see? That's what makes us all afraid when reciprocity is broken off." He wanted her to see, he wanted her or someone to warm his frozen heart. They need only to flavor his day. No more was needed, only an understanding presence, someone to touch his isolated self.

But "No," she said, "no, I don't see." Then she stopped herself and began again, "I've always been a separate person, alone inside myself. Yes yes, I guess I do see what you mean. Being one is always better than being divided. I'm certainly aware of that." Phil came to mind and their recently recognized estrangement and earlier partings. She began to walk, looked downward briefly, then raised her head, shook herself, and said briskly, "Well anyway, I'll always look at you as a sentinel of dignity in a place of putrefaction."

"Don't make fun of me," he shot back.

She cast him a look of pure affection. "I wouldn't make fun of you, Zeldon. I wouldn't make fun of you."

Mollified, he walked on.

Looking about then, she said, "Give me a tour?" Then looking about, she said as though it might be a deterrent, "There's dew on the grass."

"Droplets come from the stars. Well, where to begin?" That was a little better, he could talk about something less intense. "A tour, you need to know what you're looking at." Prompted by his own remark, he looked at her. The upswept hair, the inquisitive look, and the grace of movement encouraged him to make an effort. Diverting his own beginning, he waved at the Yarde and said, "It's a perfect job for me. Look at them, pit ponies for half a century and then they die. I see the life summation of the recently dead, and I see how the survivors express their fear of death. Everybody's naked and I'm the voyeur."

"Very educational."

That triggered his mind in the direction of the stroll around he had held with the schoolchildren, and so he began describing what was clearly visible. In his years as superintendent, Zeldon had made modifications to the Yarde's appearance, composing a wraparound design with a feeling of inclusion to all, the incumbents and the otherwise. As for the sense of a lofty escape from gravity, he left that to nature and the sky above. His gift of the clock tower simulating a church spire only raised the eye in an upward suggestion. By its subtlety, an entire theology was whispered to the unconscious in an extended harmony. By that time in his Rockwater life, he felt firmly planted; it was the Yarde that was growing about him. And he saw the Yarde as secretly exuberant in its life surge, just where death felt triumphant. In that he had already met his private-most goal as superintendent.

But all that was left to the viewer's own capacities of perception. Leaving behind the physical descriptions, he changed his tone. He had always tested a person's imaginative powers by whether he could smell and feel and remember a rose he had seen in June. He threw the test to Catia. "Imagine the road down there and the water behind it. You remember that Trinity Lake was once three small ponds that were made one lake by a dam. And you know there's a small river running into and out of the lake, you can imagine that water." He pointed across the roadside. "Is Lethe, the river that runs through the underworld. It carries things that are deep and hidden, secret, guarded things, things that hide from the sunlight, like earthlight on the moon. Or you can see Trinity Lake as Trinity Lake with its Christian reference."

"Wonderful, wonderful!" she cried. "A dead place." She paused then added, "Or a place of resurrection."

"Ye . . . es well, not altogether. One was the Roman's invention, a myth. They believed the dead people drank the waters of the river before they were reincarnated and returned to life in another form. And the other is the Christian belief in a continuation of the same person."

"Why did the Romans need their spiritual cocktail?"

"So they wouldn't remember their earlier life."

She was silent for a long while; he could see the power of myth working on her imagination. This man, she was thinking intuitively, without a lot of evidence to support it, might be mythic himself. Aloud she said, "A clearing house, where they drank to forget?"

"Yes."

"Sounds like a spooky bar." She sat down on a nearby stone.

He laughed and sat in the grass next to her. "You're right." Then he grew serious again. "Well, they weren't stupid, these people. They believed we forget ourselves, and we lose all memory of who we are. Songs erased and skulls forgotten." He paused.

"Who said that?"

"Me." Carefully he went on, carefully because he wanted no distraction there, a distraction would act as a subtraction from their concentration. "Anyway, they believed we lose our memory of who we are, but there's always that shadow self, maybe a better self, standing in the wings." He waved in the distance.

Catia went very quiet, lost in her thoughts.

Zeldon went on, "They believed that's the basis for all social intercourse. All social intercourse is a search for seeing our real selves reflected in someone else."

"Sort of everyone else becomes a Rorschach test, to see whether you're in there or not?"

"Sort of like that."

From a long way away in a slow measured voice, Catia said, "Social intercourse?"

"Yes."

"Did you say that's what social intercourse is?"

"They thought so. What do you think?"

Again she went on a long journey inward. Zeldon remained silent, not wanting to interrupt what he sensed was important work, not realizing that was exactly what she did in her own self-portraits, to find her other self. Finally she returned, presenting an undefined presence from which she whispered, "Or sexual intercourse?"

Zeldon was startled at the abruptness of the question, and its power. "Yes . . . yes, I guess so. Yes, most of all that I suppose." His surprise was obvious and his discomposure. They both were silent then. An evening sound came from the gathering darkness around them. Catia trailed her hand along the upright stone that stood next to her.

"Zeldon?" she said.

Zeldon held his breath before he answered. He knew something important was happening. She was enamored over his lecture on the Roman myth, less attentive to the Christian story. But "Yes," he offered, "Yes."

"Zeldon, will you make love to me?"

He sat motionless before her. The Yarde was always a quiet place, but just then, the silence was absolute. Her back leaned against a grave marker, her hand rested on his foot. He knew she had become a Roman woman there in the night where identities were malleable. Her request was more than carnal. It was a reaching more for herself, he suspected, than for him.

"Yes," he said, and Rockwater became Rome. He hoped his wanting a personal intimacy didn't constitute a spiritual commitment. For that, he wasn't ready, but oh, how he was starved for love.

She slid her hips alongside him, wriggled out of her clothing, and waited, white flesh on green grass. The night made no sound. Zeldon removed his own clothing, trembling, lowered himself upon her, and took what was given. Instantly he ejaculated, splashing on her belly and her thigh. He groaned with embarrassment, but she was undeterred and in no time had him erect again with her unrefusable invitations. She stroked him with moistened muscles deep within herself, a milking, draining, reaching channel that pulled from him climax after climax, more than he thought possible. All the while, she sang in a soft moan a song of craving hunger, a continuous sound of longing. He was shocked at the ferocity of her sexual appetite. She lacerated and bit him, held him with a desperate strength, gasping and crying over and over again, "Love me, love me, love me, love me . . ." But she wasn't talking to him, she was talking to herself. Even during their coupling, he knew she was reaching for more than him. There was a craving, a stretching for some goal to be found by way of his body perhaps, but what could that be? It acted like a madness trying to claw its way to sanity. It was lightning in a bottle. And that call to love her, she was without reserve, without caution. He was afraid of her. He found her compelling and matched her frenzy with his own. And why might that be? Why had he loved her body so entirely, her female perfection? It went, he knew, further than lust, beyond esthetics, into a realm of unities, something about being complete, whole.

Finally, slathered in moistures, they fell into each other, expended. Neither moved or spoke. Seeing her eyes soft in shadow, her hair lustrous in a pale shaft of light, and her rounded shoulder becoming a graceful reach from arm to fingertip, persuaded him that, yes, she was visual music.

At long last, she shuddered, cold with the encroaching night's damp. He stirred, covered her with his shirt, and finally she said, "Almost."

He knew what she meant but said nevertheless, "Almost?"

"Yes," she sighed, "there's another Catia. I almost met her." He made no answer. "In you," she said, "she's in there somewhere."

"In me?"

"Yes, there's not enough of me to be the true me." She paused. "But there is when you're inside me." To that he could make no reply. Fondling one another, embracing, caressing, they dressed. "I'm a mess." She laughed. "Folks, I'm a mess." She turned herself about in the direction of the neighboring gravestones, laughed, stuck out her tongue then laughed again more heartily than Zeldon thought discreet. The gesture frightened him. It smacked of something distasteful; it left him uneasy. There was something about the unpredictable woman that did that.

Catia gathered her handbag and jacket, kissed Zeldon lightly in an almost cavalier way, and said, "Phil is going to smell on me the musky smell of lovers. Ah well, never mind." Then tossing her parting words over her shoulder, she smirked, "Together, you and I, we're going to outwit that Roman river." Swinging her hips, she walked to the Yarde gate and disappeared. He heard her car drive away, the tires rolling slowly over the gravel. Red taillights cast a demonic glow on the underside of the leaves above.

*   *   *

What did she mean about outwitting the River Lethe? Things were changing for him. Did she mean that shared events are important, maybe more important than the lone experience? She actually made him feel the need for a social life. Formerly, he had felt that in the end people are all alone, and he was simply getting ready for it. He had changed his mind. Friends mattered. Lovers mattered. In something else, he also changed his mind. He had always thought that courting should be rhythmic. That was abrupt, leaving in its wake happiness and confusion.

The very next morning, his inclination toward entering a social life was tested unfairly, he thought. The Yarde played host to what he disliked most, the burial of a child. By then, he had managed to protect himself as Dan had taught him, from the ongoing line of the Yarde's visitors. They were an endless stream, always in grief, and he could not live with this fare as his daily diet. But invariably, the end of a child's life broke through his defenses.

That day, following the storm of emotion Catia had released in him, his vulnerability betrayed Zeldon into a deep searching of what was happening to him, elated and afraid, surrounded by battalions of impressions and responses.

He reviewed his experiences. Bryan, of course, had brought him there, and Bryan's forgiveness was still his holy grail. His inward voices had helped him retreat from normality. Although he had no sympathy for social class distinctions, he had come to recognize the vacuity of what the French so disdainfully referred to as the life of the bourgeoisie and was glad to have avoided it. So by then he lived mostly inwardly. Necessary exchanges naturally took place. His work required frequent collaboration with town officials, funeral directors and others, but by and large, he was recognized as a private man.

The public debate over the road proposal had drawn him out of his preferred environment. Nothing short of a threat to the Four could have done that. And it was a costly sortie. He had leapt into public controversy and drawn attention to himself. He had alienated powerful influences. He had met and become entranced by a married woman, married to the strongest of these influences. And then he had become her lover. Where was he headed?

The service ended, the subdued visitors left, and Zeldon followed their departure with a heavy heart. While he was having lunch on a bench, a breeze passed over the grass, bending it in a narrow progression, like footsteps leaving their imprint behind. He sensed, in a space above the prostrate grass, a presence, soft, receptive, and safe in its friendliness. Without any more inducement than those insubstantial impressions, he felt an invitation to speak.

"Someone's here."

'I saw your lovemaking last night.' It was Sarah.

"What?"

'Don't be embarrassed. To us, it were a natural and beautiful thing. We envy you.'

"You're shameless."

'Not so, sir. Women of my generation reached for something that none of us could put a word to, something womanly and desirable. Last evening I saw it in your new friend. She has delicate emotions, delicate emotions.'

Zeldon sat spellbound, his sandwich held in midair.

'I'm proud to say,' the voice went on, 'I could see you both last night with affection and admiration, and you can be pleased, you were seen by eyes that love you. I may have reached a degree of delicacy myself.' There was a moment of silence, then. 'You have come to make one shadow. I'd like to celebrate that with you.'

He had taken up residence in a place of burial precisely to
bury the pain of Bryan's death and his responsibility in it. And
there he was, exposed to the rending emotions of the real world.
Present day's dead child and Catia's tender call had stripped away
his armor. He felt the union of two worlds in the whispering on the
wind. He was naked, more naked that morning in the company
of the child than he was last night with Catia, naked and afraid.
The Yarde was no longer a safe place of death. It was a place of
life, and like all inevitabilities, there was no escaping it. "And so
the boundary of time, of my time, my lifetime," he asked himself,
"is it my given years or is it boundless?"

"O God of infinite compassion, who art the comforter of thy
children, look down in thy tender love and pity, we beseech thee,
upon thy servants . . ." Tap Andrews had intoned the obsequies
of death. Zeldon couldn't come to any conclusion over his own
question. Was he himself a live man or a dead man? Should he
step into life or continue to hide from it?

"As a father pities his children, so the Lord pities those who
fear him." The voice in his head went on, washing over the memory
of a child no longer allowed the choice. At the town meeting, he
had seen the faces of some who take their dailiness so much for
granted that they had slipped unknowingly into nonbeing, dead
men, dead women, in effect, not knowing they were. It left him not
sure just where were the boundaries of the Yarde.

He thought of Catia; he thought of the child. His impulses
wavered; he looked for guidance, cast his eyes about him. It
surprised Zeldon how the ambience of the Yarde varied from day
to day, from occasion to occasion. The light quality that day was
low and subdued as though the voice of the sun itself had fallen
to a murmur. It was a day of jade trees and soft sapphire skies, a
gem of a day. "Choose life," it said. No, that was Andrews's voice,
"Choose life." His scriptural words to the small gathering had
come as though coined for Zeldon, personally. Catia's bestowal
of herself, coupled with the heartrending observance so recently
concluded, brought everything in his life into collision, his parents,
Bryan, his carefully crafted escape from pain, and then, "Choose
life." "Choose suffering," it might have said.

That night, he slept fitfully and held the same weather system in his head the next morning. "Tragedy is the currency of our age," he wanted to shout in answer to the jogger's hello, but he only answered with a nod. That much he had learned in his years in Rockwater. Fair enough. Life reduced, life denied, life abused, undeveloped, uncelebrated—that's tragic. Resisting the tragedy must be the only way to reaffirm nobility and grandeur, the lost qualities of the past. All right, he would resist. By refusing to accept the finality of tragedy he would redeem himself in his own eyes. Not to deny Bryan's calamity, no, to acknowledge it, even his own participation in it, but to deny it as ultimate. Ultimately, loving would trump guilt.

He had been living in a small country between worlds. The Lethe—Trinity Lake—lay before him as a constant reminder. He was ready to love again, to see those worlds joined. They would seek it together in their crabwalk toward sanity.

# Chapter 10

From time to time, Phil Glover felt obliged to attend services at the local church. His position required, he reasoned, that he should appear at some funerals, weddings, and holidays. It was all part of his modus operandi—concealment while pretending self-exposure whenever that was possible by deft deflection into an affable persona. It was responsible for his social success, by degrees having created a textured and self-possessed personality. He had his ways. Primarily, he carried himself with a soldierly authority, with a hawklike glance, intimidating. Then a later inclusion would leave a person flattered, not knowing it was insincere. It was just one of the tricks that made him liked by the very people who didn't know him.

But of course, he was guardedly nervous on many occasions. He could never anticipate Catia's emotional state for one thing, but fortunately, she had never yet embarrassed him unduly. He had guarded their secret about her mental problem as he called it. There was gossip, of course. So far, he had faced that down. In his youth, he knew himself as a package of potentialities. Although he knew he would never become one of the great captains of history, there were still his ambitions to rise higher and he sometimes worried over how entirely he could hold his wife's instabilities at bay.

They were becoming more frequent, those irrational moments. One time last week he had come home from attending the burial of a prominent ex-supporter. "How was the funeral?" Catia had asked. "How was the funeral? The guests were morose, and the principal was dead. But I might have picked up a couple of votes." At first, she laughed, but a dark streak slid through her laughter.

Then she went all funny as she sometimes did, turned quiet, registered a wild, distant look, and made murmuring noises to herself. He had had to tread softly for two days around that gaffe. It was like that more often those days, self-exposures followed by quick retreats.

Following that day's service, he spotted the source of that day's worries talking over coffee with Tap Andrews, another one to be watched. Andrews was significant. He had a brain, and he had presence. Phil was never sure of his ground in the clergyman's company because he had influence in the town and was astute and subtle enough to be dangerous if he chose to be. He crossed the room to join them.

"Hello, Phil, are you holding the terrorists at bay?"

"In Rockwater, they're called Democrats."

"Ah, well then, they're encroaching." Phil wasn't sure how Andrews voted. That was one of his capabilities. He kept his flock guessing by registering as an independent.

"Catia was just asking me about Zeldon Wade."

"Wade. Digger O'Dell, our gravedigger."

"Yarde superintendent," said Andrews.

Phil noticed an uneasiness about Catia as though she wished the topic hadn't been shared. Andrews exchanged a few pleasantries with them and moved on.

"What about Wade?" Phil pretended indifference.

"Nothing, I just wondered how well Tap knows him."

"Why?"

"No reason."

He looked her over with a cold eye. Something wasn't right there. Phil's antennae rose up and told him to pay more attention. A man had to keep his wife on camera in that damned 24-7 world. What's more, deceit in their lives together had become like the wallpaper.

They greeted a few coffee sippers and left. On the short walk to their house, he wouldn't let the topic of Wade drop. "I notice the guy you and Andrews are so interested in isn't a churchgoer. I guess he's less religious than me."

"So?'

"Well, you three use an old religious trick. You identify your self-interest with God and justice and nature and then you and the Almighty will be partners cleaning up the world."

"That's a bit of a stretch."

"OK, Wade." He got right to where the itch was. "Shouldn't a fellow with his intelligence have a more important responsibility? The guy has a full-time job on a half-time salary. What's wrong with him?"

"He seems to be where he wants to be," Catia answered. "Don't you think that's using his intelligence to advantage?"

"From what I hear, the boy takes his every experience and calcifies it into a philosophy. Leaves him constipated. What does the man do with his ideas? Doesn't look like he's ever tested them in action."

"He seemed to put them into action at last week's town meeting, to your embarrassment."

Phil tensed. His wife could insert an acid remark as quick as the flickering tongue of an adder. To cover his anger, he said carelessly, "Yeah well, he put one over on the gullible that night, all right. He gave them an appearance of owning an impenetrable secret, but I think it's a cover for ignorance."

"From what I heard, he didn't leave many thinking he's ignorant."

She was baiting him. "Yes, I know, but he can be cagey. Maybe he's not so intelligent, just thinks he can avoid the complicated stuff just by being simple. God, living in a cemetery! How would he do working in the town hall or a bank?"

"A bank, making money, you mean. That's your definition of a serious man." She cast him a scornful glance. "You know that man who covered ice cream with chocolate and put it on a stick? He became a millionaire from that stroke of genius. The race to riches isn't that complicated."

"Forget ice cream on a stick. My point is that simpletons aren't simple. They're complicated idiots."

Catia hated his arguments. They threw her off balance. She covered her discomfort by becoming angry in her turn and snapped, "He's not simple. He's more complicated than you in that little shadow play you call your life." Then realizing she had said more than she should have, it became clear to her that Phil would be wondering how she would know that.

Phil was livid and made no attempt to disguise his feeling. If there was going to be any female taunting over sex with anyone else, he'd snuff it out as soon as she tossed it out. He had to be careful with the hand grenade he was married to, and he was still smarting over the gravedigger's public meddling. Under ordinary circumstances, he would simply fire the kid, but after his performance last week and given his growing popularity, that would be delicate. His venomous wife was right. Wade was making friends and had called attention to himself. So he blurted it out, "Something that's entirely acceptable and authentic in one context can be made to look pitiful and distasteful in another."

"What are you talking about?"

"I'm talking about relationships. A woman's sex life at home, for instance, or her sex life put on the witness stand."

"My sex life, on a witness stand, what on earth?"

"To you women, we men appear to be domesticated. Some even run errands and help with the dishes. Somebody has to tell you what you haven't noticed. Our dreams are set in jungles and battlefields and storm centers. So be careful with us. We can be dangerous."

Catia stopped, froze, emptied the conversation of all air, and stood before him entirely inert.

It was Phil's turn to be unsure if he hadn't gone too far, but he wasn't going to be made a fool of again. No matter what it cost him. Both resumed walking, they reached the front door, and he strode in before Catia and went straight into the study, slamming the door.

*   *   *

"How could he know? He had to be guessing, but what even made him suspicious?" Catia slipped into one of her tornadoes of nothingness the minute the door slammed. Phil could have no idea of how suddenly they could come upon her, those emptyings. Always she hoped to explain her desperate reachings for someone, anyone, before disorientation noticed what she was doing and closed her inner door. But it had all happened so fast. The falcon swept low, and then the little sparrow was cowering. That moment she was lost. The world was never as perfect as the one she carried in her head. Like the artist she was, she always wanted to rework it till she got it right. And she never could; it was always a negotiation downward. She knew what was on the way. All reason would fall away. She would drift, drift and float, further and further from any hand to reach for. Hoping for footing beneath, she would find only water. She knew she was sinking. Soon she would be as lost as the sounds of wind sailors singing their work songs. She raced to her bedroom, slammed yet another door, and slid under her bedcovers amid a kaleidoscope of emotions, hoping never to emerge.

*      *      *

Seldom had Phil sat in silence, awake and sober, for such a span of time. If it could be said that he was an introspective man, those inner moments were spent weighing and calculating courses of action, decisions to be arrived at. But that morning, his mind worked in uncharacteristic style, stemming from what he had caught in one glance, viewing his wife's face while she was talking to the padre. His interruption of their conversation allowed a flash of dismay to cross her expression as though there were inner thoughts being caught at the very moment they were being indulged in. If that event was complex, subtle, unmistakable, and confusing, they were the very reasons the moment itself was so shocking to Phil. His wife had a secret. She had been caught but at what? Her defense of the town shoveler couldn't be it. It was important to her, and so it was to him, thus the long, long silence.

They had been talking about the Yarde man. From Andrews's view, it was small talk, just coffee chatter held in the commons room after every service. But to Catia, it was not. Otherwise, why that quick flinching of her composure when he blundered in? He dismissed the young man, Wade, as irrelevant. He mustn't get too far off center there. There was some other path in the labyrinth of her mind. Yes, he knew he was too committed to action, politics, and relationships that are not real relationships. It was part of his drive, his love of the hunt, and his purposeful aggressiveness. It hadn't really mattered that he wasn't privy to the private hopes and fears and dreams of others, except insofar as they colored their public preferences. And yes, he had never probed those same qualities in Catia. Their marriage was satisfying, at least in the early years. He recalled how she had first caught his eye, walking with a certain hip roll, subtle and therefore all the more provocative. Her entire manner of movement, buried deep in her unawareness, spoke of buried erotic pleasures. Knowing how seldom those awarenesses came to him then made him dislike what she did to his peace of mind. But certainly she was a public asset at least to that point. She had never completely understood him, he knew that, but her deference seemed adequate, again at least until then, hence his surprise at sensing a sharper degree of alienation.

It surprised him into an insight about himself and about her. He had been struggling for years, first in business and then in small-town influence peddling, to increase his effect on others. And on that unmarked day among the many, he was unnerved to suspect that what he wanted all along was to be approved of and to influence people to love him, most of all his wife.

Weighing her nature anew, he admitted that in her case, assembling the small details that make up a character proved impossible. All was too fluid, too unpredictable to state hers as final. To try was like herding mosquitoes. But the mystery that those effervescent details approximated couldn't be matched for charisma or magnetism. He couldn't allow the thought to form itself: he was lacking in some essence. He knew it but wouldn't allow himself to know it. It was at that juncture that the silence penetrated even his mind.

*       *       *

Legal was drunk and angry. Phil Glover and his boneheaded town government authority had gotten too petty to offer him the place he had bargained for. And lately Phil's manner went just a little beyond his outline, assigning to him, Legal, a role of insignificance that couldn't be tolerated. What's more, he had learned some things about his sponsor's secret doings, and they didn't bode well for him. It was time to make some moves that would bring about changes. That was his style, the unobtrusive use of power, a power that came when he called on it. Legal was adept at managing the variables that others hadn't counted on.

From childhood, undersized and pointedly unhandsome, he began early through silences and pointed remarks to build a strong defense. His own counter-assaults were usually wounding and always effective. They came from a consciousness that his fellow humans are smiling, scowling, loving, killing, and weeping creatures, and who, therefore, could trust them? They gained their points of view from their various TV sofas. He had been told that law schools were centers of ambition and besides, studying law was only the natural extension of his native talents. He would be powerful, and working without fanfare would make him secretly powerful.

That early anger brought a blanket condemnation to his social relationships. All thereafter was calculation, another helpful characteristic in his chosen profession, the Law. It was his end-all-be-all, but law corrupted. The Law was a foundation that crumbled when pressed, leaving life without a center. So he filled in the vacancy with a purposeful intelligence. Justice was ephemeral. Not surprising then that revenge was the unnamed stream running through his days, all of them always. It motivated him then. He took out his cell phone and called Penelope Hentoff.

"Penelope, this is Legal. We need to have a talk." After waiting for her guarded response, he went on, "How would you like to be town supervisor?" Again getting the expected reaction, he said, "How about three this afternoon in the town park. I'd like it to be private." Hearing the excited reply, he slid the phone back into his pocket.

At three on the dot, he opened his car door for his guest to enter. It was more than two hours later that their two cars drove away.

*   *   *

For days, Catia lived with her soul turned inside out, not for the first time. She lived in her drama-filled world, some of it real, some invented. "I'm not Catia, but I can impersonate her." All the recesses of hidden fear opened. She talked to herself, slept when it was necessary, ate when Phil was out of the house, and locked her door when he was in. Words floated around her, without her knowing if they were her words, Z's, or imagined, searching words, probing. Some of them felt definitely like his. "The sun was on the maple tree this afternoon, just before dusk . . ." Yes, it was his sounds, like hands feeling their way over her. "It caught the colors in that pale, clear light that comes from the side, not from above . . ." The tumbling words looked for an opening in her, no, for one particular opening. She knew he wouldn't get into her, not again. "I wish you had been there . . ." "Why, so you could fuck me?" "What?" "Go away, I don't want you around." He was leaving. She was slipping further into her nosedive. "What are you talking about? What's wrong?" "I'm tired, just leave me alone." She envisioned swallows arching through the air, gathering mosquitoes by building concealed architectures in the sky. No, not architectures, thoughts in her mind, alone, her own words said, "I'm in trouble. I'm going to be folded up and put away while I'm still moving."

*    *    *

It had been three days since his wonderful/terrible evening with Catia, that evening that left him feeling he was inside a kaleidoscope and not a word from her. Any contact had to come from her but none arrived. He was tired after a hard day, worried, discouraged, so he went to bed early. His sleep brought troubled dreams of the strange sight of smoke rising from a graveyard. What was it, fire down below, the fires of hell? Coffins ablaze, past conflagrations lifting to the surface, the dry tinder of forgotten history aflame at the offenses of ignorant progeny. He awoke with the sound of a cry, not sure if it came from him or from the appearance of Bryan in the midst of his confusion. Gathering his senses, he realized it had come from across the road in the Yarde. Dressing quickly, he hurried outside to discover a small campfire alight in the circular driveway skirting it. A crowd of young people was milling about, laughing, clowning, tending their fire, drinking beer, and roasting hot dogs and marshmallows. Wide awake then, he could only laugh aloud, a wienie roast in timelessness. Reluctantly, he walked over and pleasantly ushered them to their cars, wishing them a good night, secretly, a good life.

The next morning as he looked over the prospect before him, it was a strange one for him. Both his anxiety over Catia and the amusement of last night flavored his thoughts. He registered his puzzlement at why others couldn't grasp his love of the place. Was it only he who recognized the largeness of death and his own smallness before it, how it held a humbling comfort and how it yielded such a quiet peace? It had something to do with the absence of struggle, of contesting and of opposition. It was not that he had surrendered himself to death, decidedly not, but that it was becoming true that he was allowed to transcend its threat. He realized that he was much closer to Tap Andrews's Christianity than he recognized. Not that he held ideas cemented in place by religion, but neither was he willing to wade in the river Lethe. Death was not his master. He could recognize its enormity but see it leaves room for love. Of Rockwater's townsmen, if they really knew him, they would think he was crazy. Some of them did. The kids of last night would know it. He wished Catia would call.

# CHAPTER 11

Eight days after their melding into one another that night, he found a note in his mailbox. It began without preamble, "I must have one really satisfying development during this sad time, and I've decided it will come through your company. Will you come to dinner tomorrow at 7:00? Phil will be away." At the bottom she had appended, "Please come. I need you."

Despite her footnote, Z found the note ambiguous, partly imperious yet modestly solicitous. After their night together, however, it was nothing but intriguing. He readied himself for what was already in place, a necessary relationship. Parallel to it though was his uneasiness, not sure their moment of happiness wasn't just another disappointment in disguise. He was, after all, placing confidence in what should come next after their life encounter in the Yarde. And the Yarde *was* his place of contradictions. With all that, he called to accept gladly, "Hello, it's Zeldon."

"You will never have to identify yourself to me again. I've heard your voice every minute since we said good-bye."

"We didn't say good-bye. You just drove away."

"You're right, our conversation wasn't over. Oh, Z, it was wonderful."

He echoed her comment with his own, but like all echoes, it came out a feebler sound than her original outburst. He hadn't meant it to be; he wanted to say she had enough life to feed all appetites.

When he arrived, he found her dressed in blue jeans and a baggy sweat shirt, hair tousled, pale, and jittery. She was tending flowers in a circle around her well, enjoying herself, humming like a happy housewife. She wore no gloves, hands covered with dirt.

She looked up. Her eyes were too bright, her motions awkward, jerky, and self-conscious. The transformation was startling.

"What are you doing?" he asked unnecessarily.

"Picking thoughts from the garden that is my brain."

"How lovely, your brain is a garden."

"Not exactly, I have to tend my head very carefully. It has a tendency to act up." She picked up a handful of violets and ushered him past the entryway portrait but not before it was able once again to pull Zeldon into a sharp, focused intensity. Her opening comments though didn't allow him to dwell on it.

"I'm moody, I admit that." Straightaway she seemed bent on explaining herself. "I know I should have called you earlier, but sometimes I like to be eccentric or outrageous. Do you ever get such wild thoughts in your head?"

"No, I couldn't say so."

"Lucky head." She stared at him, too long, disconcertingly, obviously in the company of her daylight demons then cast her eyes downward. She led him to a sofa in the living room and sat close to him with her legs curled under her. "What would our bland Rockwater residents think if they knew I was banging the local gravedigger?"

Zeldon was shocked at the crudeness of her remark and at the insensitivity it showed to his own feelings. He was not so disappointed, however, that he didn't notice the particular hip roll she displayed when she walked. Neither did he forget the modestly disguised figure hidden beneath her jeans and sweatshirt. But he couldn't help wondering what she was up to.

"They suspect pleasure," she went on, smiling wickedly. "I see it as my reward." She didn't say for what. "Well," she sighed, "I wonder how many of Phil's voting citizens are what they appear to be. Certainly not you, Mr. Z. Do you know what your reputation is here in our fair village?"

"I can't say. No." Zeldon had to confess he didn't much care.

"I can tell you. My house is a gossip-gathering center because of my Phil's chosen profession. You leave people with a confused impression, my love. They think you're a genial companion of the permanently departed. Isn't that choice? You're a gentleman gravedigger, a cemetery scholar . . . sort of a tombstone historian."

"Defined by my profession, ah well," he sighed, "I can't do much about that."

"Maybe not, but they've marked you as Rockwater's man from yesterday. Why would you swoon into the arms of the past? What's wrong with today?"

"Plenty. Yes, we've got good dentistry, but we pay for it with things like genocide." He was remembering his uncomfortable conversation with the Four over that point.

"All right, touché, but that's not all. You make people nervous. You make them feel their opinions are inappropriate for no clear reason. That leaves them disoriented and befuddled. Does that surprise you?"

He wasn't enjoying the game; she was enjoying it too much. "I don't know what to make of it if it's true."

"Oh, it's true. But there's a sort of compliment in it, too. You're the closest a human can come to serving as doorkeeper to the mysteries," she said that with a scornful smirk on her face.

For the life of him, he couldn't make out what all this was about. Then, abruptly, as though she had put him in his place, she switched the subject to the other man in her life. "My husband is an odious man. Conversation at our dinner table isn't exactly the Algonquin Round Table. He's in Albany, by the way, building his empire or something . . . some sewer convention for mayors, he said. He must think I don't know Rockwater doesn't have any sewers, just septic tanks. Maybe water pipes, or backup pipes . . . Phil-type pipes . . ." She seemed determined to reduce him. "What does my husband know? Sewer pipes, just one small inch of a very large elephant . . . septic pipes . . ."

"Storm drains."

"That's right, storm drains." She shook her head in disbelief at such a concern or at her dwelling on it. When I say, 'I must collect myself,' only you know I'm speaking almost literally."

He wished she would stop that rambling. He liked her real conversation, and there she was offering him the most reckless confidences, intimate feelings that left him feeling voyeuristic and uncomfortable. All the while, she was worrying her small handful of violets, twisting and bending them. Her building anger against Phil could become something threatening, so he tried to introduce a degree of tolerance to the vendetta against him.

"I don't think highly of Phil, but even a cold heart deserves some northern lights now and then . . ." That was a gesture of gratitude toward Phil because Zeldon knew wellbeing came when outer and inner security coincided, and Phil had at least given her half that total. "Calm down."

"Calm down? You don't live with him. Someday I'll follow that man's hearse with a dry eye. Anyway," she went on, ignoring the indiscretion of the remark, "he's out of town, and dailiness is interrupted. I hate dailiness. Let's do something."

"Like what?"

"I don't know. Well, maybe just be together."

There it was again, that introduction of a subject disjointed, unrelated to what came before.

"Phil drinks. I never made him happy, but neither did drinking. One New Year's Eve, I mixed him a drink and wished him a jiggerful of joy. Humor isn't part of his package, and he hit me. That's when the trouble started." She stroked her cheek thoughtfully. "My husband is a master of the bear hug. He embraces you to death." That was followed by a pause and then she added, "I just remembered something. I heard of one of those Hindu people, a goddess of some sort, with lots of arms sticking out all over the place . . . Kali . . . that's it, Kali. She's supposed to grant favors with one set of arms, but she uses another set to slit people's throats. And she's surrounded by skulls. That's my husband's political sponsor . . . Kali."

Finally, a reason was showing for all that conversational awkwardness. "I think, if we're to confide in each other, we should really confide. Don't you think that's fair?" There was a repeat of the overly bright-eyed stare.

"Of course." That was becoming even more uncomfortable, not at all what Zeldon had expected.

"OK, do you know I've been married before, before Phil?"

He shouldn't have been surprised at that. After all, how long had they known each other, if it could be said that they did at all. But he was.

"You're serious."

"Yes."

In any case, it explained Catia's intent to confide and to expect a mutual opening up. He waited expectantly for her to go on.

"I got pregnant in college at the University of Vermont. Had an abortion, but we got married just after we graduated." She registered a look of indifference as though the experience was unimportant to her. "It lasted less than a year, and we had it annulled." He was watching her closely then, trying to catch from her manner some of the details she was not bothering to relate. That indifference, though, was hiding what she wanted to keep private. Without pause, she went on, "That was Walt. In the meantime, I had met Jim, and we got married as soon as the annulment came through." There was some engaging expression on her face. "We didn't know it when we had our wedding, but Jim already had liver cancer, and he died before our second anniversary." She was showing her first signs of feeling over her narrative. "In our first year, I became pregnant again . . . that time I had a miscarriage. It left me unable to try again. So since I was thwarted in one manner of creativity, I increased my interest in another. You see the results of my miscarriage all around you."

During its telling, she got up, paced the room, and stood facing one of her full length self-portraits, all the while carrying the flowers. "When he died, I had a breakdown. I call it a breakdown. I was beside myself. You know what that means, beside myself. It meant there were two of me. Oh, Z . . ." She stared at herself there on the canvas. "I'm beside myself often . . . Well anyway, when I recovered, sort of recovered, I married Phil and pretended it was Jim. To my sorrow," she said while again she studied herself there on the wall, "I've had to learn to count husbands, hardly an unopened bud."

"Many times defeated yet always unvanquished," he thought. He saw that early in her frightened life she had learned the necessity of provisional loyalties and kept what mattered to her safe within her thoughts. He supposed it was necessary for her also to develop a totally self-centered pattern of defenses, without reference to others more able to cope for themselves. Maybe that was why nowhere in the house had he seen an image of Phil, not a snapshot or a painting, not even a newspaper photo. She was everywhere; it was as though he didn't live there. In some ways, she could appear to be uncaring. At times, obviously she was.

"And lovers?" Much as he was learning, he wanted to know more. He knew already she was something primitive, something vital, elemental. Then she could switch to being muffled and uncertain.

"Kali," she said, "Kali giveth and Kali taketh away." Suddenly, inexplicably, she threw her then ruined bouquet of violets to the floor at Zeldon's feet. She stared at them with intense concentration as though she had an interesting idea. But then saying nothing, she restlessly came back and sat down. She didn't answer his question, only stared at her self-image opposite. "I don't like to paint pain. I don't want to record it. But I do it when I have to, if I'm going to tell the truth."

Zeldon sat intent, wondering what else he didn't know about the curvaceous bundle of surprises. For some reason, he remembered she had said to him when they first spoke, "I don't sell my talent. I prefer to choose what I do with it." She might have meant more than her painting. And listening to the light quality in her language, he realized that she also paints luminous images with words, words, images, showing her beauty, hiding her pain, communicating in more than one medium.

"So what are you thinking when you paint?" he asked, trying to corral his confusion. He knew he was rummaging in the netherworld of her mind. The directness of his question drew out of her a reply she had never recognized even in her mind. She surprised them both by saying, "I'm coping. Every attempt is a new hope that I've found myself."

"Wonderful, like the Romans."

"Exactly, I never realized it before. I'm thinking white is a whisper and black is a shout. Except that white is a tofu color, it takes on the flavor of its sauces, its surroundings. Once, though, I wanted to paint a black that was dazzling, to show how I felt. More black than black. I got it once in a dress I wore for a mirror sitting. I actually got it. Now I can't see it . . ." she did as she often did, paused and stared into the middle distance then picked it up and went on, "I can't see it, but I've got it more clearly inside me. Well anyway, I know yellow is a song. Blue is a moan or a groan.

Sometimes it shows indifference or apartness, maybe distance. Red criticizes, orange quarrels, and pink simpers. It goes like that."

"Always the same color means the same message?"

"Except when I want to be contrary. Then I shake it all up in a bag."

Again, she was toying with him. "Now, Superintendent Wade, tell me one of your secrets."

"No, wait a moment, I need to send out for dinner. Not in any mood to cook. Chinese, OK?"

It was all Zeldon could do to nod his agreement. His head was awhirl at that chaotic exposure, and he was being asked to match it with his own recent history. While he waited, he stepped into the next room down the hall, Catia's studio. An empty easel stood in the middle of the space; the floor along the four walls was crowded with canvases piled in front of one another, some framed, some not. He tilted some of the works in front to better see the hidden ones behind. The forward canvasses showed a familiar style, with festive colors, but some of them were interspersed with subdued shades, even dark. There, sheltered by the familiar self-images, he discovered a layer of quite different pieces—darker figures clothed in darker colors, showing startling visages of a different Catia, one of them a figure of her reaching for butterflies—black butterflies. They told a different story, revealed that even when the artist was in a stable mode the ominous dangers lurked in the background. Those had to be the painful ones, telling that other truth. It was not alluring, not inviting, the work of a tormented mind, quite off-putting in fact. Additionally, he found one, only one, unfinished work. Might that have been done in a confession of confusion or self-doubt? Whatever else it meant, it exhibited a statement of the vaunted *vanishing point* in composition, where Catia herself was not to be found. That was certainly a secret gallery, hidden behind a façade of the familiar.

His discovery told him what he knew but wanted to deny. Her heart may have been a flower garden, but her mind was, as she herself confessed, a windstorm. And so the flowers died. It was his self-assigned necessity to love them back to blooming, two sides to that one person. She was the honest charmer, the loving Catia, capable also of demonic rages. He knew he was adored. Equally he knew he was abhorred, a double intensity housed in that lover-destroyer. Or in another mode, she would one day be scandalously intoxicating, vivacious, the next bury herself in an inertia that was unchallengeable.

Hearing Catia's approach, he quickly rearranged the pieces he had moved and stepped back.

"Dinner will be served in forty-five minutes. One of my specialties, direct from General Tsao's personal chef." She was talking too fast and acting unlike herself. But she brightened when she said, "I have an idea. Why don't I paint you while you tell me some of your secrets. Remember you owe me some."

He felt awkward but could think of no better way to respond, and so he nodded his willingness. "Come and sit here, facing toward the door but turn your head toward me." She guided him into the position she wanted and began to arrange her paints and brushes. Soon she was talking again, talking too much. "Z, why didn't you get an MBA and join the race to riches?"

"Not my style, really, I live in my head." He thought that should have been obvious.

"So?"

"Well, I carry everything with me. I just don't have any other life."

"You could do that and have a career."

"No, I'm a turtle. My home is on my back."

"You slipped into this life, didn't you?"

"Maybe." He thought he had explained all that to her earlier. Without telling her of his inheritance in escrow, he said, "I lead a life with little money and less love."

"I can take care of both of those problems." There it was again, isolated thoughts without reference to all the other facts. He ignored the digression. "It's such a contingent world. In the Yarde, I find permanence."

"Permanence, in a few acres of silence? I'd expect you to live in a bottomless melancholy. Why don't you?" He didn't answer. "It's that boy who died, that's why, isn't it? You think he will redeem you."

"Yes." That was foolishness. He had explained himself to her the night they spent together in the Yarde. She knew some of that, and she was only fishing for more, fishing in his inner being. But he went on long enough to say, "I don't know. I certainly know we die. And our only defense against the vast indifference of nature is to love. So when I'm spooning dirt into a grave, I get an itch in my hands. I want to be ladling out a final good-bye, some kind of reassurance, more than dirt, some . . . some shovelful of love."

With that he had had enough, so he turned the subject to something more true to their moment, "I looked over your inventory here, way more than I could get to." He didn't want her to know what he had seen. But it was enough to tell him a great deal. It taught him, for instance, that Catia was an excellent impressionist. She could give the *appearance* of a subject, in that case, herself. That was her social self, and they were the works placed about the house. Then there was what she could *see* in her subject, the underlying fact. That was something else again. She painted herself in health, her beauty, and in her illness, her demented appearance. In her total collection, she had revealed that she knew she existed in each of these forms and that she carried her awareness of that duality into even her better moments, a heartbreaking revelation. She was showing him a needy emptiness within herself, and he knew that it was the unoccupied space in a room that made it habitable, a home for himself and a safe haven for her?

"So you want to know more of how I paint? What more . . . Let's see, how can I say this? You know by now that it's a lifelong probing for my self. And I never know when I've got it right. Just a suspicion . . . a sense that I'm in the vicinity of myself. But then I might have erased myself entirely." She looked forlorn. "I'm chasing a black hole." There was a long pause this time. "You see why I'm so tentative?"

Obviously she wanted him to know her private-most self. She stumbled on. "I start with a common painter's trick. If I paint on an unprimed canvas, the surface absorbs the paint and gives a more diffused result with an indistinct outline. It softens them and gives its heavier texture. But if I work on a primed surface, the result makes its own statement. Edges are hard, clear or distinct or diffuse. They're where I begin and where I end, you see?"

"Fascinating, I never knew it was so complicated."

"You could learn that part of it pretty quickly. But then comes the hard part. I've already told you how I feel about colors. When

I'm serious about it, it's all at work down in my belly, where the instincts are. Some other days, though, I relax and let them play. Red says, 'Let's take charge here,' and then rose says, 'Take it easy, red, don't overdo it.' Black says, 'No way, I'm not mixing in this crowd,' and white asks, 'What am I doing in this painting? It's a riot.'" She shrugged and then turned serious. "You know how wide nature can reach from the tornado to the titmouse. Well, my insides are the tornado and my paintings are the titmouse. I start a painting from my insides, but there I'm all angularity and tension, so I paint the opposite. I paint my hopes. Watch for a pink, loitering surreptitiously in shadows. That's hope."

She was still in a confessional mood. "What I'd like to be. Can you understand that? I see my own life with detachment, from a height looking down. It was self-portraits that taught me that. 'There she is,' I say, 'that's her.' Then I just paint. I paint fluid, softly curved lines." She drew her hand over the air. "Myself on the outside, maybe find an attitude that makes the eye of the observer twinkle. What I'd like to be inside." She didn't quite say she had a collection that included both her angularity and her fluidity, things seen only in the corner of the observer's eye, fringe awarenesses. But then Zeldon could reach that conclusion himself; she was subtle enough not to always make a statement but offer only a captured gesture or a glance of a thought.

It was then that Zeldon fell in love with all the screaming dangers he felt around the issue. Not least of those dangers was his full awareness that from time to time, she could cast him a look that liquefied whatever resolve he had formed within himself. It placed his very core in jeopardy.

Nevertheless, he was able to say, "That's beautiful in itself," referring to that *making the eye of the observer twinkle . . . what I'd like to be inside*. In the silence, he dwelt on the thought, turning it over and over in his mind. It remained with him in his heart, indelible, till the day he died.

It didn't omit his awareness of those hidden suffering images. They told him her painted hopes hadn't come without a cost. It was becoming more deeply obvious to him that he was dealing with damaged genes there and that they served as an obligato over rational thought, leaving her governed by confusion. It looked like mental confusion and emotional confusion were her constant suffering. Or was he presuming too much? Smiling inwardly, he admitted he was confused himself.

"It's what art is." She spoke it as though it were common knowledge, her arm forming quick motions all the while with her eyes fixed intently on Zeldon's near shoulder. "So the inside . . . that's where the tornadoes are." She did some quick brush strokes. "And I've got some dangerous appetites lurking down in my tornado cellar. Want to come down into my cellar with me?" She glanced at him and gave him a lascivious smile. She was speaking in a soft voice, her crazy voice, a parody of reasonableness., All the while she worked, Catia, with guile and gender chemistry, slowly drew him to her. He on the other hand as they negotiated those impulses, saw himself as circling and circling his desire, coming closer with each encroachment to his gratifying conquest. Each of them felt the pride of the initiator.

"You," she said, holding her brush in midair, "the plumed knight rescuing the maiden from the dragon and making love to her, did you ever think the maiden might see you as two beasts? Not much to choose between?"

Offended despite that revelation of emotional instability, Zeldon said, "Am I a beast to you?" Her emerging worldview was appearing more and more to be unrooted, maybe uprooted.

"Do you remember when I said I had met you before during your tragic fire?"

"Certainly, I remember."

"The evening you were here and you were lost in my self-portraits, going over them so carefully, I thought of that again. You were in shock, and you stumbled into me. I grabbed at you, and we recovered our balance together. Ever since that night, all those years ago, I've wondered if maybe we could do that again. Catch our balance together."

Moved, he nevertheless asked, "But if I'm just another beast . . . ?"

She lowered her brush, looking crestfallen. "Zeldon, I couldn't find my balance in the arms of a beast." She was making little sense, but she went on to reveal why, "I have a curse, my darling. Once it was called religious vision. Now it's called unresolved inner conflict. If they want to be rude about it . . ." Tears flowed from her anguished eyes. "They call it psychosis. I can't connect my thoughts . . ." She looked crestfallen. "And pearls without a string can't make a necklace."

Stepping away from her work to regain her lost composure, she turned and hid her face while she mixed paints on her palette. He watched the highly intelligent woman, recognizing her concentrated inward activity. He had seen it often in her, painting, doing household chores, talking, and feeling restless. She turned then sad faced, features drawn, and said, "Your world and the world inside me aren't the same, Z. You don't know about despair. When I'm sorting out the gold and the garbage of a day and there isn't any gold . . . when everything . . . everything . . . is ultimately unimportant, that's despair. I feel that dragon writhing . . . roaring." She took a deep breath. "And snuffing and barking." There was another pause. "With the smell of my sickness evaporating from it. I know despair, Zeldon. You know discouragement." Swallowing her anguish, she murmured, "It's like taming a dragon that won't be tamed. You know how these things work. That's why I love you. We each have an inner radius of self-regard. It's our ego ownership, right? Pride . . . no, more than pride, integrity, we can't lose it, Z. We just can't lose it. Well, right now my self-esteem is on a diet. And every time I crack up, I emerge with a narrower understanding of who I am." The lost look reappeared. "It's hard to regain lost ground." She stopped then spread out her hands and said, "There, now. I've offered you my *coeur mis a nu*, my naked heart. It's all I have to bring to the party."

Deeply moved, he said, "I know about losing my self-regard, love. Keeping mine hasn't come easily. When it comes to holding your essential dignity, the world isn't going to be cooperative."

"Tell me about it." She grimaced. "I guess it doesn't come easily to anyone . . . especially when you, as I do, live with someone who has plundered your heart for years. You have to carry it about inside yourself and honor it there but . . ." She allowed herself no comfort from that truism. "For years, people have told me I should get help from those people who make it their business to teach the rest of us how to pull it off. I know about these people. I've studied them. They tinker with your brain. They'd all love to get into me, just like you. Only into a different part of me."

Offended again, he held his peace, and she went on, "Medication is their favorite plaything. Medication for all of us." She cast Zeldon an intense glance and went on, "Has it ever occurred to you that we may be the last of the randomly born generations? I mean these people are getting more influential and whole later generations could be custom-designed. You and I, my dear, would become disposable genetic experiments. That's all, disposable."

It was a little far-fetched, but he could see her crazy fears. That was all she would tell him for that moment; she fell into her habit of oceanic dreaming. The rest of it was left to his imagination.

There was more inner tempest. Did that poor woman live in a climate of total lunacy? But no, he had seen her as a female wonder, entrancing. Evidence surrounded him in that very room of an artistic genius, masterful, and able to depict deep truths about human nature and her own insight into it. And in a short while, he had come to sympathize with her, to empathize. What was his empathy drawing him into? It was no imagined fear. To him, no room was as empty as a room just after she had left it. He was forced to admit he found himself strongly attracted to the opaque child of light. And he knew in his heart, that paradox would cost him dearly in days to come. He loved her. She would be his ruin. He knew he was (he had heard it said) vanquished by the never-healing wound of love. "But suppress your instincts." He was certain. "And nature will have its revenge. Time . . . friend, enemy? Time would tell." He had a suspicion he was about to commit himself to a custodial love. How would he ever find peace of mind if he embraced that kind of caretaking for a psychotic woman and the radical ambivalence of her divided mind? How could he peer down the well of her suffering and not fall in?

"She's skating over a blue window glass of ice." He couldn't interrupt himself in that monologue. "What courage." Then he became preternaturally still. "I love her." He confessed it again; it came out as a final declaration, a no-turning-back commitment. He knew full well what it might mean; that explained the dark stillness of his realization. "But," he declared to himself, "it's the antidote to dying. It's not all one way. She has taught me how to love beyond the margins of convenience, no small gift. And she, in her most subterranean self, has disclosed herself to me entirely, exposed her final weakness and her greatest dependence. So there's no possible response but to surrender to her, in exchange, my complete self-interest."

He was conscious that he was committing himself to a deathless fidelity. It was what he chose to do, even though to their mutual peril, they were destined to experience the salient extreme of human love. There was something like despair in his eyes. There would always be the question, he knew, of when would the thread snap, that was, when, if ever, would her mind tip irrevocably? Would the day come—quite possibly it would—when he loved a mad stranger? He dared not hope for a love drawn out into old age.

Slowly the idea that would redeem the dilemma took shape. He would love her beyond her mind, behind her mind, and transcending her mind. If it remained intact, all the better. If it bent further or broke, he would love that part of her that stayed within his reach. He recalled the story of the British soldier who lost a leg in the American Revolution. Awaiting his lover's response to his news, he found his life again in her answer, "I will love that part of you that is left to me to love."

A costly intention, with all the price to pay still in the future. "But isn't that what love is," he thought, "a mortgage on the future?" It was resolved. He was at rest. His mind joined his eyes and dipped into repose, causing him to shake his head in recovery and realize that he had been thinking intensely; all the while, Catia was concentrating on painting his features with no idea of the hard work going on behind those features. Inexplicably from out of nowhere, he thought of the gracious people he had befriended with acts of kindness in the Yarde and how they had outlined for themselves a portrait of his nature. Flattering, then Catia had given that portrait a visible presence. He wondered how those two images would appear to one another, and if either resembled the true Zeldon. He wasn't to know.

Actually, although busy with her brushwork, she had jumped to a playful topic over one of Phil's business guests. "The other evening, Phil had an appointment with some money mogul in his study, but in typical fashion, his friend came before he got home, so of course I had to do the honors and offer him a drink over a stalling conversation. I hate those. Anyway, after I got him settled,

I said, 'What do you do, Mr. Prescott?' He said, 'Minerals. I'm just an old-fashioned prospector.' 'Shouldn't you have a mule and a shovel?' 'Well, not quite, I'm not that old-fashioned. I use a satellite and a computer. I find oil.' 'I have a friend who still works with a backhoe and a shovel,' I said. You must be famous, Z, because he said, 'That Yarde-man, right? Tell me about him. I hear he's strange.' 'Not so strange.' I spoke up for you, you see? And he said, 'Hangs around in the cemetery, doesn't he?' And I said, 'Yes, but think about it. The most interesting thing underground to you is oil. To him it's bodies. Who's strange?' Phil came home, and the guy was glad to see me leave."

Both of them had forgotten dinner. Catia put aside her brushes, circled the easel, and glided over to Zeldon. Caressing his cheek and shoulder, she said, "I'll finish your portrait later. I've got enough of it here." She paced before him, frowning. "I wonder if we should make love." Zeldon immediately immersed himself in the still, velvety darkness of the question. She gazed at him with her blue, sea-green mermaid eyes, sending waves of invitation. He couldn't believe his eyes then when he saw her draw a coin from a pocket of her blue jeans, study it for a moment, and toss it up before them. "Heads, the dragon-slayer wins." She began to lift her sweatshirt over her breasts. He was working hard there, and she was taunting him, teasing him. What was wrong with her, the chemical soup that gave her her humanity? Furious though he was, he exhibited his deep confusion by realizing that she was at once independent and dependent, rebellious and tormenting. "When she locks you in," he admitted, "the crowd falls away." She was Sunday, everyone else a weekday. She was red, other women beige. She was 212 degrees; others were room temperature. She was a full-fledged mature woman, who left him always foraging for happiness. And he hated her.

He was getting to know the seductive conundrum. In her cunning state with her cold eyes and her quiet manner, she showed a wild and brutal nature. She appeared at such moments withdrawn as though studying where best to strike. Svelte, lithe, with inviting breasts and promising loins, she attracted in order to destroy, Kali. Her clothing, her glances, her gestures, and speech could woo, and her lunge could kill. He knew it. She was a savage with the instincts of a viper. Hadn't she pointed to his own idiosyncrasies and accused him over his unbalanced personality? Did his own derangement match hers? Was she really mad or were her own inner spirits as real to her as his to himself? Were they fellow mad men or kindred spirits? No matter, he remembered his dilemma resolution, and he loved her.

\*   \*   \*

The next morning, the Jogger limped into The Yarde. "Hamstring," he explained. "Just taking a few days to try to walk it off." Offering his thermos, he said, "Coffee?"

"No, thanks." Zeldon didn't explain that he hadn't had a cup of coffee for over five years, ever since the night Mrs. Rodgers pointed out his coffee ring as the cause of the fire. The Jogger limped away.

Zeldon tightened his running laces and set out on his own badly needed morning run, badly needed to wipe the night's restless dreams from his head. He was no sooner underway before he realized the run was to be a continuation of the night, a review of Catia's recent sentiments jumbled in no particular order and lying there in wait for his attention. "My brain is a rollercoaster set in a bowl of bone." He ran with that for a few minutes, thinking that could be true of anyone, well, maybe a little more true for her. That brought another of her brain remarks to mind, "All right, my brain circuitry is hungry for a few chemicals, so what? When I'm running normally, I think circles around everyone I meet." True enough, he was quite proud of her for that.

Her powers of reason, when she was being reasonable, were superior. And he knew her emotions, when they were her own, were pure poetry. Reason and poetry were twin sisters who should dance together in the very harmony that she was so hungry for. But she could color it all with her eccentricities. One day he had caught her lying on her living room floor, alone. Explaining herself as though it were the most natural thing in the world she said, "Sorry, on Tuesdays I'm easily deflected. Something to do with my astrology. So on some Tuesdays I do this. I'm listening to my house. Do you have any idea what your house wants to say to you? Walls that have memory, eyes that never forget." Scenes like that were more telling than might be realized. The mental heroine showed not only her strangeness, but gave a hint of that upward surge she so often revealed, the surge that always comes with the gift of life.

A dip in the path caused Zeldon to break the rhythm of his stride, calling his attention to how frequently her world changed its rhythm. To prove the point, he smiled at one of her protesting non sequiturs, "I ignore science, know-it-all science. Those people are never around when their embarrassments bring some new disaster." She excused the avoidance of scientific knowledge by confessing, "I like being information-deprived. Look at how much idiocy in others I avoid." On the other hand, she was willing to contradict herself with "before I die, I'd like to get a toehold in reality."

While she could hold his attention with conversation like that, he noticed how she in turn listened to exchanges herself, not as others do but intently, taut, ready to spring on an idea. If one emerged that she liked, her delight showed instantly. Poor ideas, lesser ideas drew a frown, or worse, disdain. He commented on that one time, "The world of ideas is high drama to you."

"Yes," she answered, "it's like one big popcorn machine. Actually, there are two worlds, the real world, and the world that can be dreamt. I like mine better." "So much," Zeldon thought, "for getting a toe-hold in reality." She would talk to herself, refer to herself in the third person as though she were another person as another being, realize aloud that she loved her other being, sympathize with her, rail at the world for abusing her then quarrel with herself.

By then he was breathing heavily. He had discovered that before; it took energy just to keep up with her mental ramblings and the operatic scenes she created. In that, he had been indulging himself for most of an hour. He slowed to a walk, casting through her varied facial expressions, her tones of voice, her gestures, and the charismatic style that flavored it all. Shaking his head, he walked back to the Yarde and sat with his bottled water at hand. "What a waste of passion, to love a woman no longer in residence in her own mind." From time to time, at least, no was one at home, from cellar to attic. Soon unthinkingly, he began plucking away at a row of unwanted plantings. With her face in his mind, he felt determined to change the shape, color, and smell of his small world, to expand it so as to encompass the other larger-than-life spirit.

\* \* \*

Impatient over his fast-moving experiences and slowly developing realizations, he crossed to his house, made a phone call, showered, and drove to the home of a recently bereaved acquaintance, a doctor of psychiatry.

"Thanks for this. I need to hear some questions answered, and you can help," he began.

"Glad to help if I can."

"I have a friend who has all the symptoms of bipolarity. Her mood swings seem to be becoming more frequent and more severe."

"Is she under treatment?"

"No, she refuses treatment."

"That's a serious decision. Not much good will come of waiting it out. There are options open, depending on the particulars. That can make quite a difference. More than people realize it's not all hopeless."

"I'd like to convince her of that."

"We have to stay with the facts, even when they contradict each other. A recent study of eighty-six thousand Icelanders suggested that people with genetic risk factors tor schizophrenia and bipolar disorder appear to have a greater chance of being creative and of holding a zest for life." There was a pause while Zeldon digested that then "What stage is this person in, what symptoms do you meet, and how often?"

Zeldon went over Catia's history, as much of it as he knew, always avoiding naming names or revealing details although he was sure the doctor would recognize some of the situation on his own. His reassurances and professional ethics would have to suffice in order to put to rest any fears of exposure.

"The common characteristics of paranoid schizophrenia leave the patient with no psychic center," the explanation was begun soberly. "There's nothing to which experience can adhere. Consequently, there's no real sense of self. Every stimulus and memory floats in a swirling chaos of sensory impressions. Terror rules."

"My god, given life, choirs of angels, with no song to sing!"

"It's bad. Causality disappears. You can see why it's called madness. It's a staircase of separate feelings leading downward to what I've described. But that's a worst case. Mercifully, it's seldom that dark. And it's a transient thing."

"It comes and goes?" He knew the answer to that of course.

"Yes, and medication is the great mercy. Have you noticed periods of no need for sleep and then too much sleep . . . mood shifts, energy shifts?"

"Yes, of course. Terrifying all of it."

"So you can understand how the patient is left traumatized and then has to anticipate the return of the horror at any moment. Again, there's the medication, but that leaves the patient one step removed from immediacy. Many of them don't take it for that reason."

"This is the person I love," Zeldon thought, thanked the doctor profusely, and left, wondering why many others could enjoy a pacific lifetime, quieter, and balanced with their own share of symmetries. Or those others, the bad children of America, competitive, barbarous mediocrities claiming their tribal entitlements, and small world greed masters too crippled to empathize were determined to pull a culture down with them. Neither camp had the passion, the dangerous, reckless reach for boundless life, life founded in love and generosity. And the gamble was worth the prize. He who had been conditioned to think not in days or years but in lifetimes had to take the prognosis extremely seriously. Furthermore, he remembered seeing one of her paintings portraying a black sun in a somber sky. There was no way he could consider no withdrawal from such courageous suffering, despite the deep scarring it left behind.

He walked home, taking the memory of their exchanges with him along with his concession and Catia's echoing in his mind, one time, two times, and yet another. He was a lonely, troubled man harboring visions of life, a life wildly improbable and infinitely precious. Yes, such a life incorporated variability into its future. Such a threat was especially ominous in Catia's case and therefore his own. So be it.

# CHAPTER 12

Phil found himself avoiding people for the first time in his life. A new appetite for privacy drove him uncharacteristically into inventing reasons for being unavailable. He hid in his office until his excuses ran thin, went home in the middle of the day, and closed himself in his study when Catia allowed him the luxury. He even took to driving to unfrequented places to sit in his car, smoking cigars and drinking coffee. All that was to enable him to indulge in an unusual compulsion, to simply think.

He also increased the hours he spent with Merle Stanley. That was a risk, not that it hadn't always been, but then he was seeing her right there in town. Admittedly, her driveway was sheltered from road traffic by hedging, and yes, Toby's commute into the city gave her long hours of sheltered time most days, but Rockwater was, after all, a small town. Two things in their affair had been a reassurance to him—her savvy discretion and her local ambitions. What Phil didn't know and Merle herself only vaguely felt was that those ambitions reached further than present circumstances guaranteed. In the meantime, she loved her social prominence, and she would see to it that even her sex life didn't threaten that. Unaware of much of that, that day Phil threaded his way to 623 Tarleton Road.

"What a pleasant surprise," purred the Hostess Supreme. "Put out the cigar," she reminded the commanding lothario, "you know the rules." He did know the rules, no leaving behind the scent of the strong perfume from his second-favorite vice. "What brings you now, as if I didn't know? But why no phone call?"

"Just spur of the moment," Phil said, "blood high, appetite strong." That didn't surprise Merle, but he was too circumspect to act impulsively. Something else was on his mind; she was sure. He answered that question when he said, "Got some problems right now. Need to unload some baggage. Want to carry a little baggage?"

"I'm a pack mule for the heavy lifters," she quipped.

He knew that to be true. He who had never confided in anyone, ever, had been unburdening himself to his mistress for some weeks, political stuff at first then more personal worries, mostly centering on his home life. She was right, she was a born counselor, with the accompanying skill to make babbling out personal matters a quite comfortable pastime. In addition to that, having heard and accepted the most intimate of confessions about his personal life, she had the emotional dexterity to set aside all possibilities of jealousy and slide eagerly into bed. Just at that unexpectedly awkward phase of his affairs of state, as her husband would call them, he found her invaluable. Yes, he knew her to be vicious in her whispered thrusts at non-friends, but that didn't trouble him unduly. So he confided.

"Something's up with my wife, my proud catastrophe."

Merle took that in stride. "Having an affair?"

"I don't know."

"Any candidates if she is?"

"No, I don't know. If you remember a divorced lawyer, lived here a few years ago for just two or three years named Potter, good looking, smooth, he saw my money and my wife's figure and figured he could cash in. I was never sure if he got her into bed. I overheard her on the phone once. She said, 'Phil's hard to love. He lives as though he's got a key in his back.'"

Merle made no comment about that. Phil didn't notice the silence and went on, "Anyway the guy's not here anymore." He didn't elaborate, but she guessed the guy had left under pressure.

"That doesn't add up to much."

"Just enough to make me uneasy." Then he launched into a review of his marriage. "At first, things were what you'd expect . . . pleasures in bed, she played at house, and I made money. Like everybody else, we vied with each other, deciding who would hold what powers over the other and when. She was no pushover." He hated to make the admission but felt he'd better, given what was to come later. "I gradually learned what areas of our life together were a matter of indifference to her. There were a lot of those. Where she took over, with a surprising tenacity, was in her studio time, utterly solo."

"This all sounds pretty normal."

"She always went for a late evening walk. Those were OK. I never wanted to share the privilege. But the moods, I called them her moods, they got to be more often and more dark and longer. Nobody knows it, but she's got an underside that isn't friendly with rational things, forever throwing furniture out the window. That can reverse your daylight impressions. Dammit, touch that woman, and you find she's a hologram."

Phil had spoken of her moods before, but he had been guarded. Merle suspected there was more to those episodes than he let on. Obviously they made him nervous. Sure enough, he changed the subject. Not to a safe subject, but a different one. "When we had sex it was eager enough, but a couple of times, I heard her whisper the name of Jim, her dead husband. It could have been just a muscle-memory thing, but I don't know, something hung in the air around those times, and they stayed in my mind."

"Not so good. You can imagine what would happen if I called out, 'Phil!' when I had sex."

"Yeah, Toby would wet the bed. Well anyway, that didn't go on too long, those sex slippages, because they soon died. But I remember it."

Merle had become aroused herself in the midst of that, and she took his hand and led him to the bedroom. They had sex to their mutual satisfaction, but when they finished, Merle looked closely at him and asked, "Are you holding me because you love me or because you want to steal my body heat?"

Looking confused, he said, "I'm not cold." The obtuse answer didn't trouble Merle because she wasn't in bed for love any more than he was. And being no fool, she knew that a snarl lived at the center of his character and found its way to the surface at any serious provocation. Her motive was ambition, his a need to drop some tension. He showed he hadn't exhausted his unburdening and picked up his narrative again.

"Do you and Toby argue a lot?"

"Not too much. Everybody does sometimes, but I pretty well get what I want, and Tobe goes along with it. He's a wimp, you know."

Phil marked again his determination about never referring to Toby as Tobe. It was Merle's personal habit and wasn't to be known by outsiders. "Well, we started quibbling after a while, and I thought the same thing, that everybody does that. But then she started with her zingers. Cat's an expert with her zingers."

Merle laughed at that and studied that handsome face, clouded with guile. "Of course, she would have to be. She lives with a master of repartee."

With that, he felt he should explain himself. "She sees me as a hustler. Well, I plead guilty. I'm a deal maker. Any pol worth his salt is a broker between quarrelers' competing interests, that's what it's all about."

Merle's acidulous temperament had a passing judgment about a spinmaster working the credulous taxpayers. What she didn't actually know she could surmise told her that his character was the consequence of a long series of expedient choices, without principle dominating. Phil was not, in the end, an evil man but merely weak. Being familiar with that quality in her marriage, she gave it no further thought. "Your wife is beautiful," she volunteered.

"A diamond, beautiful and hard." Then alluding to his need for the confessor-priestess, he blustered, "A man has to find an outlet for his anger. We've been over-domesticated. And the outlet has to be robust and allow some outward action. We do lead with our shoulders when we walk, after all."

"We lead with our hips."

He ignored that and seemed to have a need to clear up the question of manhood. "A man today is too narrowly engaged, too many social controls. No wonder we're angry."

For Merle, that might well be Toby in bed with her, emphasizing his testosterone. Looking at the bedside clock she said, "The commuting train is on its way. You'd better take your hormones and go home now."

Phil stepped into his trousers and decided he was going to have to tackle the challenge with his own wits. Merle was OK for a roll in the hay; she was a good place to deposit a few confidences and reduce a few tensions but no answer to his problems. Not an anchorage, OK, she was a cultured woman, but unfortunately, all the culture had swallowed up the woman and left only a snob.

*   *   *

He decided to take them to Catia directly. He was more troubled by her estrangement than he might have expected to be. It even occurred to him that he might find her more important to him than he had realized, so he would accost her directly. He went home and finding no sign of her about the house although her car was there, guessed she was in her sanctum sanctorum, painting. He knocked and opened the door ajar. "Can I come in? I'd like to talk to you."

"Wait a moment," she answered and began cleaning her brushes.

That of course was to protect her rule about his intrusions into the studio, and he knew it. He paced from room to room, turned on the TV, lighted a fresh cigar, and prepared his approach. She appeared in the library, walking with her usual puma-like grace, but he knew that lately she had been acting like a puma in a cage. She looked at him questioningly, and he could tell in that first glance that she was her rational, sensible self again. It was like that lately, unpredictable with those sudden changes. Good, he felt, that would make it easier.

"What's wrong with us?" he asked.

She looked at him cooly and said, "I'm still adding up what's wrong with you. I know very well what's wrong with me. I'm a nutcase and when I'm trying to be more than that, I'm like a harpist in a military band, making music but no one hears it."

"Can we do without the melodrama?" The minute he said it, he knew that was a mistake. He wanted to talk, not to argue.

It was already too late; she was angry immediately. "All right, we'll skip the melodrama and get right to the truth. You're a noisemaker. Even when we're the only people in a room together and we talk, like now, you aren't really talking to me. You're making noise. You're a cheat and a liar."

Despite his recent suspicions, Phil couldn't know that it was pure projection. Furthermore, just when he was about to lose his own temper, an inclined beam of light struck her skin, translucent, alive. It reminded him that he truly wanted to reach the woman, that he hadn't forgotten her allure when she was herself. It was to that woman he was sensing a renewed attraction. He couldn't quite say why. Because of the vague need to change things between them, he controlled his own anger and answered mildly, "I'm not a liar. I'm a profession keeper of secrets. I wish we had fewer."

"Ah, now we're getting there. After all the diplomacy and all the lying, we're coming to the truth. We've peeled the onion to its empty middle. There's no love. There never was. You're too busy climbing your cobweb ladder." Idiot TV sounds scuttled across her consciousness, and she strode across the room to turn it off.

"Yes, there *is* love." He looked wasted, slumped into his shoulders.

She, on the other hand, was energized. "No, it was self-interest all along! Will this be good for me?"

"There were many times when it wasn't good for me. And there was always the tension."

"Well, you know I like my tensions neat, like marching armies at war rather than terrorists with their sneak attacks. Or is that too melodramatic for you? You need to lighten up, Phil. Sounds funny coming from me, doesn't it? You need to lighten up. You should learn some Bessie Smith, some 'Worn Out Papa Blues.' Listen to this, 'Your use done fail, all your pep done gone, Pick up that suitcase, man, an' travel on.' That's Bessie Smith."

"Pack your suitcase . . ." Only an hour ago, the keeper of secrets had told Merle that Cat was no pushover. And he knew that often conversations with her had no future. Nothing established stayed that way. Those days she was sand, and life with her was a house built on sand, his house. But something had happened to him that made him want to change that—if it could be.

"We need to see a doctor together."

"No," she snapped, "I won't put myself in the hands of those people. Put me on mood drugs and give me the latest designer personality, not me!"

"Come on, Cat. There's plenty of life ahead. We're not an Arab and a Jew wanting to kill each other."

Then she attacked, claws unsheathed. "Arabs and Jews? It's not the breed, my husband, it's the breeding. You make a big thing in your speeches about the social good. You have a primitive sense of the social good, and you've got a beat cop mentality yourself." As she spat that out, Phil could see that her pulse rate rose and her muscle tension increased. He saw her body language show defiance and her gestures lose their grace. He had seen that before. His wife's passions became deeply physical, negatively so, when she imagined her will to be humiliated. How had he come to know his wife so well and not find her more compelling? He was not without analytical skills, after all. He needed them in politics. And premeditation, he knew, was a luxury to such a frightened, driven soul. Rashness, suddenness of will, and impetuosity had destroyed any deliberate order to her life. There was little weighing of alternatives, only consequences. Of all people, he had to weigh consequences, and he knew full well how they left her terribly in need of love.

How could he explain himself? He found the animal endlessly exciting. Her energy carried her through time like an electrical current through a wire, constant, undeniable. But it must be allowed its constancy, never to be frustrated or like a power source, it would explode. And so it had.

His well-intentioned effort had turned into a brawl. She came out of her latest episode with guns blazing, and he was only giving her an arena to blow him away. That had to stop because after scenes like that, her absences became frequent. She would step into a hole in the social surface of things and simply not reappear for days on end. When she did, she looked momentarily disoriented, not yet altogether back. The cycle was forming itself again. Before his eyes, he could see Catia slipping back into her dementia, and he had to do something to arrest her returning descent.

With a sinking heart, he admitted to himself how much he cared for her, loved her, so he said, humbly, "You're right. I've been a bastard, maybe mostly to you. I'm sorry." Yes, he loved that frightening temperament, love her, but he had lost her.

Was that her husband, courting her favor? Far from being flattered, she hated being the battleground between two powerful admirers, if that was what it had come to. "I'm going to bed."

"It's only eight o'clock, Cat."

"Green eyes need more sleep than brown eyes." And she was gone.

He left the room hoping desperately there could be another chance. It was Noah expecting a draught.

\*   \*   \*

It was 10:00 p.m. and Zeldon was listening to the intricacies of a Schubert sonata when he heard a soft knocking on his door. Opening it, he found Catia looking sheepishly at him with tears in her eyes, her mascara streaked down her cheeks and her hair tousled. But she was herself, he saw it instantly. He gathered her in his arms, and they felt the wounds in both their spirits closing, healing.

"Once I said to someone," he whispered, "that money is muscle. If that's true, love is skeletal.

I'm together again."

"Me too. Me too." A look of anxiety crossed her face.

They rocked together a while, both remembering their talk about first meeting in an embrace that helped them regain their balance. Finally, they led one another to a couch and huddled in a physical unity, she crooning quietly in a female song all her own.

At long last he said, unnecessarily, "I love you."

She only continued her song. But then finally, she rose and said, "No, that was only a recess. I don't think I'm finished being crazy. And love has nothing to do with it. It's the chemical soup that was ladled into my skull, genetic stuff."

Zeldon went cold. He didn't know what that meant. It had appeared by then that there might not be permanent resting places with her, but . . .

She dropped her eyes and a look of sadness darkened her face. "Z, you think love can soften a hard heart, don't you?"

"Yes, I do."

"I admit it happens, enough to make us think it will always, if only the love is persistent."

"Yes, that's it."

"But some of us have been formed by lack of love. I've been ill all my life, Z, and I'm hard to love. You might have found that."

"You're heavenly."

"Well, some starlight maybe and black holes. At least I'm celestial."

"Yes, well all right, it's not easy. But maybe you've never met anyone willing to pay a price of loving you. I am."

"There are things you don't know . . ."

"I'm discovering that. But you might be discovering that I don't give up easily."

"I have to confess to you, dear Z, it's like a bullfight with me, full of exciting trumpets, but often you get gored by the bull, lots of little deaths. What I'm saying is, no matter how much I want love, my craziness won't let me respond to it, at least enough to last."

"And you have to know that sometimes at night I grapple with God in a dark room behind a pool hall. But then you show up, and it's morning, and I'm safe. No one is impervious to love."

She looked infinitely forlorn. "Words won't help. Meanings slip between the words," she continued, and her sorrowful look extended to an expression of full despair. Zones of judgment merged in her and drew apart again with a viscous plasticity, sanity seeped away as if by osmosis then returned in a flood of intelligence. Worst was the constant uncertainty, the fear of placing a foot on a floorboard, not knowing if the dancing molecules were dependable, if they could be counted on to hold together. Time was a jack-in-the-box; she never knew when it would explode in her face.

"Scatter the night for me, Z," she said, "please, scatter the night and bring me morning."

Suddenly, he remembered something, rose up, went into the kitchen, and returned carrying a jar in his hand. "Come," he said and led her to the door. Outside, he removed the top of his jar and released a swarm of insects that flew into the darkness. Within minutes, they revealed themselves to be fireflies, lightning bugs, surrounding them with sparks of cold fire. "There, I gathered these for you without knowing you would ask me to scatter the night. These are pieces of morning." He waved his hand toward his loving gift.

Then his expression changed. He showed her a face with no compromise in it. "You have a way of churning up my heart," he said. "All right, here's something that has brought morning to a lot of people. Who was Christ but a holy madman?"

Her pressing despair had pushed him to make the unprotected appeal from his innermost, bedrock utterance. He was willing to concede that Catia showed unmistakable signs of madness, yet showed every sign of wanting and giving love, given the chance to be her real self. He wanted only to be seen in a similar condition. He also understood that madness and love can contest, just as he had already seen death and love contest, but he truly was determined to prove it was she who was wrong, whatever it cost him. In his determination, he was brilliant. He recognized the only contribution he could make was to supply an element of constancy. That element was love. She must know, in her lucid times, that she was loved, would be loved when her focused self departed, and that love awaited her when she returned home to her true self. Always she was loved. She could take that assurance away with her into her darkness. Who knew when it would serve? Maybe often not, maybe never but maybe, as an afterthought.

Looking up at the night sky, they stood silent, shoulder to shoulder. In a voice almost inaudible he said, "What is more beautiful than what's given?" When he whispered those words, it made her wonder why she painted then she quickly realized that was exactly why she did.

Instead of going back into the house, they parted on that note. She was downcast, and he insisted that he could be aware of crimes, misjudgments, and illness on her part without surrendering his right as a flawed man to love a flawed woman. Muddled, he stood waiting as she got into her car, listening to the wind, the lake waters, the trees, nothing. Then after what seemed a lifetime, he heard it. The sky itself spoke, "Love her."

Fireflies sent her on her way.

\*     \*     \*

Catia drove home and quickly closed herself into her studio. There she painstakingly and with intense scrutiny finished her portrait of Zeldon. She always felt a degree of sympathetic comprehension in him, and she wanted to capture that in the work. When she was satisfied that it was complete and in judging it felt it to be one of her best works, she hid it to dry behind other finished pieces. The next day, she checked that it was dry and then carelessly dashed off over its surface a watercolor self-portrait that she knew to be only average. That didn't matter, the covering work was only intended to be a façade disguising her latest masterpiece. Satisfied, she cleaned her brushes and put the canvas aside for its second drying. Illness and strife would not prohibit her determination to speak her color-coded mind when it came to her deepest desire—to find life.

*     *     *

For his part, after Catia's departure, Zeldon entered the Yarde for his late review of the day, but that time with a sharp intensity meant to absorb those recent events. He smelled the damp earth and listened to the quiet sounds of the night with their small tics and rustlings. His hand brushed a boxwood bush, and he relished the sensation of tactility. "I'm of this world," he acknowledged, "made of dust. I love it. I want to live robustly in it." He could say that truthfully despite his recently uncovered horrors. He looked upward again at the sky, his sky—more his than of most residents of the town. No one could cherish the Yarde until he had become accustomed, as Catia would say, to the full palette of the seasons. Space, the sky, he felt like time was a gift with both of them liquid experiences, malleable, even variable as they were encountered for him, personally at least. That above him was his space, distance for him to grow into. He was ready to expand outward and upward from his limited self. He hoped to grow into that expansiveness gracefully, like a swallow's flight, not in a plodding style. And he knew the direction he would take. Catia, splintered; suffering Catia, was his direction. He would fill the space of her frightened emptiness with himself. He knew the cost—already it showed in the loss of his inner peace. But he knew although he was often defeated he was never disarmed.

The decision gave him a remarkable recompense. By surrendering his inner securities into the maelstrom of her emotions but also by embracing her in her tumultuous wholeness, he would serve them both. She, he was sure, would find at some level a value in his companionship. Even if she felt it only unconsciously, she would feel a suggestion that she was not alone, never would be alone. Saved from madness or not, never would be. His love would not be like fireworks that fizzle, it would continue alighting her nights.

And he, in his long quest for that will-o'-the-wisp courage, that gaping deficit in his character, might surely find it filled by flinging himself into her fires of torment and thereby reconfigure his dilemma and emerge intact.

But following immediately on what he was sure was a final and determining intention, he recognized an offense to Catia in such a bargain. He was not sacrificing himself to her. He was using her to gain a prize, his self-respect. No, again no, that sentiment was overridden by yet another recognition. He was given to her not for gain, not for his own self-esteem. Self-esteem be damned. He loved her. His love was a far more golden quality than mere courage. He had been chasing the wrong goal. He remembered the Jogger saying he sometimes felt like a greyhound chasing a false rabbit. Courage might come in its own good time, might already be coming. In the meantime, he would love. Love Catia.

That was not something Zeldon had reasoned out for himself. It was something he had stumbled upon. First, he loved Catia, entirely loved her. Then only then, did it occur to him that love might be an act of courage.

The deep sky in its profound depths confirmed his intuition. He walked home to finish his Martell. Under the borrowed light of a half-moon, he indulged in a confession of profound loneliness. He was aware of the busy lives bustling around him, implied by the Jogger and his stopwatch. Tap Andrews, he knew, endured a similar element of isolation, but he was wrapped about by his scriptures and their comforts. Catia, his true haven, so often vanished into her craziness. And yes, he took refuge in the companionship of the

Four. But he had to concede they were the irretrievable deceased. Shaking off the retreat from manhood, he reminded himself that "we're born alone, we die alone, and, indeed, during some moments in between, we must perform alone."

The Martell was especially rewarding as was the night's rest.

# CHAPTER 13

## The Artist

With all her joking with Zeldon over color meanings and placement, Catia was a serious painter. It showed in her work, the relationship of space to space, of space to color, to form, line, light and shadow, and shadow edges. She had studied techniques and mastered them.

Beyond technique, she was a master of emotional intent and interpretation. How else was she able to paint herself with such detachment? It was all to be found in a superior imagination. Zeldon, when he had first seen her, noted the grace of her movement, as he remarked, "Like a child, joyful in motion." And like a child, she could hear a children's story personalizing animals and thereafter "see herself clothed in fur" as they say. Although first glances could see her opus as narcissistic, a practiced eye could detect honest imagination at work, honest interpretation in effect. She recognized her own approach to that in Zeldon's fascinating description of the Romans and the river Lethe. The Romans, he said as she listened transfixed, saw social intercourse as an attempt to find themselves reflected in someone else, their earlier self, having been erased in the waters of Lethe. Or that at least was how she understood his meaning.

What had she been doing all those years in her self-portraiture? Only searching for her self, her single, integrated self in the image of a divided other. Every painting was an attempt to capture someone, herself, in this other presentation. It must be remembered that the young woman was unable to have children. Not surprisingly, she turned her creativity back on herself. Her studio was her womb, her paintings were her self/children. In one of those works, depicting Zeldon, she took him into herself then enveloped him in an overpainting. That undercurrent explained her once having found Zeldon and still in that probing for self-recognition, she pleaded with him, "See me, Z, or we will both vanish."

Apropos of that, she revealed how her mind worked when one day she said to Zeldon, "I was putting on my lipstick at the mirror, and I realized that it reversed my face from left to right. Right? Why doesn't it reverse my face up and down?

"I don't know," he replied.

"Neither do I, but there's something wrong there. So don't get after me for not being logical. Lots of things aren't logical, and you don't think anything of it."

In the face of that, all her productivity was done during those days; she could hold a brush and face a canvas. It was really quite astounding what came out of such a burdened spirit. One anxious day, one among many, Zeldon said to her with great concern and compassion, truly wanting to know her innermost difficulty, "What's it like, love? What's it really like."

Sensing his deepest desire to understand and contribute anything, anything to ease the pain, she swam in her disarray for some time, gazing into the middle distance. "Zeldon, listen to this. Some years ago a handful of archeologist found a mastodon frozen in a glacier. Now listen, he had fresh buttercups in his mouth, unchewed. Unchewed, Z.!"

Zeldon knew enough to wait, spellbound, for what was to come.

"They said to freeze a mastodon that fast the temperature would have to drop 150 degrees in two seconds." She speared him with her eyes. "Are you listening?" She knew he was, mesmerized, wondering what she was leading to. "No proof, Z, no proof, but they supposed that an asteroid collision could drive debris upward, up, past everything familiar and then fall back down and bring the outer world cold down with it."

She continued her manic stare. Zeldon could make no connection in all that with his original question.

"Sudden, terrible cold, from outer space, Z . . ." Tears formed in her eyes, softened and filled with pain. "When I'm about to eat my buttercups, it can turn cold that fast." She seemed to shrink before him, almost to fade from his consciousness. Her voice came in a whisper, barely audible. "That's what it's like."

Zeldon himself turned cold. That had left him with nothing to say, and he could understand with such eventualities waiting to pounce, why the artist's high intelligence would quarrel with realities. And as for vanishing, it made sense for the disturbed mind to believe that to be true because her illness drove her into a pre-social state where no one else matters. In the earliest days of her youthful strangeness, she merely preferred to be alone, withdrawn, watchful and unrevealing, albeit alluring. But that was true of other young people who went on with their healthy, productive lives. As her future unfolded, the characteristics changed and became seriously unsociable. No one else existed, solipsism. "It's like when we die," she explained, "and we become extra-social beings, all alone, truly alone, isolated."

When they first met, he was a quiet man, and she was all anxiety. As time passed, she brought him with her. But along the way he had, albeit intermittently and privately, given her hope. And then, that night in the Yarde, it seemed she might have been able to disprove her own hypothesis in him, in the union of bodies, of isolation overcome, finding recognition of the woman for whom she reached, herself as she said to him then, almost, almost, But almost meant the continuation of reaching over that ever-receding horizon. As the artist always did, she reached for the impossible with demonic intensity. When that failed, the intensity itself was punishment enough. And the media of portraiture and copulation, both, were failed efforts to recover that lost self. In each of them, she lived with a near miss. So far. So far. Reluctant to admit it, she had to concede that certainties to the honest mind were few and short-lived.

The intensities continued. "Light and dark, good and evil," she said, "all we can do is lean toward the light. And leaning leads to losing your balance. That's where I count on Zeldon." Without overt acknowledgment in that she personalized art's classical intent to bring light out of darkness. And as for partners, were not she and Z partners in culture, holding their balance with herself in art and him in literature?

But as for her placement in the various styles of art, she had recognized herself to be post-impressionistic, pre-Raphaelite. As time passed, she chose to supplement that identification with tendencies in another school. Her struggles revealed to her that she was also groping in the school of surrealism but surrealism with a twist. Representational in her self-portraits with the surreal present as suggestion, inference, a sideways glance of the mind, an under-the-surface hint catching only the attention of the initiate, her representation style was after the manner of the post-Edwardian painter, John da Costa, but to repeat, taking its own direction. In all of that of course, she had left classicism behind and gone her own way into Romanticism.

Zeldon without Catia's developed skills of theory and application, nevertheless held an opinion about her workings. Sur realism, under realism that is, the unconscious preoccupied her. In the vicinity of the real, working in its undercurrents was familiar territory to his troubled lover; that determined the suffering young woman. Working beneath the surfaces out of sight, looking for herself, and looking for connection to another, he sensed it was all of it subliminal, suggestive, waiting on her part for a later recognition.

As with every serious painter she was as much philosopher as technician, and like Zeldon, she was better educated than most realized. One day, when a perplexed Zeldon asked her, "Why do you love me?"

She replied, "Because the hidden harmonies are better than the obvious ones." The reply exhibited her education in the fact that the quotation is from Heraclitus. Also, her artistry went beyond her canvasses. It was visible in her surroundings, the context she had created for herself, justifying the contempt she had for the glacier-like march of bad taste in her own time.

She lived in dark days, it must be admitted, days which did not always coincide with those of nature. On her dark days, she was governed by melancholy, whatever the sun was doing. And of course, the reverse held true; but on those days when she painted from her illness, the work was depressing to look at. On one such day Zeldon had said, "When the sun is absent we must learn from the stars." Her quick reply was "No clear message comes from the stars. They're too far away. Our eyes aren't made to read such small print." She also lived in days of light, however, elated then recorded them on canvas. They said she was manic-depressive, a lazy, line-of-least-resistance description of life's adventure. To defy that dead vision of life, she painted light. Yes, her works were exactly what her life was, a searching for the light. Whenever in a scene there was something she couldn't see, couldn't understand, and couldn't grasp, there she painted shadow, used dropline shadow or subdued light, a lessened revelation of what filled that space. But what she knew, her clarities and certainties, there blazed, billowed forth objects that became perspectives of glory. And those objects were herself, exhibited over and over and over again in a house full of her presence. In that she could shout out in the primary colors, echo her joy in the secondaries and beyond, all the while knowing that warm colors come forward on a canvas, cool colors fall back. She employed it all masterfully and could find truth on canvass.

In that way, the artist was uncommon. It must be repeated, her artistry went beyond her canvasses, so much for extended influence but extended in time? It had to be understood intuitively that she, through her work, would live on in time. Like a ghost star, one of those entities shining light-years away, her work would still bring its light long after the light source, the artist, had expired and was gone.

Zeldon, when he looked on that work, was stirred, deeply disturbed by the assault on his senses, that explosive insight. Of course he had fallen in love with the artist's beauty, all men did. But his was different. Reading her inner secret spirit revealed here in her work could come only to the discerning, and he knew her instantly, recognized her unmistakably. Her careful public persona was made naked in her portraiture, but who—until now, none—could see her that way? In her framed presentation, she was truly revealed, at least as well as she was able to show it, as a woman living on the edge of light. From out of the shadows of social discretion, she stepped forth as incandescent. She was a threshold-dweller, to be recognized by her lover and in time by others, many others.

Just as he, Zeldon, lived in the Yarde, the threshold between life and death, so did Catia live in mental illness between light and dark. She lived sometimes in darkness, a harrowing place that he could only distantly imagine, but when she emerged and saw the light, the light of a living day, she celebrated it by creating those astonishing works of art. The subject, yes, was always her. She herself was what she celebrated, herself, a creature of light, a miracle, with her representation thrust into the world to shout out its joy.

Of course the woman was mad. She would have to be to contain the secret joy—and that secret terror. The two-in-one soul could not be contained within a rational framework. They both knew it. One frustrating day he said, "You're a cloud of oxygen, waiting for a match to set off all that combustion in your temperament."

Far from denying that, her reply was "Yes, I *am* oxygen. I'm heady and I feed your intelligence. You know I do, I stimulate you."

So she had to frame the darkness in her illness and her natural light in those portraits. Then and there staring at the framed miracles about him, Zeldon had fallen in love all over again, irrevocably. He knew in that first encounter in her home that the person was more than a woman, she was a life-dynamic. She was a principle personified but still a person, a woman, not abstracted, a woman, elemental.

The woman, in her younger years and despite brutal challenges to it, had harbored a buoyant personality. Her aforementioned intellect made her impossible to defraud. So men, most of them fraudulent, left her disappointed, somewhat scornful. Yet she was not a cynic and wanted no part of disappointment before the fact. Actually, Catia entered her experiences hopefully. She was an ingénue in that and endlessly expected good things from the world's next presentation to her. Given the world's track record, she needed an inexhaustible well of optimism upon which to draw, and she had it. "Life is good." She was certain. "It's just that life found it hard to confirm the belief."

In her latter years, she found it necessary to complain, "I hate it when men try to take over my inside territory."

"Do we do that?" protested Zeldon.

"Yes, always with sex as the weapon." She didn't add that Zeldon might have been the first man she wanted to do just that, with the exception, also perhaps, of her second husband. She did though add to her remarks, "I used to meet men I liked, or maybe even could have loved, but I wouldn't give authority over me even to them." She smiled at a distant memory. "I treated them carefully, so they wouldn't worm their way into my decision-making apparatus."

"Your decision . . . ?"

"I mean my freedom. So in time, these men would turn away. Cowed, I guess." Again she showed the smiling reminiscence. "I don't think they rejected me, one after the other. I think they just found out I couldn't be conquered." She stared hard at Zeldon. "You men like to conquer."

In the present, in the time of Zeldon, behind the bravado of that dynamic dwelt the howling self-loathing of the bipolar disease. The disease ruled, at least under current circumstances. And those circumstances had been decades in their formation, unspoken memories of adolescent sexual abuse by an alcoholic father, unchallenged by a cowed and defeated mother. Twisted early by those experiences, the future artist even then in her youth, had the strength of character to avoid the common hiding places of alcoholism and drug abuse. She simply suffered and waited, a rational nature with a fluctuating grip on rationality. Her high IQ stood her in good stead, but it was housed in a schizoid personality, moving in and out of tune with nature. Waiting in the wings were her own courage, the scientific knowledge of others and Zeldon's love. It remained to be seen what would prevail in the soap opera of her mind.

Those were the years when Catia confessed that she couldn't tolerate her younger self, a common symptom of the ailment in its advanced state. There had been years when there were hints of putting her under lock and key, submitting her to treatment chosen by others. She subsumed her sufferings during college years, denying the suspicions of onlookers and bluffing her way toward graduation. Sex and early marriage failed to change anything but provided escape from her father until his death. Then came a new hope in a second marriage that promised love. That love died early with the death of her second husband.

Intrinsic intelligence and compelling beauty carried her into a threatened future until she met Phil Glover, a newcomer to her home town of Rockwater, where she lived with her shade of a mother, who very soon thereafter died. Earlier, reaching desperately for some vehicle, any vehicle to carry her through her secretive symptoms, she had taken up portraiture—self-portraiture. That, too, was practiced in secret.

Glover was considered a catch by local women, but he set his eye on her. He was wealthy, more than prosperous, seriously wealthy. He came from an ill-defined business background in the City, which interested Catia not at all. He seemed just as pleased with the indifference and got on with his affairs during the workday. His proposal and her inwardly ambiguous acceptance led to their marriage with a wedding made sumptuous at Phil's insistence. Surprisingly, it seemed that he had local political ambitions and a social wedding contributed to his standing in the circles that mattered.

In the meantime, Catia continued to search for a tolerable attitude toward her self-loathing interior, seeing such tolerance as money in the bank awaiting the coming rainy days, psychologically speaking. Sometimes the attitudes worked, sometimes they didn't. Without her ever openly confessing to her silent battles, she knew Phil at first noticed and then came to realize what was happening. It suited him to be as denying of realities as she was herself. As long as her periods, as he came to call them, were veiled from public knowledge and his growing ambitions went uninterrupted, he played her game, up to a point.

That point became dangerously visible as her symptoms intensified and threatened their agreed-upon containment. In those times, the artist was as usual overwhelmed by a savage homelessness of the spirit, visceral in its effect with a seepage of sanity and leaving her drained of spirit or hope. Her latest glimmer of a tolerable future, as much as she was able to entertain one, came in the person of Zeldon, who vowed a till-death-us-do-part fidelity which he claimed must serve as her anchor to reality.

She hoped to strengthen that anchor when she one day advised Zeldon to flatter Phil, to play to his vanity. "Why," he answered in his irritation, "would I defer to a man I'm going to bury?" His seemingly ruthless reply alluded to his repeated claim that most likely he would bury a goodly part of the town's present population. On hearing him say that, she felt the merest presentiment of death, a very slight roll of the drum. Nights were more likely to deliver nightmares than to embrace her in dreams. After all, true color to that point in her life had been bleached away by an absence of religion, leaving her short of glimpsing the wondrous shape of creation.

All the while, the elemental woman loved and anguished. A common insight shared by true artists confessed that any first touch of the brush upon a virginal canvass destroyed its perfect symmetry, and every stroke thereafter was an attempt to restore it. Perfect symmetry was the very thing the lost soul's mind so lacked. And on its deepest level, the real endeavor of the artist was to hear, convincingly, that home-whispering voice that haunted every soul, to come home to the fundamental destination of a primal belonging, which was the ultimate symmetry. Her story, however, was not yet finished.

# CHAPTER 14

Penelope was entranced. Legal was rendering her all the material she would need to write her own passport to power. She had always known a Legal whose inner weather was calm, whose thinking seldom crossed the threshold of his lips, and there he was showing her his very mental center. The man had obviously had a few drinks and was uncharacteristically talkative, presenting her with the chance of a lifetime.

"I'll tell you some of the facts behind the scenes, but I don't want you publicizing where you got them."

"Fair enough, of course I won't. Just give me some ammunition." In the privacy of her mind, she knew otherwise, but she had always known that the white lie is the glue that holds society together.

"Not long ago, Phil and I went out and tied on a good one. Had to drive a few miles to get out of town, White Plains. He was going on about his wife. He'd spilled it all out long before, but this night he was wound up and far into his cups." So was Legal just then, but she wasn't about to point that out. "He had a way of doing that once in a while. 'Trouble with my frau,' he said. 'Hell, nothing new to me. Came to this shithole town after my divorces, already made a lot of money.' I knew all that, but as I said, he talked like he was educating the bartender. 'I'm going to Albany, you know, and this place is my passport. But I have to keep a semblance of a marriage to stay in the game.'"

"Divorces?"

Her treasured conversant filled her in on two divorces lost in the records of New York City and not heretofore mentioned in Rockwater. Then she followed up on another prize tidbit. "Did he mean to get out of Rockwater even when he first moved in?"

"Of course, of course, he came here to make some changes to his reputation, make his mark. The record in the city wasn't too clean. Your supervisor is a man of arrested ideas, but even he knew he needed a buffer for the old résumé. You've seen too much duplicity around to take anyone at face value, haven't you? Anyway, he said to me, 'What I don't need is a nutcase wife on my flank. I got married so fast, got to move fast in politics, you know that, so fast that no one had time to tell me she was a schizoid since she was a kid.' I didn't know that, and I said to him, no one told you? 'Well,' he said, 'not so I caught on. They were all pussyfooting around it. Talk about sexual abuse from her father and a lot of hush-hush gossip.'"

"Wait a minute." Penelope was flushed with the excitement of what she was learning. She herself knew some of the suspicions surrounding Catia Browning, but they hadn't been allowed to blossom, partly due to Glover's smothering efforts. "Sexual abuse and hush-hush gossip, I just know her to be a generous woman."

"Generous? Well, sexually maybe. Anyway, Phil dropped these remarks about her father, but he didn't follow that up. Instead he said, 'When we first got married, she was better, I mean it was better.' Then he stopped talking and had another drink, and then he looked funny and said, 'I'd like to get back to better . . . but shit, I guess I got to settle for good. And it'll be good if I can make my mark in good old Rock-fucking-water.' That's when I knew he was losing it. First time I ever saw him lose his real focus and worry about a woman. Phil has always been pretty smart, but when the chips are down, sometimes I think all mental development ended on his twelfth birthday."

Penelope ignored the rudeness about women. "He was drunk," was her reminder. She did notice, though that her reporter was also. Her own head was spinning.

"You know he was. I knew he was because he got all palsy and said how he appreciated me. 'When I go to Albany, you'll go with me. We'll make our mark up there, all right. But first here in Stonewater, Goodwater, Rockwater, eh?' I remember it all clearly, I wasn't as drunk as he was. What he didn't know was that I knew he was already laying plans to dump me before Albany."

"Cashing in on his political experience."

"Yes well, I know that unstudied experience is no experience at all. He's a smart politician, but he hasn't studied human beings enough. Neither have you. Why haven't you asked what Phil was trying to shake off when he moved to this hick town?"

"You know that?"

"I know that and a lot more." With that, Legal went on the describe to his new colleague the sordid details of Phil's transactional habits on the street, insider trading, fraudulent derivatives, pre-loaded mortgages —a shadowy record of lucrative malpractices.

"How much of this can you prove?" asked a breathless Penelope.

The tipsy informer looked offended. "You think I work without records? How far would I go without being able to back up my information? I had to do a lot of his work in my name, but I've got plenty to pull him under." That was a phrase that Penelope was to remember, but just then it was time to bring out her strongest question, "Why are you telling me all this? You know you're giving the election to us Democrats." Both of them knew it had to be explained.

"All right, in the old days, primitive men pounded your balls off, present company excluded of course." He took no credit for his tipsy humor. "More lately, they shot your balls off. But now they litigate your balls off. I could do that, but it's a long process and would waste a lot of time. So I'm going to do it my way, your way. He's forgotten how much he owes me, and he's laying the groundwork for dumping me."

"You know that?" Again she ignored the coarseness of the squalid genius. He was handing her a new life, and she mustn't quibble.

"There are signs of . . . disrespect. And I have a rule I never alter, endless tolerance of ambiguity is only sleeping with the enemy. I never forgot how oil and vinegar don't mix. Well, your town supervisor is oil, and I'm the other."

Penelope recognized the aptness of both descriptions.

The slurring narrator went on, "So listen to this, he had a mistress in New Jersey with their two children. She took a chance and waited while he went about his business, but in the end, he paid her off and dumped her. Not me. Not going to dump me. I'm going to erase him politically." He threw Penelope a jaundiced look and took his satisfaction in seeing her pleasure at the whole idea. She knew Legal just well enough to recognize injured vanity. It didn't hurt that he was loquacious enough to speak his mind. Out of character but usefully so, and she was beside herself with the story of the paid-off mistress.

Continuing in that manner, the two plotters followed up their earlier meeting as they spelled out in greater detail how best to make Penelope Hentoff Rockwater's next town supervisor with the present officeholder none the wiser until it was too late. The Republican plotter, talking too volubly and too long, gave his fellow conspirator the benefit of his wisdom, most of which Penelope had appropriated long since. "Behind the ebb and flow of social events stands the hard rock of self-interest, who gets what. That cancels out all reciprocity, and then you get our every-man-for-himself world. When cancer strikes, take two aspirin and say your prayers. You aren't going to get help. It's an instinct, built in."

Legal had never been so self-revealing, an indication of how the dangers had been closing in on him. He wasn't finished yet. "Let me point out to you, madam, who will look after you if you don't look after yourself." Obviously, he was presuming his confidant was a novice in these affairs. "There's no higher power to appeal to. No guidance, no structure, no pay off you don't engineer yourself. Left to itself, it's just one damn thing after another." He hiccupped.

Seeing his new protégée's eyes begin to glaze over, he concluded with his parting advice, "Remember one thing, an iron will can manage the lesser problems. But it's useless in the ambiguities. When things are vague, strength of will has nowhere to go. So do your homework." Despite the rambling, she would make it her mantra in the coming months. They parted with shifty, streetwalker faces.

Following their meeting, Penelope made a phone call. "Barbara darling, I'm being caught up in some dangerous political things here in Rockwater. I'm afraid, my dear, that it means we will have to be doubly discrete for a while . . . No, I can't be clear about it just yet. It's too explosive. But I need you to trust me while this is going on . . . Of course I love you, my precious, more than ever now. I need you, Barb, I really need you. I promise I'll get down to Tarrytown as soon as I can . . . yes, I will. As soon as I can, you know I will. I love you, darling, I can't wait. I can't wait."

*   *   *

"Phil Glover is a smiler. He will show you his teeth while his eyes are studying you for profit, his profit." Looks of surprise and some disapproval passed through the crowd.

Penelope was speaking before the League of Women Voters of Rockwater, New York. She meant it to be her coming-out moment before the May Democratic primary, and she needed their support if she were to supplant Phil and the Republicans in the November campaign. After her first overwhelming encounter with Legal, she had walked around in a daze, not knowing how she should act. To do nothing was to make a decision, not to her benefit, so she quietly and secretly contacted a few influential supporters. She excluded all the present members of the town board, their being Republicans, and for various other reasons, meaning to approach them over a coalition only if and when she had the backing of her personal friends. Those friends excitedly weighed the likely outcomes of each of several possible moves, but everyone knew they would grab the opportunity Legal had given them. Penelope had promptly broken her promise to him to keep his name out of it. Each person present, six of them, swore themselves to secrecy in their turn, knowing full well they would only tell their closest friends of their information and its source. Legal was doomed from the start.

"He'll show you his teeth . . ." she went on, "and he won't tell you of his two divorces in New York or his trouble with the SEC or his affairs since escaping from the city." She tossed in the reference to his affairs knowing Phil couldn't afford the publicity of a lawsuit. Besides, there were certain to have been affairs. A shocked look of hatred crossed the face of Merle Stanley, but there was no time to register the impression, and she moved quickly on. She knew Phil. And others couldn't vouch for his fidelity to the flaky wife, which brought up her next reference:

"We all know Phil's house is filled with his wife's self-portraits. We all know that's a strange approach to interior decorating, and it's raised a lot of questions over her stability and their private relationship." Mouths were agape by then, the more astute listeners wondering just how far Penelope intended to go and just how much she could defend her already rash remarks. "Their private relationship is no business of ours," she virtuously conceded, "but the stability of the domestic life of our town supervisor is. It impacts on our town matters and the concentration they require."

Penelope paused, pretending to search her notes while she let her drift sink into the minds of her abashed audience. Then she went on, "We have noticed long periods when Mrs. Glover hasn't been seen about town. No crime in that but troublesome, especially among those of us concerned for her health. In addition, Phil Glover has mysteriously and inexplicably not showed up at some important functions from time to time. Again, those of us concerned for Mrs. Glover's health have wondered if she were unwell. This has worried us, especially since it has happened more frequently in these last couple of years. We wish her well." She lifted her glance and swept the room with a worried look. It was a masterful performance thus far. There was much more information to come forth later on this point as it was needed.

"Because of these revelations, so upsetting to us all, I for one would like to hear something reassuring from our *leader*," she emphasized the word carefully. She said nothing of the documentation of those allegations promised from Legal, neither did she mention her blockbuster over the mistress and children. That would be held in reserve, strengthening her arsenal. After a few inconsequential remarks she left, saying, "I'd like to leave you now to consider what I've said and to assure you that I remain available to serve the town in any capacity you might desire." She quickly departed with a clamor of voices ringing from the walls.

*     *     *

Merle knew at once that Phil was in trouble, serious trouble, and was not sure she wanted to jeopardize her place by backing him. On the other hand, if she abandoned him too abruptly, no one knew what he might do to avenge himself. At home after the meeting, she paced the floor, looked at the clock, and decided there was time to call Phil before Toby arrived home. Velma said Phil was out and didn't know when he would return, possibly not until the next morning. She took a chance of attracting Velma's curiosity and asked her to have him call at his first opportunity.

It wasn't until after Toby's arrival that Phil called, but luckily, her husband was not in the kitchen. Nevertheless, she took no chances that time and spoke circumspectly. "Oh, Phil, I'm glad you called. You know that Garden Club presentation I asked you to make?" She was immediately glad she had taken the precaution because she heard Toby pick up.

"Yesss," Phil stammered then caught on, "Oh yes, of course. What can I do?"

"You said you could pop in and make the award. It's tomorrow morning, you know. Ten o'clock. Can I show it to you tonight after dinner? Just take a minute."

"Sure, I'm still in White Plains, and I'll come straight to the town hall. Nine o'clock?"

She was relieved because she was sure Toby hadn't hung up, and Phil had handled it wonderfully, but he hadn't heard anything yet about Penelope's attack. "Good, see you at nine, just five minutes."

Three hours later, they sat in Phil's office with Phil looking curiously at Merle. "What's up?"

She told him everything in Penelope's bombshell. She was right, he hadn't heard a word. Then he was stunned. Not wanting to confront him with any need for explanations—she needed to keep him quiet about the two of them—she let him squirm, aghast in his chair and explained that she had to get straight home. Phil was relieved to see her go; he needed to be alone.

*   *   *

"What was the Cow trying now?" Phil knew her to be the same opportunist he was and to have the same ambitions. The others on the board didn't have the wherewithal to fight him. He and his satellites exchanged anecdotes but not ideas. Whenever he wasn't calculating the political fallout of a conversation, he truly liked to share pleasure with others. But Penelope hadn't the political energies to embark on any kind of campaign against him. She hadn't the gut instincts, only the envy of the second best. Nevertheless, she had smelled blood and knew she was on to something seriously damaging. Where had she gotten her information? It was too detailed to be guesswork and knit together too skillfully to have come to her out of the air. She had a source. Instantly on arriving at that realization, Phil knew who it had to be.

*   *   *

With his Albany ambitions at stake, Phil knew he had to strike back at Legal and the Cow instantly. She could be handled without too much trouble, but Legal was big trouble. He knew everything and had exposed little of himself for public criticism. Yes, he was creepy, and everyone knew it. What was more, Legal knew they felt that way toward him, and it didn't bother him. His own goals didn't depend on public approval, and he had little to fear from his controller because he had never revealed his actions in carrying out Phil's requirements, never even to Phil himself. All that Phil knew and had never objected to. The reason for that apparent carelessness on his part, however, was part of Phil's deeply planted strategy. Some of trading secrets in his own office had been given to Legal, to be sure, but with time bombs attached to each resulting transaction. Whenever Legal sold or bought to his lucrative advantage, a paper trail was established, showing they had to have been with inside information but without revealing whose inside info. That left Phil hidden while Legal could be exposed at Phil's determination. Complicated? Yes, but all such transactions were, and meanwhile, Phil had his insurance precautions in place without their being announced. It was merely a fact of life, reciprocal weapon wielding in the alley fights of Wall Street.

It was creepy, yes, and clever, very. Legal, too, could be handled. But how to smother his attorney's whistle-blower information before he could use it? In the absence of any answer to those urgencies, Phil knew one thing he could work on while he mapped out a more wide-reaching strategy. He had to firm up his extremely shaky position at home. Driving home from the town hall, he determined to make amends with his wife, knowing that her passivity even if he could achieve it, would be unstable. First effort—regain her good will, at any cost. He could do that through her first interest, her painting. That was her life, where she took the greatest pride and would most appreciate praise and encouragement.

# Chapter 15

It was ten o'clock when Phil drove up the driveway to find the house dark. Immediately, he grew tense, fearing he would find her wrapped in a dark cocoon of depression. It was like that, every homecoming an anxiety but soon his fears turned to relief when he found her to be not at home. Of course, she would be out on her habitual evening walk. Good, he could do a little groundwork. On entering the house, he went directly to her studio, meaning to look over her recent work so as to have some detailed praise with which to greet her.

It was time, long past time, to become more familiar with the work of the dedicated artist who shared his home. Her studio was filled with her works, most of which he had never seen. That in itself should have told him how he had neglected her in favor of his own interests. He would correct that, beginning that moment. "Beginning now, yes, but beginning where?" The walls were covered with the works, some of which he had seen before. They were finished pieces, but not Cat's favorites, and so they were delegated to the anteroom, her private hideaway. Surrounding his feet though were any number of questionable pieces, mostly unframed. As he began to sort through them, he was surprised to find the second row of pieces, and those behind them in turn, to be recognizably different. They were of a different Cat, a fierce-eyed, less attractive Cat, decidedly different. She wasn't beautiful, more than unattractive, some of them ugly even—leering, snarling, spitting, and clawing!

Phil knew his wife could change in appearance when she was in her bad periods, but he had never met that woman. Those were depictions of a hoyden, a truly mad female. It took a mental pole vault to admit that those were portraits of his wife. He knew her as a combustible woman. Even with that concession, he was not prepared for that scene.

One portrait in particular caught his eye, probably because the surface paints were still wet. It was behind others, set to one side and unframed. A water color, he knew that much. He knew better than to see himself as an art critic, but that one seemed to combine some of the pictures of Catia that hung about the house with those hidden, forbidden ones in the private studio. It showed her presentable beauty, no doubt about that, but there was a fire in the eyes that was more than human. And it had a magnetic, dangerous come-hither look. The disturbing combination was all hidden behind a softness in the flesh tones. Phil was aroused by it and made extremely uneasy.

While he squirmed, he noticed a detail that didn't belong there. The water color surface was cratered and protruding, giving it a depth that water colors couldn't give. As he looked more carefully, he realized that was a freshly finished work that covered another painting below it. Her self-portrait was a mask.

He knew his actions would bring her outraged reaction. Nevertheless, he couldn't do anything but discover what was being hidden. There was so much duplicity in the air that he had to fight back, beginning with that discovery. He gathered cloths, a container of water and a spray bottle. Shooting a stream gently over the water color and carefully wiping away the discolored results, he could see the vague outlines of the oil painting that lay below. As the details began to emerge, he could see that the underlying subject was not the same person that was disappearing while he worked. It was not a portrait of Catia, like all her other paintings. It was the form of a man, gradually taking shape before his eyes. Phil's hand shook as he continued. A young man, someone familiar, someone, it was, it was Zeldon Wade!

\*    \*    \*

It was late when Catia returned. She was predictably angry when she found Phil sitting in her studio, but he paid that no mind. She saw the detritus scattered about and wondered how he could be so coldly calm.

"What have you done?"

In icy tones he said, "I've erased you." He turned the portrait of Zeldon to face her and scrutinized her expression as she reacted. First on her face, he saw surprise then dismay then the expected fury.

"You removed my water color!"

"I've removed you. No, I removed the crazy woman you've become. No, you always were crazy, I removed the girl your father broke in, and the one the others had later, the used goods that Walt and Jim and who knows who else had. And guess who I found waiting in line, your spooky graveyard guy." He sneered that last charge, and Catia knew there was no turning back from that moment, not that she wanted to.

"Whatever I might have been looking for, I certainly didn't find in you, did I?" All the vacancies of midnight swept over her anger, but anger it remained. "And for your information, Zeldon Wade is no passing impulse, not like your zipper flings."

"If he's not, that would be a first. And as far as guilt in this world goes, I'm about average. Not a trend-setter like you." He couldn't find words to spit out his fury. "Your saliva doesn't run clear, you know that? You're one step away from shaving soap around your mouth. You're crazy!"

Both were reaching deep into their arsenals of insult to outdo the other; each knew the confrontation was going nowhere. Finally, Phil lifted the portrait of Zeldon, drove it down on his knee, and thrust himself through its center, smashing it to pieces.

It would be impossible later to know what it was that snapped the restraint within Catia, her deeply offended artist's sensibility or her wounded love for Zeldon—the object, that was, the destroyed painting or the subject—but either was enough, and the future of the marriage was sunk deeper than either knew at that time. She had seen their arguments as way stations on the path to some dramatic solution to their problems, and she was always waiting for that solution. Then it was imminent. After a long silence, during which Phil realized he had destroyed what little remained between them, she seethed, "Get out!"

And get out he did, out of the room, out of his marriage, out of his past. He went to the study, lighted a cigar with shaking hands, and poured a double vodka. While he drank it he went to the patio, unzipped his insulted fly, and urinated into the well. "You'll never see him again," he whispered to himself. Then he returned to the study and made a phone call to an all-night pharmacy.

*     *     *

The next morning, Phil's telephones began ringing, but even so, it registered in her mind that they rang incessantly all day. Velma pleaded ignorance of his whereabouts, and Catia didn't answer the home phones. She had a long bath in the morning, performed her usual routines of breakfast, dressed, and applied makeup, including rinsing her tired eyes. The latter was a usual habit, but a sleepless night made it more necessary than usual. She opened a new bottle of eyewash, not remembering emptying the one before.

It was a relief that Phil was nowhere to be seen, but even so, it registered in her mind that the soul needed more room than the body. She went through the day in desultory fashion, without plan or intention. Late in the day, while preparing dinner for herself, she confessed that her eyes had been poorly focused and irritated all day. As the hours progressed, they had become painful to the point of applying more of her eyewash without relief. When she went to bed, it was a comfort to keep her eyelids shut.

It was in the night that she woke in great pain, unable to keep her eyes open for more than a few seconds. A further eyewash did nothing and as the hours of the night advanced, the distress became unbearable. As soon as the doctor's office opened in the morning, she was calling from her bedside phone describing the condition. Told to come straight in gave little help since she couldn't see to drive, but a call to Zeldon, throwing all precaution to the winds, brought him over shortly. By one o'clock, she was admitted to Rockwater Hospital, had had a diagnosis and some relief from the pain. Her eyewash was the culprit, containing a contamination that had done serious damage to her sight. Within two days, as her eyesight deteriorated, it was determined that permanent damage had been done, and it appeared to be irreversible. The calamitous development left a devastated patient and a helpless Zeldon, both of them in despair.

"What am I to do?"

"I don't know, Catia. I don't know." He was the picture of defeat.

"I won't be able to paint." There hadn't been time to grasp the full extent of the devastation. "I won't be able to paint!" She broke into sobs, which irritated her eyesight even further. "Oh god, Zeldon, I can't even cry!" she wailed, dabbing at her face.

Zeldon, having slept in a chair during most of the previous three nights, held her in his arms and murmured, "We will look after each other. We will." He looked into her eyes as he said it but could see only a cloudy vacancy. His despair deepened.

Suddenly, Catia grew still. "My eyewash, my eyewash, the doctor said it was my eyewash!"

"Yes, so what?"

"Z, will you call the Rockwater Pharmacy and ask when I got my last order of eyewash?"

"Well, sure," said a perplexed Zeldon. "I know John Mason, the pharmacist."

"Now, please, now?"

Looking confused but glad to have some chore to break the helplessness, he departed. Ten minutes later. he returned a changed man. Grimly he said to Catia, "John said on Monday night he had an emergency call to give a bottle of your eyewash and an order for rodent poison. It struck him as suspicious, especially given the hour of the night, but . . ." Zeldon paused, swallowed, and said, "but the order was for Phil Glover, so he filled it quickly." He looked at Catia with confusion, fear, and deep distress.

The pitiable woman on the bed stiffened, began to speak, halted, and began again, "It was Phil." She said no more, setting her face in a rigid expression that wasn't to change for hours.

\*　　\*　　\*

After his discovery in Catia's studio, Phil wasted little time in anguishing; matters had gone too far to lament his new position.

His enemies were exposed, caught dancing together on black ice. He dealt with Catia that very night and took the train to Albany first thing on Tuesday morning. There he called in some old chips owed from previous dealings in exchange for a prosecutor's promise to level insider trading charges against Legal. He then produced memos and trading sheets revealing his buried evidence in support of the charges. Actually, Legal had no proof to the contrary, which would nullify any counter claims. The crafty attorney was not the only dissembling participant in that sordid history.

In those bargainings, all of them verbal and in privacy, Phil was sacrificing a strong political position for a weakened one. His coconspirator, the state attorney general, knew he was gaining leverage in certain circles through Glover's sponsorship and at Glover's expense. But those were the moments opportunists waited for, sometimes for years—a desperate trading down by a power-broker in trouble.

That would take care of Legal. Next, the Cow had to be butchered. That was going to be a pleasure. In his files, Phil had letters, photographs, and tape recordings of Penelope's lesbian history dating from college days to current passions indulged in only forty miles from Rockwater. For him, Penelope had all the menacing insincerity of a scarecrow. Scandal—money in the bank, politically—was seldom useful on its discovery. Its value was compounded as it sat quietly in a vault awaiting its moment. Phil was a practiced expert at recognizing those moments. All his life, he had held a conviction of his own significance. It had propelled him in business and beyond into politics. He took pride in his admittedly local successes because they gained for him just enough notoriety to satisfy him for the moment. And they didn't command too much of his attention. He needed to be able to carry on his quieter endeavors, silencing past threats and managing a hidden fortune gained in past questionable practices. Few people took the trouble to discover why successful politicos were successful. Phil could teach them. Penelope Hentoff would soon learn why she was an also-ran.

And then there was the Shoveler. Wade had no idea what he had been shoveling or how deep he was in it.

# CHAPTER 16

He knew it. He knew it. From his first sighting of her, probably from that first staggering embrace at the Mrs. Rodgers' fire, it was destined that one day Catia would hold him in the palm of her hand in that movement between certainty and uncertainty. Yes, he loved her. He had declared it over and over again, and from its first declaration, he knew he was never again going to find that ridiculous sensation called closure. Once he had been comfortable with the silence in his own head, no more. That was back in a time of risks never taken, and emotions never felt. Yes, one penalty of loving her was the knowledge that any closure thereafter would be contaminated, finales that would never finalize. The firefly would never be caught in a bottle.

That day he found her in her reduced version, inconsolable. She lay in her bed, whispering out her death song, her mumbled lyrics telling the story of her blinding and her doom. "I have tried really hard. I am always pushing toward the light, but I keep seeing my black butterflies, only black, only black."

He had met those black butterflies in her studio among the hidden paintings. Listening to her, he could imagine all her yesterdays, the horrors and the beauties, gathered into memory and making her into who she was. Lifting those memories into her tomorrows should have given her hope and expectation. Instead, there she was, a blind painter, rocking in her own embrace, obliged to live by instinct instead of by experience. His heart was broken, never to be repaired.

At the bottom of the deep well of his mind, he could almost feel a vague kinship with the villainous Phil, the other victim of her disarray. He was rapidly gaining a sharper awareness of both good and evil and the distinctions that separated them. But then he was staying in Phil's house with Phil's wife, feeling he belonged here more than his unknowing host. The distinctions were not always clear, but his capacities for recognizing uncommon nuances of morality were also developing. He did though wonder if that was sophistry.

"It's in there," she was saying, "it's in there, and I dance to its music. The way of the world is not nice. Your world is user-friendly. Mine isn't."

She had said that to him before, and he knew she was singing of her illness. It was her style, assembling that poisonous air mass that was her mind, setting its mood, and then presiding over it. But that was beyond her doing. From his earliest days in the Yarde, he had found death acceptable, even reasonable, notwithstanding that he loved sounds, smells, sights, tactilities, and the world. He never forgot he was made of dust. Yes, he loved the earth; he lived robustly in it and was deeply rooted in its tangible things. And yes again those were the things that brought him both pain and joy as Catia was enduring. He was clearly open to both, committed to the present as a valuable gift and yet accepting of death as well. If nothing else, it gave value to time. It was acceptable and reasonable death, except when it was a theft of life, and Catia's life was being stolen. He thought his years in the Yarde had left him not inured but accustomed to common suffering, but Catia was his Achille's heel. Through her, he had learned Dan's ability to be detached but not indifferent in a kind of shielded empathy, except then. Her destruction left him outraged—the grand cheating. It was even worse than the larceny of Sarah's ending. She at least was bearing another life, Catia was, wait, wait, Catia had created a portrait of him, of himself. She was blinded because she had created a portrait of him. But must she die because of it because surely she was dying before his very eyes.

And so Zeldon anguished as his love anguished. Had he not married himself to her fate, made it his own? Catia, his love, and the truths he had discovered in the Yarde, those were the goldfields of his mind. They had exchanged the most intimate confidences, shared a lifetime in a month. Yet he was learning every day how much more of her there was to discover. Looking down on her, he saw her as poetry, and she made all his thoughts rhyme. Her auburn hair trailed out on her pillow, wisps of color, shining copper strands. All the earth could have lost its beauty and that sight alone would be enough for him.

"You're my center," he said, "the rest of me is only part of the circumference."

"That's not me, the person you're talking about," she mumbled. "It's a case of mistaken identity."

He crept into bed with her, cradled her in his arms, and joined in her suffering sounds. "I need a place to rest," she murmured.

"I know, I know."

"Mmmm . . . will you let me rest in you? Just hold me and let me be still?"

"Yes."

"Mmmmmmmm . . ."

Soon she was asleep, in sleep's withdrawal from all relationships, a legitimate vacation from others. Sleep was like her mental flights from reality, her mental vacation from the tyrannical requirements of reason. He loved her cleanly then, asleep, his heart no longer in conflict with itself. But that was only a confirmation of his earlier determination, without its challenges. Couldn't he also learn to live her other withdrawals? Weren't they as necessary?

He joined her in her vacation.

*   *   *

They slept the night away together, and in the morning before breakfast, Zeldon went for a walk in the woods. When he returned, he met yet another unexpected surprise. Hearing him about the house Catia awoke with her faculties intact, at least to a functioning degree. She was indeed depressed, but that struck Zeldon in his hurricane world as perfectly normal and entirely welcome.

"Am I really blind?" she asked over the coffee he had prepared. Words squirmed about in her jangled temperament, but no answer came, neither to him.

"It looks like you are, for the time being," he stammered.

She stared unseeing into the middle distance, a picture of sorrow. "I won't paint again, will I?"

He couldn't answer, didn't dare try.

"My DNA is telling me to be a pussycat over that." She straightened, sipped at her coffee. Then she said, "You know, Z, you're more strange than I am. I never could get it, how you want to live in the Yarde. But now I'm blind, and I'm beginning to see. You love life so much you want to discover its boundaries. You live there, don't you, because it's the frontier, between time and space?"

"Yes."

"Ummm, undiscovered stuff at your fingertips, right?"

"Yup."

"Yup, if you're going to lead the human race, couldn't you be a little more articulate?"

"I don't mean to lead anyone." He was stirred, hopeful even that he was hearing a touch of the old Catia in her playful mode.

"Well, God gave us shoulders, so they say. He also gave us burdens." She shook herself, felt her closed eyelids with her fingertips then struck a pose of quiet contemplation. "I can still have my dreams, can't I? My own dreams inside, where no one can blind me. I guess that's why they're internal." She thought about that for another moment then added, "Dreams are the paradise of the poor. Now I'm blind . . . poor."

It was time to confront the unsaid and offer some kind of hope to the subdued despair, so he offered, "I remember a child's story where a prince was blinded, and his sight was restored by the heroine's tears. Turn around the genders and make the tears my simple grief, and there you have your dream."

"I like that. I have another one to go with it. A child lives near an imaginary forest full of dangers and threats. But living there gives her a chance to play at its edge. She can experiment and prove her strengths and gain confidence and grow."

"I like that one too."

"But she's still blind. And she still can't paint."

Not to be defeated, he said, "It's still a dream. There's still room for a miracle."

"There you go again, being religious. But . . . you're right."

"Cat, I read somewhere that there's no word for no in Swahili. Not yet is their closest term. Will you give *me* some hope by agreeing that our miracle is just a not yet?"

"OK, a miracle but not yet."

That was all Zeldon was to be given at the moment, but it was enough. Nobody expected miracles anymore, he conceded that, but he was willing to believe there was one in the neighborhood. He rose and began to clear away their tableware, and the morning picked itself up in a series of necessary tasks shared with a tender solicitude between them.

When they had finished, Catia sent unmistakable signals of desire to Zeldon. He knew she had a sexually freighted mind, and that she frequently studied him through that prism, so he gladly responded and led her into her bedroom. It was a time for walking on eggshells, delicately dangerous, and that was, he reminded himself, Phil's house and Phil's wife, wonderful, no remorse, wonderful.

Later, at Catia's unexpected insistence, he went home, presuming he would hear from her later in the day. She demanded, however, that he should not return until he heard from her even though that may not be until tomorrow. Again he wondered what she had in that labyrinthian mind.

\*          \*          \*

Rockwater's local newspaper, the *Patent Trader*, was a weekly and came out on Thursdays. Most of its coverage was of committee doings, auto accidents, and obituaries, but on occasion something developed that was attention-getting and just enough beyond gossip to make it acceptable and newsworthy. The week's news was a step up in its interest level. "Town Supervisor Attacked" read the headline, leaving the reader to pick up the paper to discover if it reported a physical assault or an unseemly aggression politically. The first paragraph clarified the issue immediately with Penelope's charges and innuendoes laid out for all to see. Of course, it produced the intended effect with allegations guaranteed to sweep through the town. There were statements requiring proof, lest there be lawsuits, which planted the impression that proofs must surely be forthcoming. The community stood on tiptoe awaiting developments.

A prominent leader below the fold announced Phil Glover's response, accompanied by a photograph of the supervisor quickly pulled from old files. It showed him cold, handsome, with eyes lowered in disdain. It was taken in St. Mark's Square in Venice, in bright sunlight with no squint, only his hard features prevailed, not a public relations view of the officeholder. In some circles, his stature shriveled into posturing. The text was a carefully crafted statement denying the offensive claims and throwing a bone to the scandalmongers by confessing his wife's incapacities to be more extensive than had been known before. It was a calculated move, leaving the shelter of political correctness, but he pleaded guilty due to an overloaded work schedule caused by the private requirements of being a caretaker in his home. Catia Glover's bipolar condition was admitted to in cleverly nuanced phrases, leaving Phil as the unheralded but heroic caretaker.

By way of providing a further sensation, he announced that he had that day delivered to the district attorney evidence of insider trading and predatory illegalities in mortgage foreclosures perpetrated by a town council member, one Murray Hubbard. There were also questions raised over Penelope Hentoff's sexual orientation, but they were left ambiguous enough that legal action would not find any solid grounds for a lawsuit. By the end of the article, the information awarded the supervisor a record enhanced rather than damaged by Penelope's ill-advised criticisms.

It was the most important printing of the *Patent Trader* in its publishing history.

Reading it and seeing her opening salvo against Phil Glover so subdued by his reply showed the challenger she was then thoroughly dependent on Legal's' documented material. A hasty phone call to him was far from reassuring.

"Penelope, good to hear from you. I thought I might."

"Yes well, we knew we would stir up a hornet's nest, so that's to be expected. Now it's time to bring out our bigger guns and substantiate some of the facts. What can you do?"

"Substantiate, isn't that for you to do?"

Greatly taken aback, Penelope stiffened at the first hint of being left hanging. "What do you mean?"

"I mean you've opened a door. Now it's time to walk through it. So just walk."

"Wa . . . walk . . . I don't know what you mean." She could feel Legal's distancing actions before they were formed. He was going to protect himself from Phil's charges by throwing her to the wolves.

"Dear woman, you might recall when we first talked that I wanted my name kept out of this. You remember?"

"Sure, I remember, but you said you had documentation to . . ."

"And now according to some of my informants, I'm being touted as the source of your accusations. How do you suppose that happened? Do you suppose your friendships are all a forgery?"

Penelope went cold, realizing her own foolishness. It was her first mistake in politics on an elevated plane, trusting her friends and supporters. There would be more mistakes to come, but they wouldn't matter much if she couldn't overcome this gaffe.

"I can guess what you mean. I'm sorry, Legal, and it won't happen again. What can I do?"

"You can live with your own doing as far as I'm concerned." He was going to twist the knife, that was obvious.

"You know if I'm hung out to dry now. I'm finished. We're going to have to stick together. Isn't there anything I can do to make it up to you?" She didn't try to hide her desperation.

"If there is, I'll get back to you." With that, the conversation had nowhere to go, so Penelope said good-bye with yet another apology and hung up hoping he had something in mind that would keep the situation in play. But it looked very much as though it was going to be the three of them, Phil, Legal, and herself trying to destroy the other two. In truth, it looked very much as though she might have surrendered her future to the sharks then and there.

# CHAPTER 17

After delivering his statement to the paper, Phil showed up in his own home like a fugitive in hiding. Catia's fury, Penelope's public attack, and Legal's betrayal had him turning nakedly, hanging in Rockwater's eye. He made his best effort in the news release, but he knew that wouldn't hold up for more than a few days then the ax would fall. He was startled to hear Catia moving about in her studio. What could she do, alone and blinded? Merle had told him of his success in that foolhardy act of vengeance. Yet there she was, bumbling about in her hideaway. He tiptoed into his own den and poured a triple scotch. He wasn't even going to scheme his way through this mess until he could get thoroughly plastered and face the music tomorrow, if then. Just then nothing mattered.

\* \* \*

Catia groped her way about her familiar studio, feeling for locations, shapes and textures until she had the materials she had in mind. Then she set laboriously to work for over an hour and in the end took her work out of the room to its intended destination. With that, she went to bed.

\* \* \*

It was four in the morning when a lurching, stumbling Phil shuffled his way out to the patio, fumbling with a cigar. He fell down—no, he didn't fall down, the world fell up—picked up his cigar, and shambled further. His clothes were in disarray, he slurred obscenities to himself as he finally got his lighter out and lighted his smoke. Drawing in a satisfying drag, he plopped himself heavily down on the well cover only to feel it bend and collapse beneath him, sending him bottom first down the well shaft into the cold water below. The shock of ice water was enough to partially clear his mental confusion but only partially. He was able to feel himself jackknifed head, feet, and arms over his midsection. He was totally immersed, and there had been no time to fill his lungs with air. He swallowed water and writhing, choked painfully. Frantic struggling did no more than hasten the end, leaving time only for a bubbling, incoherent crying out of his wife's name. No one will ever know if they were a cry of accusation or a cry for help.

The man drowned not in water but in a deep sense of insufficiency.

*     *     *

Friday morning, Zeldon received the call he had been awaiting every hour since he had left Catia to her own devices. He hurried over and found her puttering about the kitchen, functioning by rote memory for coffee and cereal. Taking over, he soon had them seated across from each other eating breakfast.

"No sign of Phil?"

"No, he's not able to show his face." She lowered her glance and smiled.

"He'll show up sooner or later. We're going to have to tell him it's over for him here."

"I think he knows that." Again there was the funny smile. "Actually, I think he's left the neighborhood."

"Tragic."

"It's not tragic," she said. "The death of a dolphin is tragic. All that joyful splashing and leaping ended . . . that's tragic."

It was hard to find any sign of grief in the young widow. "Well, all we can do is carry on in the meantime. We'll wait to see what happens with the doctors and what we can do about your eyes." Phil was not his greatest worry, except insofar as he had caused this dire situation.

The first thing he had done to confirm and clarify Phil's formal declaration of Catia's malady was to find a medical definition of bipolarity even though he was sure he knew it. "Bipolarity," it said, "a disease of the prefrontal cortex of the brain." It went on to explain that the prefrontal cortex yields two characteristics, symbolic abilities and virtually all mental illness."

The irony for Zeldon, among all the cheap ironies of life, was that Catia was paramount in employing character empathy in each of her varied self-portraits. And then of course, there was the bipolarity. Busy little cortex, how much more did he need to know?

But there was more. The brain had one hundred thousand cells that made serotonin, he had been told, that being a mere .0001 percent of the brain's neurons—all that grief from such a tiny, tiny aberration. On top of all that, he was very familiar with Catia's scornful reference to the source of such facts, tenured foolishness, credentialed lunacy.

All those things he knew. He was brought up short when Catia took him out of his thoughts and said, "I think until some of this gets cleared up, you should make yourself scarce here. I can manage as long as I stay in the house. You might have to bring me in some groceries and things, but we can do that at night."

"What, you can't manage on your own. I won't go." It was his second dismissal in a few days.

Her face hardened. "You must. I don't want a scandal, not yet."

What did she mean, not yet? What could change with any passage of time? And she certainly did need help during the day. It was unsafe to do anything else. But she was adamant and again because that was her home and not his even without Phil's claim, he was forced to concede that he should go home. She promised to phone. So home he went.

And true to her word, she did phone, the next day and the next but only to report that she was managing. By ways of reassurance, she explained that she felt his afterglow, ripples in her pond from his recent presence, and that all was well. He could only accept her wishes.

There was still no word from Phil while the political gossip swept the town. Everyone wondered where Phil had gone. Finally after four days, Catia reported to Phil's office that she was worried, she had seen his housecoat floating in the patio well, and it frightened her.

Promptly two local policemen appeared and peered down into the well, looked at each other, and called for backup. Within the hour, they had recovered Phil's body and inquiries were underway.

"When did you last see Mr. Glover?" asked the police chief.

A distraught Catia wrung her handkerchief and stammered, "I have to think, several days ago. When he had the trouble that was in the newspaper . . . political things, he just drove out the driveway." She stopped, felt at her eyes, used her handkerchief, and bowed low, unconsolable, "I thought he would be back later in the day, but he didn't come back. I wasn't alarmed, except I knew there was trouble and he was very upset about it."

"What day was that?"

"I don't know. The middle of last week, I think. Yes, maybe Wednesday . . . No, maybe Thursday."

"The paper came out on Thursday."

"Well then, I guess it was Thursday I saw him. As I said, he was very upset, and he just drove away."

"And you never saw him again?"

"No, he was just gone . . . like a kite whose string was broken." She looked extremely distressed, and soon was in tears.

The medical examiner reported the obvious, death by drowning with no unexplained marks on the body. Shreds of a cigar were present between the teeth. A high level of alcohol was present in the blood. The police noted that the well cover leaned against the side of the well.

A preliminary police report gave the facts with a general presumption that an inebriated Phil Glover had come out to enjoy a cigar before going to bed, a common habit of his and had sat down on the well cover but the cover had been removed without his noticing, again an unsurprising accident. No further inquiries were held. Questions of a possible suicide were never answered. Phil Glover had had his moment of fleeting fame, but then he had been found at the bottom of a well where his past could not touch him.

\*    \*    \*

Zeldon and Catia spoke daily over the telephone during those crucial days, and when the news of Phil's death broke, she insisted and Zeldon agreed that they must each stay below any untoward attention, especially in any close relationship. Throughout, Catia presented herself as the grieving widow, exposed then as emotionally unstable. Because of that perception, she was spared any unwelcome scrutiny.

Of course, the next issue of the *Patent Trader* surpassed itself in its sensational coverage of the story. Statewide news of Glover's remarkable death only emphasized the importance of the local news sources. Citizens were gratified at their break from small town boredom and submitted themselves willingly for interviews with nonlocal reporters, both print and TV. Penelope Hentoff expressed outrage over the unsubstantiated and irresponsible innuendoes over her personal life and had to live with the shadow left by the exchange. It inhibited her already delicate political advancement, but there would be further developments on that score.

Public attention, in its frenzy, turned to Murray Hubbard with its superlative accusations over financial fraud. Showing a commendable prudence in preparing a case against Legal and revealing his sense of the dignity of his office, the district attorney expressed dismay that a leak from his office revealed Phil Glover had provided substantial proof of the charges he had leveled against Hubbard. Much to the public's satisfaction, it appeared that the accused would be indicted and found guilty. In the meantime, he too had disappeared, taking his congealed resentment into hiding with him. Those fast-moving events provoked from Penelope Hentoff, town council member, knowledge of Murray Hubbard's criminal collaboration with Phil Glover in his illicit financial dealings. She confessed to having only Hubbard's conversation revelations of the guilt of both men, without documented proof, but the witness might prove useful during the prosecution's inquiries.

With all that to digest, the citizens of New York's lower counties showed little interest in the by-then boring discussions of Penelope Hentoff's political and personal difficulties, only in her knowledge of the skullduggery of others. Otherwise, she was more or less left to herself as being dull potatoes in the sumptuous feeding frenzies of the past days.

# CHAPTER 18

One fine morning, Zeldon was sure he heard '88's whistling on the wind. In the fast-moving events of the past weeks, he had mulled over the developments with his immaterial friends. They had, of course, comforted him in his distressing periods and required information from him as the drama unfolded. Throughout, they had stayed in character themselves, offering their support even when Zeldon was preoccupied with his fears and sorrows. With Sarah's taking the lead, sympathy for Catia was paramount in their concerns along with a common watchfulness over his fragile person. One day Zeldon's burdened mind envisioned the conversation.

'We have to watch over him,' cautioned Harold. 'We of all people know that he can only be found from within. That's how we met him, from within.'

'Yes,' agreed Sarah, 'all of this outside trouble can only confuse us if we let it.'

'He loves his wench, that's the nub of it,' the gravelly voice of '88 showed his concern for their incarnate friend. Together they were gathering their perspectives into one point of view. Hope was silent for the time being, not sure of what all those rapidly emerging events meant for Zeldon or for themselves for that matter.

'He hasn't spent much time in the Yarde lately. I guess he's had too much going on outside.' '88 answered Sarah's remark with a wish that they could spend more time with Zeldon than they had been privileged to lately. A strong-minded onlooker might suspect that gradually the spider web of relationships woven into his life might very well by then have obviated Zeldon's need for ephemeral companions. Town ties had multiplied, lessening solitude and filling his life with substantial associations. Yet he remained aware of a rich imagination's tendency to evaporate. That therefore was not to say the Four no longer mattered, only that they no longer occupied a vacuum. So they conspired that one of them would stay attuned to the vicinity at all times or as much of the time that world-awareness was available to them. That on the chance that Zeldon would appear soon, no one mentioned it, but they all wondered what would happen then to the threat of their disinterment. Meantime, Zelda's musings drifted off.

And appear he did, being required to prepare for the burial of Phil Glover. With Catia's indifferent approval, he chose a site of some prominence and opened the plot awaiting the ceremony that was held three days after Phil's death. It was a single plot, that at Catia's insistence, indicating there was to be no Yarde-induced reconciliation between husband and wife. A service of remembrance was held at the church in the hamlet, conducted by Tap Andrews and attended by several hundred people, most of them seeing the ritual via remote TV projection. A heavily veiled Catia was lost in the numbers. She carried a small bouquet of violets, which she placed on Phil's grave.

When the crowd arrived at The Yarde, Zeldon took up his usual unnoticed station and listened to the solemnities given forth by the Rev. Dr. Tap Andrews. "You're accustomed to hearing me say we are all sinners depending upon the mercies of God. You are also accustomed to agreement without undue breast beating over the issue. Most of us therefore carry on with our trivia, our tiny scandals, secret betrayals, little corruptions, and justifying ourselves by castigating the others. Any town, ours no worse than others, is a cauldron of gossip and each secret keeper is as airtight as a screen door on a submarine." No one had heard Andrews as sharply candid as that before. But he went on, "At the same time, while all this is going on, each of us carries visions of the good, thoughts beyond the everyday. And our characters are decided by what we do with these transient indicators. If we haven't learned it yet, Earth must learn that its Creator incorporates variability into its imagined future, where freedom has a tendency to evaporate and memory forgets voices that were extinguished long ago.

"Phil Glover was one of us. Now we commit him to the Yarde, where his character will present itself to a loving and merciful God as will you be so presented someday." He concluded abruptly with a benediction, "May the Lord bless you and keep you this day and for evermore. Amen."

A stunned and silent mass of humanity dispersed itself, moving in small knots to their cars and departing with few exchanges to diminish the effect of what they had heard of what they had to take away into their subsequent performances.

\*   \*   \*

As it so happened, the very confusing events the Four had referred to precipitated yet another development that had benefits for Zeldon and indirectly, for them. And without their raising the question directly, it came to be discussed without an indelicative move on their part. The issue of the road relocation and the disinterments that proposal would have initiated became moot. Without the hidden agenda held by Phil Glover, the proposal died of its own weight. Too much divisiveness threatened to allow it to be espoused by others.

As their prominence in his affairs diminished, Zeldon was obliged to scrutinize their role in his life, their very substance, if that term could be used. Certainly in his early days in the midst of their world, he found them real enough and crucially healing in his transitory period. During those times, he steeped himself in reading about their historical periods over their century and a half. But then he found it impossible to grasp that first sense of substance. That of course illustrated his difficulty—spirits had no substance to begin with. And then in their fading participation, he saw it exemplified in his—there it was again, that word confusion. Had they grown out of his extensive reading of their historical contexts? He was aware of the desperate need of his early days in the Yarde. And if they were purely invented, a product of his post-Bryan neuroticism, he had to have invented even those conversations that had among themselves; In effect, it didn't really matter. To him, they were substantial in the full sense of the term, and then that his tangible relationships were so constant and so fraught with importance and his days so eventful, it wasn't surprising to him that the spirits were retreating into silence.

He must have been more disturbed than he had realized. But that of course was in the nature of the neurotic or the psychotic— not recognizing its presence. Hadn't Catia proved that?

In addition to Zeldon's personal debate, the public saw with Zeldon's happy endorsement, Dalton Sumner's coming forth with his offer to develop the town park as a memorial to his wife, Hazel. In response to his letter addressed to the town council, making his formal proposal, that body consisting then of only three members, called itself into executive session thus avoiding public scrutiny and public input as it deliberated. Toby Stanley, the vice chairman, presided, precluding his hiding behind his crosswords.

"Well, we three kings of orient are . . . .going to tackle this mess. Matt, any ideas?"

In response, he heard what anyone would expect to hear from Matt Purdue, "Of course not, there's no way to clean this up."

"I don't know, somebody has to make a start." Penelope was far from surrendering her chance at leadership.

It was like crows quarrelling over a robin's egg.

Ms. Hentoff pressed her point. "When our esteemed head fell into the well he took himself out of it. And our other valued councilor is running from the law he represents, so who is left to govern our fair city?" Penelope was far from surrendering her chance at leadership. "We need to take a position before the electorate that put us here. I think we could do worse than start by accepting this town park offer. It's generous, it costs us nothing, and it bounces back from all this trouble with a positive proposal that gets things moving again. It makes us look good."

It was politics as usual, opportunism plus good timing. Penelope was being true to form and her two rubber-legged companions could only admire her perspicacity. And they couldn't care less if she were a lesbian. It was quickly decided that the road plan was to be postponed for further study, code talk for dropped like hot coals, and the offered gift was to be unanimously recommended before a town meeting scheduled for late June, again perfect timing for Penelope's resurgent ambitions. Toby presided over a few traffic sign decisions and a review of the assessor's report to help cover the paucity of substance they had raised on their own initiative, and they adjourned at 8:15, pleased with themselves.

*  *  *

When the town council announced their decision and the planned agenda for an upcoming town meeting, Zeldon quickly took the news to the smoky residents of the Yarde. Predictably elated, they held excited conversation among themselves and praising Zeldon for his admirable championing of their hopes and desires.

"Your real praise should go to Mr. Sumner, and I know you can't tell him yourself, but I'll tell him he has secret admirers all over town, which will be true, and it will include you."

'We will be part of the town!' cried Hope.

'We already were part of the town,' sniffed Sarah, 'but you're right, we had a victory without having a vote.'

'Zeldon for President,' called out '88. 'Who needs a vote? We elected him ourselves without a vote.'

Suddenly, Harold noticed the drawn and haggard look on Zeldon's face. Pleased as he had to be with the public progression of events, his personal situation was dire and devoid of any sign of improvement. All hinged on Catia and her state of health. 'I with our vote could bring you a victory, friend,' Harold said, his strong emotion whispering on the wind. 'I wish we could return to having a say in your world. It would make a difference the same way you have made a difference in ours.'

The expected chorus of support clamored silently around him as their friend and sponsor walked slowly and silently to his house. As hushed and unobtrusive as a breath coming to one of his specters, a realization slipped into Zeldon's character. It had come to him at Phil's burial service as Tap Andrews was outlining their quandaries and the forgiveness that accompanies them. That was Sarah's conviction and Andrews's. Without noticing it, it had become his as well. In midstride he understood he was at one with them, Christians. No fanfare, no pool of light falling about him, he went on home to carry on his acts of love and forgiveness.

* * *

Zeldon tiptoed his way through the days as tense as Catia was rigid. That was the pattern during her times of cliffhanging unpredictability. He was becoming uncomfortably at home in the familiarity with the uncanny. In those past years, he had seen the seasons evolve with spring slipping into summer, summer into fall, fall collapsing into winter, and as events progressed, with all their changes and even surprises, things had been taken as normal social history. But the uncanny had become the posture du jour for too many days. Just part of his contract with the devil, so it was with relief he saw her one afternoon playing her hand in the Yarde fountain, looking dreamily into its pool. Sensing his presence and leaning gracefully in his direction, she peered in his general direction with a loving glance. He stood at a slight distance, shadowy in the late summer half-light with the silvery mirror of the pond water behind him. "Why," she wondered, "did he never seem a somber graveyard man, never dark but always a sign of life and light?" On such occasions, he seemed ageless, a vivacious, legendary man, Prometheus. Both his bearing and composure fed into an understated magnetism. In her present period of equanimity, she could bask in his presence and his predictable support. Despite all their variables, she felt he was growing in her grasp of affairs. But she had a disturbing message for him. "Z," she said, "Z, there's something . . ." She spoke tenderly, aware of the delicacy of her announcement. "There was an item in the local radio news, did you hear it? Mrs. Rodgers died yesterday. You knew her quite well, didn't you?"

Unable to speak, not trusting himself to speak, he realized the many spaces between people that silence filled when sound and noise were absent. No, he didn't know the private details of Mrs. Rodgers's life, but he recognized one of those spaces just then. And that only emphasized how much more true it was when applied between people who loved each other. His inner being leaned toward Catia's, carrying Mrs. Rodgers with him. So he made an effort by trying to express for her and for Mrs. Rodgers something the moment called for. Apropos of nothing but his sad exposure to the disappointments in the air, he offered a gift of his emotions to her, "I heard of a religion in Asia that believes when a person dies he or she becomes a rainbow."

She took her time hearing his remark then a longer time before replying, "Do you think," she stretched her words out slowly, "do you think Phil is a rainbow?" She paused again. "Because if you do, I know enough to unweave the rainbow;"

His gift was crushed. His own colors died in his mouth. That was his punishment for loving a damaged, dying woman. She magnified the cost by saying, "Do you know I'm looked on as the local terrorist? I was the weak person who's always beaten by the rules, and Phil was the rule enforcer. So I changed the rules. Now everyone is afraid of what I'll do next." She smiled her sinister smile and went on to make things even worse. "Often I fall through the bottom of appearances into a dark underworld. Just like Phil, he fell through a cardboard well cover, and I fell through . . . through this accident of . . . the biochemical circuitry in my brain." She retreated to her deep interior, features slack and disengaged.

A cardboard well cover? She was in the same quicksand as he. A cardboard well cover? She had capitulated. He had his immaterial friends hinting, but without accusation, that he—no, they, Catia and he—were pitted against an unworthy time, a time when power had gravitated to the least noble among them. But those friends proposed to him that by learning from the best of his time and the best from theirs and by giving respect and admiration to worthy subjects as the sun today was lending its light to the moon, beauty could return. Had she capitulated? A cardboard well cover? No, it was nothing. She was only trapped in the cycle of illness that reached beyond her own capacities. She had not and he would not; he would not capitulate. A cardboard well cover?

To fight back, to face the ominous suspicion in the only way that was honest, the only way that could serve, he had to look the devil in the eye. "What do you mean a cardboard well cover?" his voice shook as he asked it.

"Did I say a cardboard well cover? I meant a well cover."

Zeldon remembered the police report. It said the well cover was propped up against the side of the stone perimeter. A cardboard well cover? A vague suspicion, one that would have gained no attention had Catia been in a normal state of being, caused him to catch his breath. She was not in a normal state, and what was more, she had every reason to lust for revenge on the man who had blinded her. Even blinded, it would have been a simple matter to— but no, he refused to go down that logic trail. He dismissed the fantastic imagining as the result of so much lurid drama in the air during their recent days. He dropped the question.

His eye fell on a shaft of sunlight striking his small asparagus garden. Needing time to rest his overloaded self, he said to Catia, "I'd like to weed this little patch of garden over there, do you mind? Won't take more than a few minutes. Can you bask in the sun for a while?"

"Good idea," she said, stretching out her legs and raising her face to the warmth. He walked about, stretching out his own limbs, surveyed the surroundings with gratitude then ambled over to his plantings. Mrs. Rodgers. Bryan. Dan. Phil Glover. Catia had once said to him she had had to learn to count dead husbands. "It's true," he thought, "she lacks the spider webs of relationships that give people's lives shape and meaning." And his own body count was rising in his young life. Desultory weeding gave him the privacy he was so badly in need of. He heard Catia humming to herself. It had been a long time since he had heard her so at peace, and she chose the queer time to tell him her demons had retreated, at least for the time being. He recognized it as good news, whatever its anomalous timing, flowers in bloom, shade trees cooling their neighborhood, and birds singing to the dead as they spread their angel wings.

Then her humming stopped, and he heard her say, "Did you hear that, Phil? I slipped up and told Z about the cardboard cover. I think I was able to hide the mistake, but I'm afraid he isn't sure. We can't have him in our little secret, can we? Privacy between husband and wife, right? Ah, well . . ." She went back to her humming.

Kneeling down not far away, Zeldon realized she thought he was further distant than he was hence the candor.

Little attention was paid over the cause of Phil's death by Rockwater residents beyond the earlier presumption of an accident, probably caused by a drunken misjudgment. The few further suspicions laid the death to the possibility of suicide, given the encroaching suspicions over Glover's secretive financial dealings. Any deeper probing that might have taken place could only have come from Murray Hubbard, his former and then estranged business partner. That curiosity was of course preempted by Legal's disappearance. That left Zeldon as the sole participant in the affairs to withhold a satisfactory answer to all the questions that had been in the air. Besides that was the wife of the deceased. If there were more to the story than that, only she could know for sure, and she was in no mental condition to be a trustworthy factor, case closed.

But no, not for Zeldon, what was he to do with his overheard information? Was it truly information or only hallucination?

\* \* \*

Zeldon slept fitfully. His dreams made up of wreckage from the waking day. Phil's death occurring in the very midst of the disinterment controversy left him at a loss over his feelings and disoriented as to what to do next. The indecipherable Catia, his growing loneliness, and then the rearrangement of the only public issue he had ever entertained, the Yarde—and that at the behest of his ephemeral friends and then of course the park—it all made for a restless discontent. His mind was a highly charged engine, not knowing what load to pull. One thing he knew, in all the assaults he had to hold enough of himself in reserve, "don't let everything pass through so there's some depth to what remains. Let the beaver build his dam." In his agitation, he rose, dressed, and crossed the road into the Yarde. He sat there all night, building his dam.

The next morning he was to be found seated on a bench beneath the Yarde clock. The fountain splashed its tumbling water in one voice while crickets sang in another. The sun generously lent its light to an early morning moon hanging low in the eastern sky, over Trinity Lake. Its waters stretched before him like a large wet patio. On his backhoe nearby sat Catia, who had come by taxi, of all things, that early in the day. She sat then staring sightlessly as though she were still looking for him, wearing dark glasses over her blinded eyes. It was moments like that when he could relish the earth's beauties and she could not that his heart weighed most heavily in his chest.

Into the sweep of sorrowful gratitude for the beauties about him and the accompanying heartbreak of their affairs, she spoke. Her first greeting on sending the taxi away had appeared almost reassuring, normal, "We have some weather coming, did you hear?" He hadn't, but it wasn't important. The weather that morning was too perfect to think of anything different. It didn't matter to her either. It was just an introduction to chatter. Quickly though, she revealed that day's form of the shape-shifting person she had become, the person she had brought him that morning. "Do you remember when we first made love here?"

"How could I forget it?"

"That night my name was Lovinia."

"Lovinia, who is Lovinia?"

"In *Titus Andronicus*. Shakespeare. I thought you were educated. Lovinia was raped on top of the body of her murdered husband."

She was at it again, in the sway of her kaleidoscopic emotions. "What are you talking about?" He remembered that that night her name was Lethe.

"You raped me on top of Phil's body."

"Catia, stop it! I didn't rape you, and Phil wasn't murdered."

She stared at him, again that tiny smile under her taunting eyes. He felt that remembered chill sweep over him. Whenever she vanished into her illness, part of him was gone as well. Raped, murdered, his ordered mind staggered under the assault of that thrust. If there were any thread of reason in what Catia was implying, it would be more frightening than a complete absence of reasoning. That was how madness worked. He knew it, by pulling away all mental linkages. He had heard her say it herself, "Pearls can't make a necklace without string." She hadn't been raped; their coupling had been eagerly consensual, even joined at her request. But that reconstruction of the deed left her the resisting victim.

And that was nothing compared to the role assigned Phil, the murdered husband? Paralyzed, he fought off the hint she had hurled at him. The second, after the cardboard well cover, but he wasn't murdered. "She hadn't m . . . she couldn't . . . .No, that wasn't right, this new madwoman could have." A confusion of a few days earlier came to his remembrance. She had been telling him of her discouragement when she alluded to "sinking into my deep well of sadness". Then she caught herself, alarmed, and stammered, "What did I say?" He recognized the awkward metaphor but couldn't explain her consternation. He didn't like those dangerous suspicions.

She was speaking again; he wasn't sure if to him or to herself. "Phil was a big man. He crushed me when we were making love, and he crushed me more when we weren't." A look of hate crossed her face, hard and vicious.

He tried to avoid the lovemaking image but couldn't.

"I had to get out from under him. He made it impossible to fight the illness."

His disquiet increased. "What do you mean?"

"I needed to be free of him so I could fight the disease. My sickness was second in line after him." Zeldon saw the confusion in that thinking but made no comment. "Well," she concluded, "one out of two isn't bad." From his sudden intake of breath, she sensed Zeldon was startled at the faux pas. She added, "I mean now I only have one problem left." Having said that, she retreated to the place deep inside her disease and pictured a scene no one would ever know occurred. In fact, she herself would never know if it occurred or if she merely conjured it as yet another imagining. In her scene, she was standing outside herself, watching herself watch her husband, fascinated with his panic deep in their well. She stood there remembering all his abuses, his gurgling cries ringing in her ears. She was not indulging in simple revenge; that was enjoyment. Then the visionary caused the scene to fade.

She appeared pleased as though she had accomplished something difficult. Something cold passed over Zeldon. He felt its death rattle but consciously avoided the shiver that wanted to move through him. "Stop this," he snarled at himself. First of all, the new madwoman wasn't Catia, at least the Catia he had held in his arms and consoled that night. Was she? *Was* she? He looked again at her leering face, allowed himself to shiver once, turned, and walked away, his own face drained of all expression. When he felt there was no more dread to confront, there came one more terrible hammerblow. Her low obscene chuckle followed him as he tried without success to distance himself from that manmade hell.

\* \* \*

As he wended his way from the hamlet to the Yarde and through the grounds to his home, Zeldon reviewed the phases of the drama he was living. Phil, closeted in the Yarde, had spent his life struggling with the positives and the negatives of the world of finance and the world of politics. Those struggles consumed him. Catia, artist, aesthete, Phil's ultimate love and Zeldon's, carried on her magnificent struggle with life itself, all under the burden of the bipolar curse. And he, Zeldon, philosopher and analyst, interpreted all that transpired. Each viewed the unfolding phenomena from the center of their respective viewpoints. Each alone made a story, separate and distinct. Even as he trod on, carrying those heavy thoughts, he felt his consciousness expanding. So too was the weather system. A wind had sprung up, and the sky had a yellowish color. Then he remembered some broadcast warning of coming disturbance. Never mind, he liked strong weather.

But his widened perspective couldn't escape an awareness of the ambivalence all about him, Catia's, certainly in the extreme to the extent of her bipolarity, Phil's in his private/public personas, needing to win elections then finding himself unsure of just what he had accomplished and how secure he was, and his own, with his straddling the grass line, his awkward and conjured attempt to see beyond. All of them, Phil, Catia, and himself, yet they were in the end unified in their hunger to love and be loved. How many philosophers before him had challenged the walls of mortality? That was his heaven, punishment for his audacity.

With all this searching and reaching when, he wondered, in the slow accumulation of a soul, was a person finished, complete, a creation accomplished? Was Phil, in his last days of Faustian desperation, a concluded creation or was his an interrupted existence? What lifetime could he, Zeldon, and Catia anticipate? He couldn't conceive of their old age after decades of a progressive mental deterioration. Love, he had come to believe, emanated from God, but pride intercepted that impulse and deformed it.

The ominous forecast of their aging years could only be softened by eroding the hardcore pride that fostered it. He would make working toward that goal another gift he would present to his soulmate.

The night, though, showed no interest in his heavy philosophizing. It had an agendum of its own. In the afternoon, Zeldon saw dark nimbus clouds scrolling over the horizon. By evening, they were overhead, bringing with them the weather they had promised. He wasn't allowed his night's sleep; wind gusts, wild then wilder, shook the house. By early morning, they graduated beyond gusting into a steady howling that left sleep a thing to be forgotten. As he gave it up and dressed himself the constant moan outside moved to a shriek as though it had become anguished over what it was destroying. Then came the rain, always welcome to Zeldon's nature-thirsty heart. But the rain was punitive, not nurturing, being driven like bullets by the tearing wind. Limbs snapped, trees bent, some could be heard breaking, and others simply surrendered and fell, roots and all. The storm lover relented and thought of the wildlife out there in the dark. He had a dimly felt affinity for all sentient beings and ordinarily could take comfort in knowing that creatures' have their self-adapting defenses. But that was hurricane weather, savagely tempestuous, and normal defenses were insufficient. He could do nothing about that. It was becoming a familiar awareness of helplessness.

Clothed then, he considered his responsibility as Yarde superintendent and decided to step outside to view the damage being done. Almost constant lightning lit the acres as though they were a stage. What he found was beyond what he expected. Trees down, that wasn't surprising, but the number was a shocker. Crisscrossed over each other and interlocked with broken and twisted branches, they formed a web of destruction that crushed bushes, dislodged monuments and markers, and left him wondering how he would ever bring the Yarde back to normalcy. Streams had formed themselves to drain the floods to lower ground and dug deeper channels for themselves as he watched. Bulldozers would be needed as well as all the tree companies he could commandeer in the competition for their services.

The churning sky disgorged its fury without any pause then. The gusts had given way to uninterrupted, sideways, galloping air. It was as though God, the sky dweller, shook his shoulders in a black-clouded fury at the depravity he found living below him.

Zeldon's clothes were drenched, his boots were filled with water, leaving him gasping to catch his breath. "Nothing to be done out here." He opened his door to go inside. It was wrenched from his grasp and smashed against the inside wall, another task— repair or buy another door. By the time he could force it shut, his floor was puddling, water saturating the rugs and forming indoor streams. He leaned, chest heaving, against a wall, slowly, slowly reorienting himself to normalcy. There was no point in trying to make a meaning for such a display except to recognize it as approximate to his loving Catia in her madness.

# CHAPTER 19

During the days that followed, public attention was allowed to digest its feast of drama, both social and in nature's temper tantrum, by a return to the mundanities of small town life. The tormented land was deeply injured by the hurricane. In his compassion for animate beings and inanimate nature, the Yarde superintendent showed himself again to be perfectly fitted for that work. However, neither he nor Catia was allowed that relief from the ongoing intensities. Zeldon's cleanup responsibilities demanded that Catia have some oversight at home, oversight that he would otherwise have provided. In their desperation, he thought of calling upon Phil's secretary, Velma Nelson, to stop by whenever she could. Velma responded willingly and quickly, much to Zeldon's relief. Catia's new impossibilities of functioning demanded her total attention, which strangely seemed to call forth in her an indifference toward her instabilities. Whatever the explanation as her physical disability asserted itself so completely, her mental climate stabilized. Her transition to normalcy arrived in her habitual style as a sudden surprise. It happened that way.

Things were indeed calmer, but before the celebratory climate had any consistency to it, he said one day, "I could feel a lot better if I thought you would make good use of these quieter days." She turned to him with a swirl of her skirt, perfectly at ease in her center of gravity, as sure of herself then as she had been entirely scattered shortly before.

"All right," she responded, "give the bird a chance to sing. What would you like me to do?"

He was dumbstruck by the change, but he pounced on the opening. "Good, just give us a chance. We can't reconcile all our contradictions, and we can't transcend all our problems. Everyone lives with some. So just give us a chance."

"OK, Z, I'll cooperate. But that's a short-term promise."

"What does that mean?"

"It means I'll be good until I change my mind."

He read her playfulness nevertheless to take some hope in its serious intent. The current turn of events came just in time. He was being destroyed in the lunacy of their recent deluges. In an additional surprise, things on the central issue were much relieved by the unexpected appearance of Velma, coming from Phil's office to Catia's aid. The seismic change in the emotional landscape of the household may not have been from her arrival alone. A new hint of stoicism in Catia's nature may have contributed to the phenomenon. In any case, Zeldon indulged himself in new determinations.

An entirely new side to Velma revealed itself. Long divorced, living alone, and lacking a busy social life to occupy her time, the lonely woman found in Catia and her needs the perfect calling for her domestic skills and energy. Not surprisingly, things in her office were dormant with the exception of the few routine duties that took half the hours of a normal workday. Phil's energies had made her work a busy full time, no longer. For that reason, his former factotum was to be found relocated in the supervisor's home rather than his office, all on a personal basis of course.

To everyone's further surprise, the two women hit it off from the very first visit. That occasion came on Velma's initiative, where she found Catia trying to do the laundry; she promptly set about helping the stumbling laundress. By the time the ironing was done, a new friendship had sprouted and blossomed with daily visits thereafter. Much of their conversation had to do with unflattering anecdotes about Phil, a source of amusement to both. One observation that gave them wry agreement was that Phil had disrespectful eyes. Each seemed to notice and neither seemed to disapprove in the other of an absence of sorrow over the man's demise. The friendship was cemented when in an early moment of indiscretion, Velma confessed to Catia that she had followed Phil's hearse with a dry eye. The trust became mutual when Velma saw her employer nod her head with a confirming smile.

Arriving one morning, Zeldon found Catia still in her bed and Velma, nude, just stepping out of the shower, to their mutual embarrassment. He retreated immediately with abject apologies. She seemed to recover her poise quicker than he with even a hint of coquettishness about her. There came a nanosecond flash of what if before it died aborning. There was time, even in that flash of imagination, to think that Velma, far from unattractive, was a thin broth of a woman when held up against the substance of a flesh-warm, rich woman like Catia. But that of course was no reflection on Velma. It held for all of womankind. He tiptoed into her bedroom and heard her whisper in her sleep, "Zeldon . . . Z . . . .Zeldon . . . love . . ." With a lump in his throat, he chose not to wake her, leaving to make coffee.

With Catia being less dependent upon his household assistance, Zeldon was able to attend to his own duties at the Yarde, but it did nothing to assuage the continuing anxieties that followed him in his movements. Yes, he did find after an initial mutual guardedness between them a welcome companion in Velma's presence. Catia, as a sympathetic mediator, saw to that. And the town buzz seemed not to be offended at his sudden visibility in Catia's life. In that, Velma's appearance diluted the novelty. But new concerns could not be silenced, and they all had to do of course with Catia. Although she was functioning unexpectedly well under the circumstances, Zeldon knew those circumstances would evolve, bringing back much of the undercurrent in their lives. There was no such thing, he knew as a future without variables.

The sharpest goad to his peace of mind continued to be that reference to a cardboard well cover. It had to be admitted, there was little doubt as to what it implied over Phil's accident, if accident it was, and over Catia's suspicious relationship to it. Then there were those telltale smiles and sinister witticisms following the trouble, not to mention the lack of the presence of a grieving widow in the scenario. Others knew none of that. Velma saw the lightheartedness of the bereaved but seemingly found it acceptable because she knew Phil so well and could understand her companion's response. Actually, Velma was filling in the dots as well as Zeldon and was not as unknowing as he suspected her to be.

No, his fears were his own. He was circling the truth as if he were walking around the outskirts of the ring road within the Yarde, too frightened and too compromised to make a sharp turn into the very heart of the matter. Without that turn and without the truth, it was as though Phil had crossed the waters of Lethe with no one left behind from whom to disengage.

\*    \*    \*

And so things transpired as the days progressed. Normality or what passed for normality dominated the popular attitudes of the populace. Under Velma's friendly influence, Catia moved into one of her extended periods of normalcy. Her inner life grew beautiful once again. She met and made love with Zeldon, she took lessons in Braille, and she gossiped and giggled with Velma like a schoolgirl with a new summer friend. Zeldon saw the sordid happenings of the previous months drift into wonderings and conjectures then slide further into ambiguities and forgetfulness and gradually become a conversational topic over town history that could have been just a further example of the vagaries of the human story, all in a few months.

But not for himself, there was too much at stake, and he knew too much or suspected too much to take it all in his stride. Phil remained dead, Legal remained in limbo, and the general attention moved on to less dramatic but more immediate matters. Such was the attention span of the public; memories of the recent past leaked out the windows, disappeared when the lights went on. Nevertheless, he couldn't forget "Just like Phil. He fell through a cardboard well cover and I fell through . . ." Catia's words were ingrained indelibly into his mind and were repeated in his memory endlessly, endlessly. "Just like Phil. He fell through a cardboard well cov . . . a cardboard well cover . . . a cardboard . . . ."

It was several weeks later that Zeldon was helping Catia and Velma clear away some of Phil's office materials. His personal effects, clothing, and miscellaneous items had been disposed of earlier, but then it was time to be more thorough. Velma was a big help in knowing which official papers had any importance. One afternoon, when the two of them had taken a supply of correspondence to be filed in the town hall, Zeldon rummaged about looking for unimportant papers. Needing a larger wastebasket, he wandered into Catia's studio on his search and began to clear away what appeared to be trash. One item burned itself into the back of his eyelids, causing him to freeze in horror as soon as he recognized it.

\*    \*    \*

The days of late summer and fall unspooled themselves until it was October. Phil Glover had owned the Republican committee, which on his disgrace was scrambling to manage the disarray left in his wake. The morose smoke of their mood drifted among them. It was Merle Stanley, through Toby's parroting her ideas, who quietly planted a strategy hoping to save face and pave the way for a return to prominence later. Merle had at long last found the moment when she could employ her latent, under-expressed ambitions, going beyond the impotent powers of the garden club chairmanship. Influenced by her mouthpiece, pliant committee members decided to concede the year's election to the opposition.

"Give place to the Democrats by way of a breather," advised a surprisingly assertive Toby Stanley. "People have short memories and at the next election we'll come storming back." He didn't say under whose leadership, but he had his suspicions, and they made him fear even more the woman he had married.

And so in November, Penelope Hentoff was the newly elected town supervisor, replacing the deceased Phil Glover. She had won a closely run race against her uninspired opponent, Toby Stanley. Toby had been all but commanded by his wife, Merle, to run. With that impetus and the despairing approval of the Republican committee, he pretended, unconvincingly in the opinion of many, to want the job. Only the traditional preponderance of his party made it a race at all.

Penelope knew she had only a short few years to establish herself as more than an aberration, and she set about doing so by meeting promptly with Dalton Sumner in getting underway with designs for the Hazel Sumner Town Park. She meant to make it her signature achievement with Sumner paying all the bills. Old threats seemed to have been put to rest but weighed heavily over her future as dangers presumed to be no longer dangerous. She served with her fingers crossed.

\*    \*    \*

Over the summer, Velma had managed to help Catia develop some competence about her house. Early probate returns had assured her of an astonishing inheritance from Phil's doings. That led her to believe that her sole name on the will meant Phil had given little attention to his expected life span. Not that it mattered to her. She would gladly exchange the millions to regain her eyesight. The unacknowledged sorrow was the loss of her studio hours, along with the always present fear of the bipolar curse.

Her eyesight had become a settled question. The blindness was irreversible as suspected. That calamity had the unpredictable result of galvanizing her determined character into a steely announcement that she would never again succumb to black despair despite her questionable mental health status. From the first day she met him, Catia had found in Zeldon a still point in her turning world more than she ever thought possible. It was not just her new dependence on the people about her; it predated and went deeper than that. He had introduced her, for instance, to the image of Trinity Lake as the waters of Lethe. That made her recognize that she had indeed been searching for herself, her real self all along. But then she saw that to him that was merely an attractive myth. In fact, he was finding the perspective of Tap Andrews more compelling every day. All on her own, without Z's tutelage but because of his inclination, she began to envisage Trinity Lake as the Sea of Galilee. To that point, it went no further than that.

All that, along with his consistent presence, made her succumb to his pressing her for a professional approach to her illness. So she actually began treatment under the best medical specialists in the city and complied with their directives like a doctor's dream patient. Velma quit her job in the town hall, much to everyone's chagrin, and became an overpaid companion, doing more than Catia could prescribe with verve and imagination.

In none of that did Zeldon take great satisfaction. He continued his duties at the Yarde with his old efficient gravitas, but his heart and his mind were elsewhere. Catia's devotion to him continued unabated, and his to her, but a veil of uneasiness hovered between them. On Zeldon's part of course was his awareness of the ebony-dark secret buried in Catia's disturbed mind. He couldn't put out of his mind that discovery while they were clearing away discards in her house of that crinkled cardboard replica of the well cover. As for the lighthearted days that had made up her past summer, Zeldon couldn't take them seriously, knowing that her mental health was not circumstantial but rather chemically determined. That was not to say he couldn't keep a glimmer of hope in her new treatment regimen. But it was prudent. He then knew the truth.

She on the other hand persuaded herself that all the deepest suffering was behind her, drowned in a cylinder of water in her front yard. She sustained the delusion despite the fact that it stood a few feet from her door, facing her with every sunrise and moistening the air through every night. It was her subterranean soul shadow.

Into the fragile fantasy time came word of another probated will, that time that of Mrs. Rodgers. That gentle widow of no family and little estate had bequeathed to Zeldon her newly constructed home with all its furnishings and a bank balance of fourteen thousand three hundred and twenty-eight dollars.

"I won't accept it!" declared Zeldon. "It's the fire house where Bryan died."

"It's not," cried Catia, "it's her new house with no history of memories. You can create your own memories to put in it the same way I'm using Phil's money."

"No, it's the same house, just with new lumber on the same lot. It still holds all the old house's memories. Including Bryan's . . . including . . . I'll burn it down." He waved aside any further conversation and that ended the question for him. Velma quieted Catia and took her to another room where they could reassure one another and wait for another day.

\*   \*   \*

Christmas came and went with an exchange of presents and an atmosphere of seasonal music taking the place of any visual celebrations that would have been lost on Catia. Velma continued to prove her sensitivity to Catia's debilities and her skillful assistance in all practical matters. Zeldon came from his home daily to check on Catia's welfare and to present as much of his affection for them both as he could muster. In the case of solicitous caring for Catia, that was the usual cascade of love, albeit filtered through his new knowledge. She felt the latter but read it as disturbance over the question of Mrs. Rodgers' house. She hadn't forgotten his vow to burn the house down to remove it from his nightmares.

The more she thought about it, the more Catia became worried over his fulfilling that intention. Her blindness had the result of driving much of her consciousness into contemplation and reverie and conjecture. She became sure he would act on his threat, which in turn became a certainty that he would be charged with arson. Soon the conclusion demanded a preemptive act on her part. She loved Zeldon. She would protect him from himself. And who would suspect a blind woman of arson? She determined to do something about it the next day.

\*    \*    \*

Despite all the adventures in his life with Catia, Zeldon had continued his daily duties in the Yarde, multiplied then by the commencement of work expanding and landscaping the town park, hence the refurbishing. The day was unseasonably warm, and perspiring from an excess of enthusiasm over the project, he decided he needed a break. His work habits were always hard on his boots, and he was particular about keeping them in good repair. So he walked into town to pick up his favorites, their having been left with the cobbler to keep them that way.

As he walked the driveway circling the Yarde, he thought of how infrequently he visited with his friends there even though he was in their vicinity daily as before. The sound of a fire truck's blaring reminded him of his first days among them. It seemed the more he was invested in his breathing relationships, the fewer his contacts with the non-breathers. Concerning the park, he knew

they were gratified at the progress on behalf of the townspeople—
they continued to hold their attentiveness to the well-being of
their historic progeny—and appeared to be somewhat somnolent
over longer and longer periods of time. As he became more and
more absorbed into the breathing world his vaporous companions
became more vaporous still. Awaiting their day of resurrection,
he was sure.

"Good morning, Mr. Yardeman," Shoemacher greeted him.
"You have mistreated your best boots again, and again I have made
them your best boots." He placed them on the counter with pride.

"Yes, it looks like you have," Zeldon answered, "they're old
friends and with a new tread I like them better than ones that
have never seen a day's work." He also liked Shoemacher. They,
too, had become old friends without frequent meetings. They saw
eye to eye, so to speak, even though the shop skulked there below
sidewalk level.

He removed the boots he was wearing. As he stood in his
stockinged feet, Shoemacher, peering with his deep-set eyes at
Zeldon's old dependables waiting on the floor before him, said,
"that faithful leather has trod over the unsaid and circled a past
that can't be erased."

Puzzled, Zeldon looked up at him. What did he mean? How
could the old mystery man converse about such personal, such
private experience? The unsaid? That left layer upon layer of
unexpressed thinking. Did he mean his, Zeldon's thoughts, or
everyone's? A past that couldn't be erased, that could allude to the
interred and their contributions or that and even earlier doings
back before the Four, back when Trinity Lake was three mud
ponds, back, back, back. That was so profoundly ambiguous that
he hadn't even an idea of how to ask Shoemacher what he meant
by a past that can't be erased. Something was going on there that
he couldn't understand, except that his beloved boots had walked
his Rockwater journey with him.

Giving it up, he bent over and stepped into his old dependables,
ready to wear them into further unspoken offerings and outline
a small piece of history, whatever, whatever, whatever. Just as he
was tying the laces, Shoemacher's telephone rang. After a minute

the old man with surprise in his voice said, "Yah, he is here, he is here." He turned and handed the phone to Zeldon.

It was a breathless Velma who said, "I'm glad I found you. No one's at the Yarde, and I knew you were going to . . . Zeldon, there's trouble . . . Catia is missing, and the fire trucks have just pulled up to Mrs. Rodgers's house. I'm there now. I know what she's done."

So did Zeldon. "Sometimes," she once said, "it gets so frightening I just choose to leave the world. It's less painful than staying." Without a thank you but with a glance that said much more, he thrust the phone at Shoemacher and rushed out the door and up the steps.

"Sometimes . . . I just choose to leave the world. I dreamed I saw the stars," She had gone on, "They glimmered and went out one by one." He couldn't drive it out of his mind. "Sometimes," his jangled thoughts panted, "a piece of music will leave its key and wander into dissonance, but the satisfying resolution is in coming home, coming back where it belongs, notes settling down into their appointed locations." "Dear suffering Catia, maybe it is time to come home for good." Heavy breathing, he was after all a breather. "We're exhausted from reaching for love in a hall of mirrors." He remembered that first day he met her properly in her own home, how he had realized it would take more courage to love unconditionally than it would take to wait endlessly for forgiveness. Stumbling, he accosted the waiting Velma.

"She is in there, isn't she?" he gasped.

"I'm sure of it. I'm sure of it," she repeated, trembling.

That was all the confirmation he needed, being sure of it himself. Without hesitating, he plunged past the milling bodies, loitering onlookers and busy firemen, and amid angry shouts from the latter to get back, he sprinted into the smoking entrance. His jogger's lungs served him in good stead, allowing him to hold his breath to great advantage. At first, nothing could be seen but smoke and furniture. He felt rather than saw the flames off to his left so he veered right and crashed into a piano. Calling out Catia's name, he heard a gasping, choking answer from down the hallway. There all seemed aflame and a scream came from her on the far side of the orange heat. Again, no thought, he worked with a knowledge that existed beyond words, with cerebral control relinquished. Had there been time for mental review, it would have been clear that he and his love would never know the slow decline of life. It was to be as the bubble he saw burst of the back of that child's hand, all to pieces at once, all at once and nothing first, Catia's disease and his confusions, love trumping guilt, all at once.

His young history, by loving her, had let him see both life and death in their full power. In that awareness, he dove into the licking fire and came out the other side with his pants legs ablaze and his shirt smoking, ignoring the pain in his left leg and reached for Catia just as she collapsed under his reach. He felt her without seeing her. His eyes were closed shut and his hair afire. Pain had no interest for him. He lifted the limp body of his love and fell against a wall, which collapsed under their weight. Adrenaline-fed strength lifted them both to his feet again just as he most assuredly caught sight of Bryan's features mouthing the name "Zell-donnn," but that time with a smile on his face. At another removal the Four clustered before him in a cloud of flaming smoke. Smiles lit their faces as well incongruously but had the calming effect of giving him a weightless, floating feeling not at all how he occupied his space.

Fire cleansed as it refined. In a final whooooshhh, the house collapsed on itself with a rushing screen of flame. All who saw it reported a center of swirling orange and red that lifted upward and dissipated itself in a tower of sparks. They claimed to have been left themselves with an impression, a sensation, a mere inclination dancing before them in the firelight—no harm, it conveyed no fear. All was well. Some then saw a surreal finale portraying the brush of God's hand as he stooped to his half-forgotten star to take up a handful of souls and raise them to a new blessing.

\*       \*       \*

Rockwater was astonished to discover how many theretofore silent residents surfaced with their saddened recounting of the Yarde superintendent's accommodations to easing the heartbreak of their personal losses. Statement after statement was elicited by the *Patent Trader* in researching their longest obituary in years. The unknown fact of Zeldon's personal contribution to the Yarde's transformation through plantings, the installation of clock and fountain, and the placing of memorial stones where paupers were buried surprised everyone. It was obvious the publishers themselves were touched personally by the community setback.

Anticipating the immanent completion of the Hazel Sumner Town Park, her husband Dalton was determined to sponsor a second memorial of importance to the town of Rockwater. He commissioned a modest but tasteful monument to his young friend, Zeldon Wade. Its low silhouette, two plaques on granite bases, stand in the near vicinity of Hazel's plot overlooking Trinity Lake.

A third, center plaque reads:

The Creator sifted the population
to find its finest seed, one
ZELDON WADE
to live beyond the consensus and
to tend his treasured holding pen,
The Yarde.
This stone was the doorstep of his
Partner-in-Courage
CATIA BROWNING

Flanking the center stone the two markers stated simply:

| ZELDON WADE | CATIA BROWNING |
|:---:|:---:|
| 1986–2015 | 1981–2015 |

Printed in the United States
By Bookmasters